Death From Above

By Don Weston

Copyright

ISBN: 978-0-9968647-5-6

DEDICATED TO READERS

This book is dedicated to all of the active readers in the world and especially to you, dear reader. I read to my kids when they were but toddlers and also had the good fortune to read to my grandchildren.

My youngest grandson, Ian, looked at a Christmas cloth recipe book a few years ago and blinked. I had made up stories for him from the brilliant Christmas figures of animals, drummer boys, and wooden soldiers. It was his favorite picture book and still is today, even if it wasn't a real storybook.

Reading to my kids and grandchildren are among my fondest memories. You can make a difference too, by taking the time to turn off the T.V., put the iPhones away, and simply spend intimate time with a child.

SMART, stands for Start Making A Reader Today. There are volunteer opportunities in your neighborhood. It is how I first came upon the book Captain Underpants, the favorite book of my SMART reader in the fourth grade.

Chapter One

The sign outside my office reads, *Billie Bly, Experienced Private Investigator*. An experienced P.I should be ready for anything at any time. This time, I wasn't.

It happened on a Saturday morning while I was out for a run. At four-thirty a.m., during the month of April, the sun is about two hours from making an appearance over Mt. Hood. But there was just enough light from streetlights and storefront display windows to safely navigate the sidewalks through downtown Portland, despite our typical cloud cover.

On this particular morning, I couldn't sleep so I decided to get up and resume my running routine knowing a nap was possible when I returned home.

I stood on the sidewalk across the street from The Marriot on Southwest Broadway Avenue and bent over to suck more oxygen into my depleted lungs. As I get older—I tell my friends I'm twenty-nine, but I've been over the trifecta mark for nearly three years now—I find it takes less time for me to get out of shape. I quit running two weeks ago because I was embroiled in two cases and couldn't find the time.

I heard a whirring noise from somewhere down Broadway and, at first, I mistook it for an early-bird shopkeeper clearing the sidewalk in front of his store, maybe with a leaf blower. I was deciding whether I should walk the three blocks to Pioneer Courthouse Square to see if Starbucks might be open or to turn around and head home when the noise closed in on me.

The buzzing sounded like a swarm of angry killer bees. I squinted down the sidewalk, illuminated enough by ambient light to make out shapes, but not enough to help with depth perception. So, when the whirring object came at me from seemingly nowhere it sent me reeling backward.

I lie there for a moment, trying to figure out what just happened. A loud metallic object, spinning a bunch of blades, nearly took my head off. As I did a back flop onto the pavement to avoid decapitation, it occurred to me the crazy contraption zipped up and over my head at the last second before it jetted up the street.

Jetted? It was still dark and the image was blurred, but it looked like a miniature helicopter about the size of a Chihuahua, with six or eight blades whooping above it. I rolled onto my stomach on the sidewalk and peered up the street. It was gone but the whirring sound was strong enough that it couldn't be more than half a block ahead.

I jumped to my feet and began pursuit before I could really formulate a plan. All I knew was the thing nearly took my head off, and I was mad. I'd gone about a block at full speed before I attained a rhythm in my stride. The damn thing was still making noise somewhere ahead, and I saw its shadow as it zoomed through a lighted crosswalk a block away.

We'd passed Pioneer Square, an open-court place of assembly for special events, street performers, and a place to generally hang out during lunch. The huge brick-laden city block is like a sunken living room with steps rising on one side similar to amphitheater seating. A sleek brick building on the West side contains a Starbucks, a split-level TV Studio, and an underground tourist information chamber.

Abruptly, the beast accelerated, and I heard the buzzing of what sounded like a nest of bees flying high above me and toward the river. I stopped and squinted upward, relying on the hundreds of glimmering neon lights of a fifty-foot-high *Portland* sign adorning the front of the Arlene Schnitzer Concert Hall.

It was hopeless. Hell, I couldn't even hear the maniacal machine anymore. I walked breathlessly back to Pioneer Square in the off chance the Starbucks might be open before sunrise. When I reached the Square, I noticed a solitary individual kneeling in the middle of the bricks. My first thought was of a street person bundling up her belongings to begin a new day of panhandling. My interest in the figure quickly waned when I realized Starbucks was open, a sign proclaiming service began at 4:30 a.m.

I jogged to the glass door of a small building on The Square, which also housed a local TV studio for on-the-spot newscasts. Inside, I faced a not-so-cheery-eyed female barista, with pink hair and half-a-dozen piercings in each ear and gave her my order. As I waited, I noticed the street person still huddled over the bundle at the opposite corner of the block-long plaza. If I'd been outside, I might have been forewarned. As it was, I was caught flat-footed for the second time in the same morning when a small flying object alighted in The Square.

I watched the figure grab the flying toy, stuff it into what appeared to be an aluminum shelled carry-on suitcase, and run across the street.

"Wait," I cried, running through the front door of the Starbucks and out onto the plaza. The woman or small man scurried across the street, ran down half a block on Yamhill Street, opened the back door of a black SUV, and placed the box on the back seat.

"Wait a minute," I shouted. "I want a word with you."

The figure turned toward me. She wore dark jeans, a sweatshirt, and a black stocking cap. It was too dark to see her face from a half block away, and she didn't wait for me to get any closer. She slid into the driver's seat and a few scant seconds later the black SUV roared out from its parking spot and sped down the street and through a red light. I tried to get the vehicle's license plate, but its light bulb was burnt out.

"Someone should tell the SOB not to fly that thing around people," I hollered after her. "You almost killed me."

I walked back toward Starbucks to fetch my latte, grumbling all the way. When I entered the store's door, I turned and gazed back toward the spot where I'd seen the figure kneeling.

"I wonder if she's a regular?" A Sunday morning would be even less crowded than Saturday, I thought. I continued through the door and spotted three people in line for coffee. I looked at my watch. It was four-forty-five. "Good thing I got my order in when I did," I muttered.

Ping Lau stopped at a light a few blocks from Pioneer Square and flashed back to the sequence of stunts she had achieved with her modified drone. She had sent it up to a height of four-hundred-feet and down to West Burnside from Pioneer Square, or about ten blocks. The helicopter found its target easily. Powell's Bookstore a mega-level building at Southwest 10th and Burnside took up a city block. The bird zipped around the store at street level with no incidents. It was early and few people were out so her baby had clear sailing.

The success encouraged her to follow through on part two of the mission--a ten-block jaunt up Broadway at eye-level along the west sidewalk. Ping Lau had staged some obstacles in the drone's path. Its software-controlled sensor located the objects well ahead of time. It avoided two newspaper boxes stacked atop each other in the middle of the walkway, evaded a parked bicycle, and easily pirouetted around a storefront gate opened onto the walkway. Healy, her name for the helix drone, relayed its successes to Ping Lau using a sophisticated camera to send real-time video to the special pair of goggles she wore.

But the real triumph, she thought, was when it came in contact with a human. Its speed had been 20 miles-per-hour and, although its sensor had been hampered by the absence of good lighting, Healy reacted magnificently by taking a last-ditch course around the woman and returning to its scheduled route.

The stoplight changed to green and Ping Lau turned and sped down Sixth Avenue a few blocks from Pioneer Square, still marveling at Healy's ability to do so much in low-light situations.

Ping Lau chuckled at the memory of the woman chasing her after the drone nearly knocked the troublemaker over. The sight had shaken her too because the video goggles made it look as if *she* was colliding with the woman. Ping Lau and Healy both bobbed and weaved in unison.

Once she realized Healy had taken evasive action, Ping Lau used the remote control to take command of the drone and turned Healy back to check on the woman's status. She must have been uninjured because she jumped up from the sidewalk and started chasing the helicopter. Ping Lau led her on a merry chase for a few blocks and then took Healy up to 400 feet and out for a victory fly-by over the Willamette River.

She thought about her near exposure as she cruised down Sixth toward West Burnside. The woman had found her at The Square and yelled at her as she packed up her equipment in her Ford Escape. She might need to find a new base of operations. She chose Pioneer Square to familiarize herself with the area in preparation for an assassination. If something went wrong during the evening training sessions, it would be easy enough to hop in her car and retrieve Healy before arousing suspicion among the few people who might be up this early.

But now that she had run a series of successful tests with her homemade drone, she felt she could trust it not to crash and burn. And its brilliant maneuver with the woman told her she was on the right track with what she wanted to do. It proved she could fly Healy through a crowded sidewalk, if necessary, and it would take evasive action and continue to its target. If something got in its way, whether an object or human, Healy would find a way around them.

Ping Lau pulled up to the stoplight at Burnside and glanced to her left. She was next to Big Pink, a forty-two-story pink-shaded granite building, which hosted the Portland City Grill. A Union 76 service station's lights shone against it and revealed a slight hue of the building's pinkness from across the street and she shook her head. During the day, the sun renders the entire building with a salmon blush.

She looked again and noticed it was under construction. She remembered reading a newspaper account of how the owner of the five-hundred-thirty-six-foot office building was renovating the inside to attract new high-tech firms wanting extra space to provide play areas for their twenty-something geniuses.

Maybe I *should* think about working here, she thought. Big Pink captured her imagination. If there were a way to get access to the roof, it would be a great base of operations for the tasks she would have to perform.

I finished my coffee, sitting on a tiered brick bench at the Square and thought about what had happened. Some nut flying a remote-controlled helicopter was just one of the latest weird things I had encountered in Portland.

People panhandled on streets and freeway entrances and exits around I-405. Mental cases threatened to beat up non-existent people and swore loud enough to be heard two blocks away. Once a guy knocked me down after robbing a store with a cucumber.

Every day is a new adventure downtown in a city where the unofficial slogan is *Keep Portland Weird*. Honest. It's painted on the side of a brick building across the street from Voodoo Donuts.

I don't know why I thought someone flying a remote-control helicopter downtown should be unexpected. The woman flew it in the early morning hours on a weekend when the streets were nearly empty. It was different to see a woman operating a remote-control aircraft, but why should it be a man's domain?

I took the last sip of my coffee, disposed of the container in a nearby trash can and jogged home. It was five-thirty and the sun still hadn't made an appearance so I showered and returned to bed to get my beauty sleep.

As I lie in bed, I was struck by one odd thing about my experience. It was how that helicopter missed hitting me. I had watched it in what seemed like slow motion as I swayed back, eventually collapsing to the sidewalk. It wasn't my actions that kept it from crashing into me. The thing had stopped, climbed six inches above the top of my head, and sped over me in one smooth motion. It was like it had taken evasive action as a human might. Almost as if it had a brain of its own.

Slowly, tiredness overcame my troublesome experience and my caffeine-filled latte, and I drifted off to dream of devilish aircraft circling around me, waiting to move in for the kill.

Chapter 2

Are bad dreams portents of something ominous about to happen? I awoke feeling unsettled with a vague recollection of a nightmare, the elements of which were fleeting. Something about being chased, I think. I remember running away from black thunderous clouds bearing down on me, but I couldn't escape them. I hate those kinds of nightmares.

I awoke at lunchtime and shook off the cobwebs of my dream. I put on my makeup, got dressed, and walked to a local Starbucks to buy a latte and some coffee cake. Because it was Saturday, my assistant, and best friend, Angel, had the day off. We'd both put in a rough couple of weeks, so I didn't want to bother her. I knew she would be spending time with her boyfriend, Chris, and I was on my own.

My problem was, I wasn't seeing anyone at the moment. I recently broke up with Steve Thomas, my boyfriend and former partner with the Portland Police Bureau, for compatibility reasons. We had great sex, but there was no emotional connection. After sex, we merely went back to our own individual work lives.

I spent the afternoon by myself at Powell's City of Books sifting through police procedurals and Stephanie Plum mysteries. Occasionally, my mind drifted to the helicopter which nearly took off my head. I wondered why it was being flown downtown and by whom.

Eventually, I found myself in the aviation section looking for books about remote-control helicopters. The closest I came was one on drone aircraft used by the United States in combat in Pakistan, Yemen, and Somalia. As near as I could tell, drones were full-sized, weird shaped, stealth aircraft designed to strike terrorists without putting soldiers at risk. The downside is that they don't discriminate whom they kill with civilians often included among casualties.

A clerk told me to look in the *Hobbies, Crafts, and Leisure* section where I unearthed books on model making and remote-control aircraft. I uncovered pictures of several remote-control helicopters like the one that attacked me.

It seemed like many of these smaller drones were used to spy on others or take aerial photographs. Law enforcement used the high-tech drones to search for illegal marijuana plantings in Oregon forests before the state made the drug legal. I read an article which said drones are used to monitor wildfires, search and rescue operations, and by farmers to check on their crops.

It occurred to me I knew someone from high school who used to fly remote-control airplanes. Brett Wright was a skinny nerd then with thick black-framed glasses and, yes, he did use white tape to mend them after a football player mistook him for a tackling dummy in the hall one day.

I arrived at Pioneer Square an hour earlier the next morning. The helicopter thing occupied more space in my brain than I cared to admit. Maybe it was because I didn't have a man in my life. Probably, it was boredom.

My therapist says I try to make something out of nothing to keep excitement in my life, so I don't have to live in the present and deal with my real problems.

Maybe she is right. The mysterious drone lady hadn't shown up yet, and I do tend to avoid the present if I can.

Whatever the reason, I found myself tucked behind a small brick building on Pioneer Square with my bicycle propped against the building's wall. I'd brought it in case I needed to chase the helicopter. I looked at my watch. It was four a.m. and the moon battled to escape from behind the cover of dark, menacing clouds.

The lights on the Portland sign chased each other above me in an attempt to ward off the gray, gloomy mood on the streets. I strained my eyes and ears searching for the helicopter, but there was no one on The Square. Had I arrived too early—or too late, maybe?

Five more minutes ticked off my watch and a lone pickup truck crawled up Broadway. It stopped at a light, engine revving. The *Walk* sign chirped the *Go* signal for blind pedestrians. The impatient driver of the pickup burned rubber through the red light and disappeared up the street. Ten minutes later a white Ford Mustang cruised down Sixth Avenue at the low end of The Square. It didn't even slow down for the red light. And that was it for Sunday morning traffic.

I shivered under my light gray running suit in the night air. The only sound now was the steady humming from a nearby freeway along the Willamette River. I wondered if maybe I was OCD to be out here in the early hours of the morning listening for things that buzz in the dark. I swung my leg over my bike and was about to push off when I heard disruption in the otherwise calm morning.

It was the faint buzzing I'd encountered early Saturday. It echoed up Broadway and I squinted to see it. A futile effort because I remembered it was black in color. I began peddling down Broadway toward the sound. Gradually the noise became louder, and I realized it was on the other side of the street flying along the sidewalk.

I stopped at the corner and glanced over my shoulder toward the bricks on Pioneer Square. Where was the operator? Before I could explore further, the helicopter entered my intersection. I pedaled across the street toward it and it sailed by effortlessly.

My bicycle idea had one major flaw. The drone was flying up Broadway on a steep uphill grade. I'm in pretty good shape but I can only pedal so fast uphill. I chased it and only fell behind a little at first, maybe a block after a two-minute chase.

Fortunately, this time it did not shoot straight up and out towards the Willamette River. Maybe because this time the pilot hadn't realized I was after it. After reading one of the books I bought, I realized the helicopter probably had a camera and its operator might have seen me yesterday.

It veered left and cruised downhill along another sidewalk toward Sixth Avenue. The descending route enabled me to close on it a bit, and when it turned left again, the terrain was definitely in my favor. The drone cruised along at about twenty-miles-an-hour and I tagged along about fifty-feet behind.

At intersections, it would zip up about fifteen feet and drop down to eye level at the other side of the crosswalk. I guessed it did this to run red lights without getting creamed by a car or truck.

The drone hovered at Alder seemingly waiting for the light to change. The light changed and the helicopter did an about face. Suddenly, it zoomed at me. Holy crap, I thought. It flew within a foot of my face, darted up and around me, and attacked again from behind.

I swatted at it but missed. It shot up thirty-feet and dive-bombed me. I hopped off my bike to use it as a shield.

The bat from hell swooshed around me and my bike in a tight circle, as if sizing us up. Its operator was either trying to get a close-up of my face or preparing to come in for the kill. I covered my face instinctively hoping to prevent my likeness from being stolen for future retribution.

The helicopter responded by doing an about-face and its six rotary blades, propelled it down the street like a hummingbird in search of the next flower. It took me a minute to realize what had happened before I could jump back on my bicycle and give chase down the middle of Sixth Avenue. The drone swerved from the sidewalk and soared down the middle of the street a block ahead of me, extending its lead.

When it achieved a three-block advantage, it shot upward and disappeared over the forty-story U.S. Bancorp Tower's Big Pink. I coasted the final three blocks hoping to spot it or its pilot and rode around the towering building, looking for the black SUV I'd seen the morning before, or the damn drone.

I saw nothing and decided to expand my search to a three-block radius. If it had gone much further I was out of luck. I was on the outermost fringe of my search when a pair of headlights flashed on in the Chinatown area a few blocks across the street from Burnside Street and Big Pink.

A black SUV peeled away from the curb and trained its bright LED headlights on me. I swerved away from the blinding luminosities as they barreled down on me. I retreated and tried to stay out of the path of the same black SUV I had seen the night before. My pounding heart told me the SUV wouldn't stop until it plowed over me.

I felt the heat from the roaring engine breathing on my neck. The lights washed over me. I twisted the handlebars to steer away from the monster and the tires of my bike jarred me as I bounced up over the curb.

I struck the wall of an Old Town cement building and swayed back toward the lights. The SUV pounced on the curb and sideswiped me. I careened against the building again and flopped onto the sidewalk. I heard the grinding noise of the SUV's fender meshing against the building and a thud as the runaway beast recoiled back onto the street.

I watched helplessly from a prone position and saw the driver's door open and a large gun pointed in my direction. Three shots rang out in rapid succession as I hugged the sidewalk. Another set of headlights flooded the SUV. Its door closed and I heard the SUV's tire rubbing against a bent fender as it drove off.

The second pair of headlights stopped in the street in front of me and a man got out. "What the hell?" he said. He walked carefully to me and bent over. "What happened to you?"

"Apparently, I wasn't making something out of nothing," I said and passed out.

I hate it when people make a fuss over me. The problem with being an ex-cop is when you get shot or hospitalized, the alert still goes out precinct-wide.

Before the doctors could patch me up, half of the Portland Police Bureau was sitting in my little curtained-off area in Emergency. Okay, so I exaggerated a little bit. It was only my three cop brothers.

"The doctor will be here in a minute." A flaxen blonde nurse looked over her bifocals at me distastefully. "Don't handcuff her until after the examination, please."

"I'm not under arrest," I said, as she left. "These are my brothers!"

"You look like crap," Jason said. Jason has always talked straight and never worries about hurting feelings. In other words, he's a lot like me. He also has the Bly's blue eyes, Mom's sandy blonde hair, and a fair-colored thin mustache you must look at twice to see.

"Thanks for noticing," I said. I had multiple scrapes and bruises on my arms and face and a slight shoulder sprain where I'd gone against the building, but thankfully no gunshot wounds.

"We heard about your little, uh, mishap on the police radio," Dan said. "I thought, 'it couldn't be Billie. She's stayed out of trouble for– how long now--three weeks?' The radio said a car chased a woman on a bicycle up onto the sidewalk, and I knew it had to be you."

Dan is my older brother, slightly balding on top, slightly bulging in the stomach, and slightly sarcastic all over. He also raised me when my parents died so some of his snarkiness is parental.

"*Of course,* it had to be our sister." Dagwood bent down to me, so I didn't have to stretch my neck looking up his six-foot-seven frame. "Who else could make someone angry enough to chase them up the sidewalk in a car? What did you do to piss him off, Sis?"

"It was a woman, and I didn't do anything." Their grins told me they weren't buying it. "Okay, I was following someone who nearly ran me over with a helicopter."

"A helicopter?" Jason said. "It was a helicopter chasing you onto the curb?"

"No. I was following a helicopter."

"In Old Town?" Dag asked. "What was a helicopter doing in Old Town, and why didn't we hear about it?"

If things weren't bad enough, Detective Steve Thomas strolled in to join the Inquisition. My ex-boyfriend was the last person I wanted to see at the Emergency room with me looking like road-kill. It had been several weeks since I'd seen him, but he flashed his boyish smile and bright blue eyes at me and nodded at my brothers.

"I just can't let you out of my sight," he said.

"She was just telling us how she was chasing a helicopter in Old Town," Jason said.

"It was a small one," I said. "Remote controlled. I was running up Broadway yesterday morning and this Black Ops type helicopter, with a bunch of whirly-gig blades, almost took my head off near Pioneer Square. The person operating it was inside The Square and I chased her, but she got away."

"Is this legitimate?" Steve took out a notebook.

"I swear. It's the truth." Tears dribbled down my cheeks, and I realized I wasn't keeping up the tough P.I. facade.

"We're sorry," Dan said. "We didn't mean anything."

"We just didn't understand," Dag said.

"Hell." Jason's face turned red. "Quit your bawling and tell us about it."

I laid out the whole story from my first encounter with the helicopter Saturday morning, to my attempt to chase it down this morning. Steve dutifully interviewed me and said a forensic team was in Chinatown surveying the scene for clues.

"We found three shell casings," he said. "They look to be nine-millimeter. Maybe from a Ruger, but the lab will determine the make."

It was nine o'clock before Steve drove me home and tucked me into my bed upstairs. My brothers had a roll call and couldn't stick around. Steve made small talk for a while and left. That's why we broke up, really. We have nothing to talk about other than the weather and cop stuff.

I thought about getting up early Monday morning and going down to Pioneer Square to confront the drone again, but my aching muscles talked me out of it. So did my mangled bicycle laying in a heap on my front porch. I knew how it felt. I, too, had spent a restless night, with a twisted shoulder, unable to find a comfortable position to rest.

The only thing I could half-smile about was the thought of seeing Brett again. I'd run into him at a wedding a few years ago, looking nothing like his former geeky self. He had grown into his body by lifting weights, replaced his glasses with contacts, and somehow became ruggedly handsome with curly brown hair, matching bedroom brown eyes, and a dimpled square jaw.

He had brought a date to the wedding or I would have flirted with him. Okay, that didn't really stop me from making a play, but he seemed more interested in the big-chested blonde he was with than me. I wondered what he was doing now. Probably married, I guessed. All the good ones were. Sometimes I wonder if I'm destined to remain single.

Maybe I should call him anyway. I'll tell him I'm working on a case involving drones and ask him for some advice. It would only be a small fib. The episode yesterday morning pissed me off and anyone who knows me knows I couldn't let it go.

Is it time to revisit the romance department? Hell, why should I be the only single female in Portland without a date on Friday night?

Chapter 3

Two Weeks Earlier

Ping Lau gazed over the top of the menu toward the elevator. In a few minutes, her life could change forever. No more contract jobs. She would have a chance to retire and see the world.

She had been successful in her profession so far, partly because of her physical appearance. She was a diminutive and attractive Chinese woman with long raven hair, which usually cascaded precariously around her large breasts, framing them like a painting. Because of her looks, people tended to underestimate her and sometimes they tended to be dead.

She was waiting for The General inside the Portland City Grill, thirty floors above Fifth Avenue. She had texted her prospective employer and changed their lunch meeting location a few hours earlier after thinking about using the Big Pink for a base of operations. It might give her a chance to scout it out a bit.

As she gazed out the window, she knew she'd made the right decision. The view was magnificent. Below, the Willamette River, a few blocks away, meandered through Portland. She could see five bridges, Chinatown, Old Town, Voodoo Donuts and half of Portland's East County with Mt. Hood looming in the background.

Ping Lau had arrived a half hour early and spent the time chatting with her waitress, a dishwater blonde named Cindy. She told her of an impending job interview and of being nervous.

"This is a great view," Ping Lau said to the buxom waitress. And it would serve her purpose admirably, she thought.

"It's the main reason people come here to eat," the waitress said.

"I wouldn't mind working here, Cindy. I'll bet you get some good tippers."

Cindy narrowed her eyes, scrutinizing Ping Lau. She had dressed for a job interview with The General, in a slinky black dress, dark hosiery, and high heels to make her look taller. In her stocking feet, she was lucky to measure five-foot-four inches, and she didn't want The General to think she was too weak for the task at hand.

Just to make sure he took her seriously, she wore a pushup bra to show maximum cleavage and brushed her hair back so it didn't block The General's view. She didn't really need the pushup, but she wanted him to be thinking about her boobs when she hit him with her price for the job.

"You're a waitress?" Cindy said.

"I've been known to," Ping Lau said. "And if my meeting with this potential employer doesn't go well, I may need to take it up again."

"We have an opening," she said. "But it's evening work. Happy Hour and dinners. You wouldn't be done until after midnight. You'd be closing."

"That's okay," Ping Lau said. "I'm a night person and the tips are probably good. I'll have a better idea after I meet The General here today for lunch."

Her eyes blinked. "A real General?"

"He's retired," Ping Lau said. "Now he's senior management in an investment firm."

An older man stepped up to Ping Lau's table. He wore a conservative business suit with a blue tie. His silver hair glistened in the sunlight streaming through the window. His face was thin and sallow and covered with age lines. His mouth looked puckered and sour.

"I'll be back in a few minutes to get your orders," Cindy said. She looked back at the man as she walked away and visibly shuddered.

"Miss Lau?" he said.

"General?" Ping Lau said. "Please sit down."

He slumped into a chair and sighed. "I got into town early this morning from New York," he said. "I took an early morning flight and I didn't get much sleep last night. Can't sleep on planes, even in First Class.

She nodded and leaned forward to glance at the menu Cindy left. She noticed The General glanced down too, but he wasn't looking at the menu. He had noticed her pushup bra. She practically pushed the girls out onto the table when her breasts bumped against the countertop.

"I, uh, have to be back tonight for an important meeting," he said, still ogling her.

"That's too bad," she said. "I would have liked to show you the town."

"Have you been here before?" he asked.

"My first trip." She took a sip of water leaving a splash of her scarlet lipstick on the rim of the glass. "But I've been here for a month now, scouting the area in advance of our meeting."

"And how do things look?" His sunken dark eyes reminded her of a ghoul on a late-night movie.

"I think things will work out for us if your side is committed," she said.

The General scanned the room pensively. There were three tourists seated six tables down and two businessmen at the bar twenty feet away in the opposite direction. It would be at least thirty minutes before the lunch crowd would wander in.

Cindy had told Ping Lau earlier the lunch crowd was small and she offered to seat people as far away as possible so her interview wouldn't be disrupted. Ping Lau had ensured their privacy by tipping Cindy twenty dollars.

"We can offer ten million," he said, when he was sure no one was close enough to eavesdrop. "That's five up front and five when the job is done."

Ping Lau smiled and leaned forward over the white tablecloth, thrusting her cleavage forward. "That won't do, General. I want thirty million, half up front. Ten for the first two projects and twenty for the POTUS candidate."

"That's ridiculous." He scowled and glanced around for another reconnaissance of the restaurant. "We're not prepared to pay that much," he whispered, through clenched teeth.

"That's too bad because it's non-negotiable," Ping Lau said. "What you want me to do is going to bring so much heat, I shouldn't even consider it."

"If you know what's good for you, you'll take the money and be happy."

Ping Lau considered his gaze and what she saw put her off for a minute. There was no soul in his eyes, and she knew he would just as soon have her killed as the three individuals he wanted her to terminate.

"Look, General, you stand to make a hundred times what I'm asking to be paid if I'm successful and I will be," she said.

He considered her for a moment. "I could just as easily have *you* terminated," he drawled.

"We're done here." She slammed her fists on the table, stood up and waved away the startled Cindy. "You can find someone else. And if you make a move on your threat you'd better have your wife, your mistress on Thirty-Eighth Street, and your seven grandchildren well hidden. Because I *will* find them and it won't be pretty when I do."

She got as far as the elevator when he caught up with her. He made the mistake of grabbing her wrist and she twisted his arm back behind his back and shoved him into a wall as the elevator pinged.

"Please," he said. "I came to apologize."

She released her grip as the elevator door opened and two men in suits stepped out. Both eyeballed her, taking in the show meant for The General. They stared for a short time and smiled at her. Meanwhile, The General grimaced and rolled his shoulder.

"Let's go back and finish our lunch," he said. "I'm sorry. I forgot with whom I was dealing."

Damn right, she thought. Of course, her actions had all been calculated in advance. She wouldn't take any shit when he balked at her price, and she would demonstrate her abilities if she got the chance.

"I *did* have my heart set on their turkey and avocado sandwich." She offered a playful smile, partially to let him know she wasn't angry, but mostly to keep him off balance. After they had eaten, she broached the price again and he sighed.

"I have a consortium of sorts from whom I must get approval," he said when they were seated. "We all know of your reputation, but it's a lot of money."

She shook her head. "It's peanuts compared to what you spent to finance the Tea Party movement, which didn't really work out well for you did it?" The General's face reddened and she could see she landed a solid blow to his pride.

"So here is how it plays out." She took a pen out of her purse and doodled on a napkin. "The first target goes down here. She drew a big square and added an *X* in the middle of The Square.

"The second target will follow in a week over here." She drew a dollar sign in the first letter in the word Seattle and circled it twice.

"You will be notified before each operation goes down. Shortly after the second contract is completed, I will drop out of sight for a while. A month later, when things cool off, the crucial target will be dealt with."

"How will things cool off? I mean, you're going to have the federal government standing on every street corner in the downtown area, searching for you. And our main target will likely cancel his appearance."

"If we can't do it here, I'll find another place to make it happen," Ping Lau said. "This is a new concept for me, and I need to have a few practice sessions to make sure it will work for our main target. I have a plan in place that should reassure the Feds that Portland streets will, once again, be a safe place for all concerned."

He brushed some bread crumbs from his sleeve and peered through the window across downtown Portland. "If you could just tell me how you plan to accomplish this, I might be able to sell your price to my group of, ah, investors."

She leaned toward him and whispered into his ear and he smiled. "That should work. Yes, that should work."

Chapter 4

Angel came to work about nine Monday morning, while I was nursing my third cup of coffee. I heard the front door open and the thud of her oversized bag making contact with her desk in the lobby of my office.

Angel is thirty-something and stands five-foot-four inches in heels. Her eyes are green and it's about the only color I haven't seen her hair. It's been pink, orange, raven with purple highlights, blonde with orange streaks, cherry, and any other color you can find in the rainbow spectrum. Not green because she says that would clash with her eyes.

She usually packs about three guns on her person at a given moment and has a dysfunctional smoking problem. She quit.

"Billie, I'm here," she called. "Where are you?"

"In the kitchen," I said.

"OH, MY GOD!" She cupped her fingers to her mouth. "What happened to you?"

I must have looked a sight. My bruised arm was in a sling and I had sidewalk rash on my chin and a black eye. "I got buzzed by a toy helicopter and shot at by a crazy lunatic." I adjusted my left arm in the sling.

"When did this happen?" she asked.

"Early Sunday morning."

She threw her hands up in the air. "Why didn't you call me?"

I shrugged and grimaced at the pain. "I figured you would be busy. I've been working you long hours during the past few weeks, and I knew you and Chris haven't had much time together."

She blushed. "We weren't busy. Well, if you don't count all the hours we were in bed together."

"See. I didn't want to bother you."

Angel sighed and adjusted my sling, which stopped the shooting pain spasms. She ushered me into the front room and made me sit back in my leather recliner.

"Now tell me what happened and don't leave anything out," she said.

I told her about my run early Saturday morning and my encounter with the remote-controlled helicopter on the sidewalk. And about the repeat performance Sunday morning with the added bonus of being attacked by the drone, run down by the car and shot at by a driver I couldn't see.

Angel shook her head. "Why can't you ever let things go?"

"Because the damn helicopter almost decapitated me and I wanted to get even."

"What are we going to do about it?"

That's my Angel. She's probably the second toughest woman I know, next to me.

"I'm not feeling much like doing anything about it right now," I said. "Steve said he'd have a patrol car cruise by Pioneer Square a couple of times this morning, but I doubt they'll find anyone. Whoever it was, wasn't in The Square yesterday, she was down by Burnside somewhere operating the drone by remote control."

Angel's mouth gaped. "It was a woman? Billie, you can't just let this go."

"I think the person responsible for the attack on me was flying her contraption on the weekend because the streets are empty in the early morning. On weekdays there would be more witnesses downtown, even at four or five."

I shifted my arm to a more comfortable position. "I called an old high school chum this morning. He's agreed to give me a tour of his drone factory later today and educate me a bit on the technology this woman is using."

"That's it?" Angel said. What about the crazy drone woman?"

"What can I do? Maybe next weekend we could stake it out again."

"Why did she shoot at you?" Angel asked.

"I would guess because she didn't want me sticking my nose into her business."

"That can't be a good thing," Angel said.

Senator John Stanton stood on what looked like a red, white, and blue square trampoline in the center of thousands of people in Four

Freedoms Park on Roosevelt Island in New York City. The stage was fifty feet in each direction with television cameras and media members entrenched in a moat-like wall around him.

Stanton was not one to be dwarfed by the huge stage or crowds. He stood six-foot-six inches tall and talked in a steady, confident, booming voice, which easily carried to the far corners of his audience. His black hair glistened in the sunlight and his blue eyes sparkled enough to be seen ten rows back.

"We have spent too many wasted years arguing over issues that have no relevance in our society," Stanton said. "Hatred, bigotry, and other messages designed to make some people feel better at the expense of others have torn apart the fabric of America and hurt the very people who are repeating this hate-speak.

"And where has it gotten us. We are falling behind the world in so many areas because our government cannot agree on one thing."

The crowd cheered.

"Seriously, when is the last time you felt like you were getting ahead in life? Each generation hopes their children will be better off financially and educationally than they were. But this may not only be the first generation where our children are not better off than we are, it may be the first time many of *us* are not better off than our parents.

"We only have to look at the plummeting middle class and compare it with the ultra-rich one percent of our population to realize there is something wrong with the Capitalistic system which used to promise a financial reward for hard work. Today, those of us who are working hardest can see our reward going . . . to banks, to investment firms, and to insurance companies."

The crowd roared its approval.

"There is something wrong with an economy that takes from the hardest workers and gives to the largest corporations because they make the rules."

Stanton had to pause while the crowd cheered again. "It is time for us to change the laws to benefit the American people."

The crowd surged toward the stage and Stanton smiled. He looked over the masses and could feel the adrenaline coursing through his veins, as the audience cheered. He couldn't believe a year ago he didn't stand a ghost of a chance to get the nomination for president. Somehow his common-sense ideas resonated with a majority of the

Independent Party faithful in the primaries and a month ago he found himself in a two-way race for his party's nomination.

His messages were earnest and sincere. The Republican Party had achieved nothing during the tenure of the last President, and the Democrats achieved little more. The country had been at a stalemate for the last twelve years and voters were irate.

His messages sounded trite, but he believed in these idealistic goals and it appeared his sincerity had won over voters from both major parties.

It was odd to see some No/Republican Party signs being held in the crowd along with hundreds of No/Democratic signs. He learned these people were disgruntled Republicans and Democrats ready to switch to the Independent Party to vote for him.

He had connected with a moderate wing in the Republic party, which up until now had been considered all but dead, and he had even attracted some Conservatives with his messages of inclusion.

"Billie? Have you got a minute? I think we have another case."

You would think after my recent ordeal I would deserve a little time off, but Angel apparently had other ideas. It was Friday, and I had made it through most of the week without doing any physical activity, but my body still ached at times.

"Can it wait till next week?" I asked. "I need more rest."

"Well, I wanted to talk to you about it," she said. "Chris and I are going to take the licensing test for private investigators next month, and I thought maybe we could take this case."

Cripes, that's all I needed. Angel and Chris have been bugging me for the past month to give them some field experience. I've been putting them off, but I should have flat out told them no.

The last thing I need is to get Bonnie and Clyde together again and turn them loose on an unsuspecting public. In one of my earlier cases, they decided to scout out a home they thought some Facebook burglars might hit. Problem is, the homeowners were out of town so Chris and Angel let themselves in.

Angel brought back an expensive antique bracelet and Chris lifted a Rolex. I had quite the time returning the items and promised myself then I would never let them go into the field again. But what could I do if they took the licensing test?

Chris was arrested once, but later he successfully sued the city of Portland and one of the conditions of the settlement was to have his record expunged. I still don't know how he pulled it off.

"I don't think so," I said.

"Come on, it's a simple case. Mrs. Andrea Green wants us to follow her husband and catch him doing the nasty."

"Then absolutely not," I said. "We don't do those kinds of domestic cases. It's beneath us."

"Speak for yourself," Angel said. "It would give me great satisfaction to nail her bastard of a cheating, low down, snake-in-the-grass, husband."

Angel was a little jaded here because her ex-boyfriend Earl, who still persists in hanging around, cheated on her. Earl's a P.I. and part-time tow truck driver, and he claimed he was working a case but no one bought it, especially Angel.

"It's an easy case and Mrs. Green will pay a $500 bonus if we get pictures."

I glared at her.

"Okay, okay. I'll tell her we don't do domestics. Chris will be disappointed. I sort of called him and told him you would let us work it. He was going to go to a pawn shop today and buy a camera."

"Angel!"

"Well, you can't blame a girl for trying." She closed the door behind her and I hissed a sigh of exasperation.

Angel patted her hair, which was a cross between orange and pink today, ostensibly to keep it in place. "Mrs. Green?" she spoke into the phone. "Billie is tied up on another case right now, but she's authorized me and another operative to take your case."

"Will that cost me extra for two private investigators?" Mrs. Green asked, at the other end of the phone line.

"Not a bit," Angel said. She hoisted her hand to her mouth to take a phantom puff of a cigarette that no longer nestled between her two fingers. She had quit smoking after nearly twenty years, at Billie's insistence, but old habits die hard. Under stress, she still resorted to old routines and she hated it.

Lying to Mrs. Green and disobeying Billie's wishes made her want to light up. Chris sat next to her desk and whispered suggestions.

She caught him smirking at her ghostly drag and made herself put her hand on her lap.

"We'll come by with some papers for you to sign later tonight. Will that be okay?"

"Sure," Mrs. Green said. "My husband, Gerald, called earlier and said he wouldn't be home until late. But maybe we'd better meet somewhere else just in case. How about the Starbucks near your office?"

"Fine, let's meet at seven," Angel said. "You can fill us in."

"Did we get the job?" Chris asked, smoothing his gelled hair back with both hands.

"Yes, but I don't feel good about it," Angel said. "I don't like lying to Billie."

"She'll get over it when she sees how good we do," Chris said. "We have to prove ourselves to her so she'll have more confidence in our abilities."

"I suppose," Angel said. "But I still don't like it."

Chapter 5

A Month Ago

Ping Lau stepped out of her rented Lexus and surveyed the factory. It was located in an industrial park in West Linn and took up about half a block. The sign overhead had a graphic of an airplane flying upside down over the words *Flying Circus Aeronautics.*

Soon a sign would say *Out of Business*, she thought.

She had scouted various drone technology plants on the web and had been impressed by the inventiveness of this one's creator, Brett Wright. Off to the right of the building was a paved circular pad painted with triangle, circle, and diamond shapes. A man and woman set two miniature helicopters on the pad and appeared to be adjusting the drones' blades.

Inside, Ping Lau was met by a receptionist sitting behind a small desk in the lobby. The woman had vibrant red hair and wore bottle glasses, blue jeans and a gray polo shirt with the *Flying Circus* logo.

My name is Kim Wu," Ping Lau said, not wanting to use her real name for this meeting. "I have a two o'clock appointment with Mr. Wright."

"Brett will be with you in a moment. He's just finished up a conference call." The receptionist never looked up at Ping Lau. She drew something on an iPad with a stylus. Ping Lau crooked her neck at an angle to watch. The receptionist's fingers danced around the frame, dotting certain points on the iPad with an index finger and lines magically appeared.

It appeared to be a schematic of an airplane, Ping Lau guessed, although it looked more like a futuristic spacecraft with short stubby wings hugging the body. When the woman finished, she narrowed her eyes at the design and smiled.

"Quite a drawing," Ping Lau said. "You are very talented."

"Oh, this is only one layer," the other said. "I'll add in the motor, wiring, and battery compartments on a separate design layer, with individual schematics of the engine, camera, other power sources, and cables to operate the wing and tail flaps. Altogether there will be fifteen layers and twenty individual mechanisms."

"That's quite impressive work for a receptionist," Ping Lau said.

"I'm an aeronautical engineer," she said, offering her hand in a greeting. "Jessica Nelson."

Ping Lau shook her hand and offered a puzzled look. "Oh, I thought you were a receptionist."

"Just filling in," Jessica said. "Nan is taking a late lunch and we all help out wherever we're needed."

A few minutes later Jessica ushered her into a small office where Brett Wright sat behind his makeshift desk. It consisted of a door straddling two saw horses. On it were miniature plastic pieces, circuit boards, wiring and a shell of what looked to be a remote-control helicopter.

"Miss Wu, a pleasure to meet you," Wright said, extending his hand. Strands of sandy blonde hair crowded his boyish face. He wore casual brown slacks, a white shirt, and a loosened blue tie with icons of airplanes and helicopters. She noticed his muscular arms and trim stomach and guessed he worked out regularly.

"I hope this isn't too much of an inconvenience." She clasped the fingers of his hand and shook them.

"I like to show off our facilities to visitors, especially visitors as lovely as you." Wright had received a call from a Riley Jones in the defense department, who asked him to show Kim Wu around his facility as a favor. He didn't know Riley Jones, but he had several government contracts up for consideration, and he wanted to do anything that might assist him in the process.

Ping Lau offered a demure smile. "This isn't an official visit. I'm not a member of the government, but a friend there looked you up in their database and referred me to you as a favor."

"Oh?"

Wright seemed more than a little perturbed. He had probably spent a rushed week getting the factory cleaned up in preparation for her visit, hoping it was a prelude to getting government business.

Ping Lau had come ready to meet disappointment. She wore a tight-fitting red dress with a short skirt and a plunging neckline. The girls were halfway to freedom and her shapely legs had already caught his attention. She brushed her silky raven hair off her milky white neck and smiled at him.

"My friend said you were the best drone builder on the west coast, and I couldn't go wrong visiting you," she said.

"Just what can I do for you, Miss Wu?" A smile grew on Wright's face. His crinkled forehead relaxed and his boyish enthusiasm returned.

"I hope I'm not being an imposition." She reached across his desk and put her hand on his forearm. "I'm afraid I'm no more than a retail customer."

His face reddened and Ping Lau could see her flirtatious gestures were having the desired effect. "I had hoped to buy a drone from you for my niece in Maryland. She's kind of a nerd and is really into remote-control aircraft. She says she hopes to someday become an aeronautical engineer."

"I see," he said. "What did you have in mind?"

Ping Lau pulled a sheet of folded paper from her oversized purse. "I have a list her mother gave me." The folded list added a bit of realism to this lie, she thought.

Wright took the paper and read it. "A programmable quadcopter, controller, camera, and goggles with first-person viewing, and an autopilot system?" He looked up from the page at Ping Lau.

"She wants to be able to change her remote-controlled helicopter into a drone," Ping Lau said. "She said she could fly with her drone and see where it goes and even control it with the goggles."

"This is a fairly high tech for a child. How old is your niece?"

"She's turning sixteen next week." Ping Lau said.

"I'd say she's a pretty advanced student," Wright said. "With an autopilot system, she can drop the module into any remote-controlled aircraft and it becomes a programable drone."

"I was hoping to keep the costs under two thousand dollars," Ping Lau said. "Oh, and a friend said you can get these kits that will break down and fit into a suitcase. Is that possible?"

He tilted his face and smirked. "That's pushing it. Three thousand would be closer in the retail world, but I can probably make you a deal."

"Oh, I don't want any favors," she said. "I insist. I will pay the full freight."

He spent the next hour showing her through the factory, and she saw a robotic-powered assembly line, a design area with people in white coats squinting at iPads, and a playroom for employees with ping pong tables, food, and video games consoles.

He took her outside to a small helipad with painted triangles, showed her how to put her kit together and even gave her a flying lesson. They laughed at her amateurish attempts and, at one point, he had to wrestle the controls from her to avert a crash.

She had him right where she wanted him. She had flown quadcopters before and was close to being an expert flyer. But she needed his designs and gullibility to make her plan work.

"Will this quadcopter be able to navigate around objects by itself?" she asked. "You know, if it started to crash into a mailbox or something—would it be able to take evasive action?"

"Not really," he said. "I have one that can do that. It's just gone up for sale, but it would add a hefty price hike to your birthday present. "

"Oh," she said in a deflated tone. "How much more?"

"Probably another five-hundred-dollars."

"I see," she said. "Why so much?"

"It's a new prototype just released to the market, called the Bat-One. It uses sonar device technology to avoid objects even in the dark. It can stop the vehicle on a dime and change course in a millisecond. We're working on another model, the Bat-Two, to be used in delivery technology. Amazon, Walmart, and UPS have indicated a desire for such a model."

"My niece will be disappointed that she isn't up on the latest technology but she'll live," Ping Lau said.

"Let me give it to you at no further cost," he said. When she started to protest, he touched her arm and smiled. "She can give us reports on how it works. Tell her she would be a Beta tester."

"But isn't it already available to the public?" Ping Lau asked.

"Yes, but we're always interested in getting feedback to learn how to make things better. She'll be doing us a favor."

"I don't know how I can ever repay you for your generosity," she said.

"How about dinner tonight?"

Back in her rented Lexus, she let herself relax and recall her achievements. She bought a complete drone package, which was now in the trunk of her car. He had given her step-by-step instructions on how to put it together and disassemble it, so she could carry it in a small carrying case.

She had paid him cash instead of using a traceable credit card. The deal came with a dinner date with him that night at the Portland City Grill.

She pulled off of the road a mile away from Flying Circus Aeronautics and dug into her purse, retrieving a very powerful credit card scanner. The Vivotech RFID credit card reader, she bought on eBay for fifty dollars, had wirelessly read and recorded twenty-four credit card numbers.

She would use a $300 card-magnetizing tool to encode that data onto blank cards and purchase whatever she needed on counterfeit cards on the internet or in retail stores. Ping Lau read down a list displaying 24 credit card numbers on the scanner screen, complete with expiration dates and CVS numbers.

The credit card numbers were automatically captured during Ping Lau's tour of the factory. But there were only three credit cards she wanted. They belonged to Brett Wright, sole owner and proprietor of the Flying Circus Aeronautics firm and she planned to put them to good use.

After Angel and Chris left for the day, I sat in front of my fireplace watching the gas-fired flames lick the window and contemplated what other young single women were doing on a Friday night. I was feeling sorry for myself because I was alone and wondering if I made a mistake cutting things off with my ex-boyfriend. I thought about calling Steve about a hundred times after we broke up, but I wanted more than meaningless sex. I wanted intimacy, something he couldn't offer.

I got up and put on a light coat, deciding to go for a walk. I settled on strolling down Southwest Twenty-Third Street with its restaurants, bars, and retail shops. I watched young lovers coming and going, holding hands and standing in line at some of the more popular eateries.

Sigh. If only *I* could find Mr. Right. Was he looking for me too? I shivered in a cool breeze and headed toward Starbucks to get a Caramel Brulée Latte. I needed something sweet in my life.

I stood outside Starbucks, looking in through the window at the menu when I saw them. Chris and Angel, sitting cozy-like at a corner table, nursing a couple of lattes. Shit. Another romantic couple. Was I the only single woman without a date tonight?

I decided not to bother them and turned away. McMenamins Rams Head was a block down the street. I decided to trade my latte for a beer. Or three.

Mrs. Andrea Green returned with her coffee and sat down with Chris and Angel. She was in her mid-forties, tall, with raven hair, and cold blue eyes. She slid her fur coat onto the back of her chair and glared at a couple of hipsters looking sideways at them and her coat.

Angel was surprised Mrs. Green would venture into the Pearl District in a fur. She remembered a furrier had been established in Portland for fifty years and how it had been driven out of business by PETA demonstrators. Portland was a magnet for vegans, animal rights activists, and micro-breweries.

"Let's get down to business," Mrs. Green said. "I'm going to a concert at the Schnitzer later and I don't want to be late. You have some papers for me to sign?"

"Let's talk about price first," Angel said. "Our rates are $500 a day with a three-day minimum for this type of work."

"That seems a bit steep," Mrs. Green said.

"It's a standard rate," Angel explained. "We'll be working long hours of surveillance during the day and night."

"It can be dangerous too," Chris said. "You never know how a subject will react if he spots someone watching him."

"I would think you wouldn't get caught if you were any good," she said.

Angel wished Chris would keep his mouth shut and let her do the talking. "It can happen when we get close enough to photograph him or get him on video."

"Oh, I see. Do you think you can get him on video?"

"Of course," Chris said. "We guarantee it."

Angel stomped on Chris's foot with her four-inch heels.

"Ouch!" Chris tried to regain his composure, and Angel gave him a dirty look.

"What Chris meant, is we'll do our best. We can't really guarantee anything. It depends on the situation."

"I think I'd like the video of him and his girlfriend," Mrs. Green said. "Get them in the act and I'll pay a bonus of one-thousand-dollars."

"It's a cinch," Chris said.

"Chris!" Angel said.

"What? We can do it. I have a few ideas."

"Then it's a deal," Andrea said. "Here's three days in advance. If it takes longer, I'll pay as we go." She handed Angel fifteen one-hundred-dollar bills. Here is a picture of Gerald and his bimbo girlfriend, Veronica. I got it from her Facebook page."

Angel opened a manila folder and scanned the pictures. Gerald was a charmer. He had wavy sandy-brown hair, a wide grin, blue eyes, and wore a blue suit in the photo. "It's his Real Estate photo," Andrea said.

Angel nodded and picked up Veronica's picture. She was an attractive blonde, green eyes, cute nose, long face and she wore a red blazer. Andrea rolled her eyes. "She's a receptionist at Crowe Realty, where Gerald works."

"Why do you think he's having an affair?" Angel asked.

"A friend of mine is a Realtor with Swanson Realty." She dabbed her hanky at her eyes and stifled a sob. "She says it's common knowledge. She saw them at an opening, a few weeks ago, pawing at each other."

"He works out in the Woodstock area?" Angel said.

Andrea nodded. "He used to work closer to home, but about a year ago he up and switched offices. That should have been a tip-off. It's where *she* works. Realtors change offices periodically, but usually to get a better split on their commissions. Gerald couldn't give me a reason for leaving Springbrook Realty. He just said he needed a change."

"I've got the perfect cover," Chris said. "We go in as husband and wife and tell him we want to buy a house."

"No," Angel said. "It's better if he doesn't meet us. If we bump into him during surveillance, he won't know us."

"I don't know. I think it would be a good opportunity to interview him about his habits and stuff," Chris said.

"We can talk about it later." Angel lifted her phantom cigarette to her mouth and began to wonder if she made a mistake teaming up with Chris. He was a sweetheart but had no intuition about how to go about being a private investigator.

"I'll leave the details to you," Andrea said. "Just be sure and get the dirt."

"Don't worry," Chris said. "We'll bag the baddie."

Angel glared at him.

"What?" he said. "I've heard you use that phrase several times."

She sighed and stood up. "We'll get to work on this first thing in the morning. Will he be in the office tomorrow?"

Andrea thought for a minute. He doesn't normally go in on Saturdays, but I think he has buyers coming in at ten. He said he has two or three houses he wants to show them."

"Good." Chris winked at Andrea. "We'll pick him up at the office and follow him."

Angel gave Chris a stern look. "I think we'd better pick him up at his home. You know, in case he is lying about showing homes to buyers tomorrow."

"Oh, yeah," Chris said.

"He usually leaves around nine when he works on Saturdays." Andrea sniffed and put her hanky in a tan, pebbled Tory Burch satchel purse.

Angel wondered if she was worried about her husband or the end of her extravagant lifestyle if Gerald dumped her. That's why she's hiring us, Angel thought. To protect her investment.

"We'll be there at eight," Angel said.

"Yeah. At eight," Chris said.

Chapter 6

But Angel and Chris pulled up to Andrea and Gerald Green's home at seven-thirty-five the next morning in her lime green VW Beetle. It was not exactly a good car for a stakeout, Angel thought. When she bought it, she hadn't planned to use it for undercover work. Becoming a P.I. had only recently become an option.

"I don't know why we had to get here so damn early." Chris juggled two coffees and a bag of bagels in the passenger seat. "Andrea said he never leaves before ten."

"She said he usually leaves at nine for work, and I'm not going to take a chance on missing him the first day of our new job." Angel took a coffee from Chris and fished out a bagel from the bag on his lap. "Stakeouts may be the most boring part of being a private investigator, but they bear the most fruit."

As if on cue, the garage door cracked open and a red Ford Escape backed down the driveway.

"It's him. Hah, he's leaving earlier. I told you so." Angel dropped her bagel on the floor and slipped her coffee into a cup holder.

Chris grumbled something about going home to bed as Angel shifted the little green car into gear. The Escape was two blocks ahead of them before she managed to get the VW into third gear.

"Don't get too close," Chris said. "We don't want to be spotted."

"No problem. He drives like an Indy car driver. I'm just trying to keep up."

"Don't lose him," Chris said. "He's getting away."

Angel rolled her eyes, stomped on the gas, and took a corner on two wheels, resulting in Chris squeezing his coffee cup to the point the lid popped off.

"Shit, I've got hot coffee all over me. Damn! Slow down, you're burning me."

"Speed up, slow down. Make up your mind." Angel took a hard left and more coffee spilled onto Chris. "Sorry." This is more like it, she thought, heartened by the near high-speed chase and chuckling at Chris.

A minute later, they caught up to Gerald, who apparently decided not to run a red light, braking at the last second.

Unfortunately, there was no traffic and she pulled up right behind him. Angel could see Gerald glancing in his mirror and she turned away toward Chris.

"He spotted us," she said. Chris was mopping up spilled coffee from his lavender-striped long-sleeve shirt and gray slacks with a single napkin which came with his coffee.

He looked at her helplessly. "I say let him go. It's too dangerous riding shotgun with you."

A few minutes later, they saw the red Ford Escape pull into a driveway of a modern one-story building in the Woodstock area. The sign on the building said Crowe Realty.

Angel drove slowly past the building, pulled into a bank parking lot across the street, and parked behind a small shade tree.

"Hey, he went to work," Chris said. "I thought he was going to pick up his girlfriend."

"She's a receptionist here," Angel said. "Maybe they're hooking up before the office opens."

"Yeah. Maybe he's going to do her in the boss's office." Chris reached into the cramped backseat and retrieved his camera bag. "I wonder if I can get a shot through a window."

"I doubt it," Angel said. "Anyway, I don't see another car in the lot. He's probably alone."

Twenty minutes passed as the two waited anxiously. Chris wanted to play around, but Angel kept him at arm's length. At first, it was playful with some giggling. "Stop, Chris. Be serious." Eventually, it turned into a demanding "Stop it!" and Chris spent the next 10 minutes sulking.

At eight-fifteen, a blue Honda Acura pulled into the still empty parking lot and parked next to Gerald's Escape.

Chris sat up in his seat. "Is it her? Veronica?"

"I don't think so. Angel peered through binoculars. "This one has red hair." She lifted a photo Andrea had given here. "According to her

Facebook photo, she's a blonde. Also, the redhead has a thinner face and build. Veronica is curvier."

"Maybe he's cheating with more than one woman," Chris said.

"Or she's another real estate agent going into the office," Angel said.

Chris opened the car door with his camera in hand. "I'm going to sneak around the building and see if I can catch them doing the nasty."

"Chris, don't . . ." But before she could finish the sentence he was bounding across the street like an awkward gazelle.

"Hi, Gerald, sorry I'm late." Betty wore a knee-high blue dress with tiny white polka dots. She adjusted its hem and smiled. Will this do for looking at houses? I mean, we aren't going mucking in the mud or anything, are we?"

Gerald laughed at her sense of humor. "I think it will do just fine."

"Where are we going today?" she asked.

"We have three homes to tour. The owners will be gone for an hour at each one. We should be in and out before they return, as long as we stay on schedule."

"Okay," Betty said. "You're the boss."

A few minutes later they exited the building and climbed into Gerald's Ford Escape. If Gerald had looked in his rear-view mirror as they pulled out of the driveway, he might have seen a man, with a camera dangling from his neck, tripping over his feet on-route to a lime green VW Beetle.

"Hurry up, they're getting away," Angel said.

Chris stumbled into the passenger seat and closed the door on his foot. "This damn –ugh-- car is too small."

She put the car in gear and they lurched out of the bank parking lot, Chris bumping his head on the ceiling and Angel cursing under her breath. The Escape was three blocks ahead and leaving them further behind. Angel swore again and put the little Beetle into fourth gear. The engine revved loudly but they didn't go much faster. Angel cursed the four-cylinder engine.

"I think we lost them," she said. "I don't see their car."

"Turn right at the next block," Chris said.

She did and spotted them at a stoplight three blocks ahead. "Did you get anything?" she asked.

"They weren't inside long enough. I got a couple of shots through a window, but it was too dark. I don't think I got anything." He raised the camera to look at the LCD screen.

"The next time you might try taking the lens cap off," Angel said.

"Oops."

"This home is owned by a young couple with two children," Gerald said, as he accessed the lockbox and opened the front door with its key. "I should warn you, they have nanny cams in several rooms in the house."

"Okay, I won't steal anything," Betty joked.

"What would you like to see first?"

"Oh, the kitchen," she said. "I need a lot of counter space."

"Okay. There are no cameras in there, so feel free to check it out."

"Woohoo! A kitchen island," Betty said. Now, this is what I need."

She reached down and pulled her skirt up over her head, revealing a sexy lace bra and matching panties. "Will you help me up?"

Gerald dropped his pants and wriggled over to her. He lifted her up onto the counter and smiled. His goal was to boink Betty in three houses in three hours and it actually was going to happen.

Betty smiled at him and tossed her red hair back playfully. "All aboard."

The two would-be P.I.'s sat in the car for the first few minutes puzzling over what to do. They decided to take a listing flyer and snoop around outside like potential buyers. They snooped into the windows, they snooped around back, and they even snooped through basement windows.

But they couldn't find Gerald or the redhead. In the end, they decided to go back to the car rather than attract the attention of the neighbors. Angel drove around the block and parked further up the street.

About fifteen minutes later, the couple came out of the front door looking very proper and very professional. The redhead pointed back to the house and appeared to ask a question, which Gerald seemed to answer.

They got into the Escape and drove off.

"I think he's showing her houses," Chris said.

Angel sighed and lifted her fingers to her lips and sucked on a phantom cigarette. "You think?"

"Yep. He might be flirting or thinking about having a thing with her, but he'd have to be careful. If she's a client, he could wind up in big trouble."

They followed the Escape to another home about ten minutes away. This one was a ranch style, which offered more possibilities to spy than the two-story home. Angel didn't attempt to pass the house. She pulled up to the curb a block away and parked.

They got out of the VW and walked up to a plastic box hanging from a post near the curb. "This one has less square footage," Angel said. "Fifteen hundred versus the twenty-two hundred at the last house had. Don't you think that's odd?"

"Not really," Chris said.

"This house is so much smaller and it's fifty thousand dollars less than the other house. Seems to me a person would settle on a range of square footage and price that's not so lopsided."

"Maybe she's just starting and not sure what she wants," Chris said.

"Yeah, but if she's single why would she want a big house? And if she's married or has kids, you'd think this house is a tad small."

"Let's check things out." Chris pulled the camera out of the bag.

"Make sure the lens cap is off."

"Oh yeah. Good idea."

They spotted Gerald and the redhead several times, going through different rooms in the house. Once, Angel thought the redhead had spotted her and she ducked under the window. At that point, they'd been in the house about ten minutes and Angel thought it might be a good idea to clear out before they finished.

Chris followed her back to the car, looking at the LCD screen on the back of the camera. "I didn't catch them fooling around, but I did manage to get a good picture of the redhead. Maybe Mrs. Green knows her."

After touring the home, Betty found the perfect spot. Gerald followed her into the two-sink bathroom, with a tub and shower and plenty of counter space. The door closed behind them and Gerald reflected on his good luck.

If Chris and Angel had hung around a few minutes later, they might have heard the sounds of ecstasy coming from the partially opened bathroom window.

It was another thirty minutes before Gerald and the redhead bimbo came out of the house. Angel decided she must be a bimbo to want to spend nearly an hour at each house. Couldn't she see everything in twenty minutes?

The next stop was a mammoth home in the ritzy area of Eastmoreland. Homes here started at over six hundred thousand dollars. The Escape pulled into a circular driveway and Gerald and the redhead walked up to the front door.

A minute later Angel cruised along the curb and stopped in front of a poster-board sign giving the details of the home. "Seven-hundred-fifty-thousand dollars, thirty-five-hundred square-feet, master on the main, hardwood floors."

"It's across from the tenth hole of the Eastmoreland Golf Course," Chris said, motioning across the street.

Angel gazed at the late thirties Mediterranean white-brick home. "Why in the hell would they be looking at this house after the other two dumps?"

"Rack 'em up," Betty said. She lay naked and spread-eagle on the billiard table in a game room with a fireplace and more windows than walls. She liked the fact that any minute a neighbor could happen by and watch their little game.

Gerald was naked too. He shot a white ball between her legs and she cried out: "Doesn't count. You didn't call your shot."

"Eight-ball, center pocket," he said, and climbed onto the slate table.

"Looks like we got nothing to tell Mrs. Green," Chris said.

A police car had passed, as she was reading the listing sign, and Angel decided they stood out too much in this neighborhood. She had parked around the corner on a side street and watched from the car. The bimbo redhead came out about forty minutes later, followed by Gerald, and they tailed the Escape back to Crowe Realty.

Chris wanted to shadow the redhead when they returned to Gerald's office, but Angel thought they should stick with Gerald to see if he had a date after his showings. The Realtor, to their dismay, took them back to his house.

"This was a wasted day," Angel said.

"I can think of a way to salvage it," Chris said.

"What did you have in mind?"

"We could pull over to that wooded area. It would be kind of exciting to do it in the back seat."

"And a little dangerous after following dull Gerald and his bimbo client all day," Angel said. "I'm in."

Chapter 7

I didn't feel very attractive when I drove up to Brett's drone shop in West Linn. I used concealer over my bruised eye and took my arm out of its sling after swallowing a couple of Vicodin.

I opted to wear a sexy green dress with short sleeves, so my banged-up arm was out for display. Well, I just couldn't show up in jeans and a long-sleeve shirt.

"What happened to you?" Brett asked when he ushered me into his office. He stood by me and his boyish smile became serious, his face caring.

"Just comes with the job," I said, trying to sound matter-of-fact.

"Come and sit down." He took me by my good arm and led me to a cushioned office chair. His blue eyes pierced me like an arrow slung by cupid. Was I in love? I hoped so and I hoped it might be mutual. It would be a nice change of pace considering my dating slump.

He pulled a chair close to me and rested his elbows on a desk made from a door and two sawhorses.

"Pretty fancy décor," I said.

"Nice things don't remain nice when I'm working at my desk. I use glues and paints so this setup tends to be more productive."

"I didn't mean anything by it." I smiled sheepishly, realizing maybe I had criticized him.

"No problem, Brett said. "You aren't the first person to remark on the work environment here. This is a factory site. We do everything from designing the remote-control aircraft to building it, testing it, marketing our products. We're small so we rely on our employees to broaden their multitasking skills."

We toured his factory, and I had to admit it was impressive. Outside, I noticed two employees flying an odd-looking beak-nosed plane about three-feet in length with barely any wing to it. They pointed it down a very short runway, maybe twenty feet, and the silent motor barely hummed.

"This model is more like what you might see in war zones," Brett said. "Many of the so-called drones being marketed in the United States are really just remote-controlled toys with a slew of bells and whistles added."

"This one isn't?"

"No. This is Grade-A U.S. military stock. It's a scaled-down model. We're testing it for weight bearing capability. The military would want to add cameras or munitions to it if we succeed in winning a contract."

One of the employees, a petite blonde in blue jeans and a long-sleeve plaid shirt, held a gray remote with two miniature joysticks. Her colleague, a bearded hipster type, tossed the aircraft and it spiraled straight up a hundred feet, hovered momentarily, and zoomed several hundred yards over a green space.

"We own twenty acres here for testing purposes," Brett said.

I nodded absently. "You said many of the drones sold today are actually remote-control toys? Do you think I was attacked by a remote-control toy?" I asked.

"It wasn't a drone for sure," Brett said. But I don't know when you stop calling something like that a toy. From what you described over the phone, it was being controlled from a distance and it had a camera, so the operator could see where it travelled. The fact that it flew at street level means it must have been programmed with an avoidance system."

"Yes. I told you how it just missed decapitating me before suddenly shooting up and over my head. And I saw it cruising up about 15 feet at intersections downtown. I assumed that was meant to keep it from running into a car or truck at the crossing streets."

"That would be consistent with an avoidance system," Brett said. "Likely the drone—yes because of the technology involved—we're going to call this a drone—it is likely this drone was on a pre-programmed route with the operator wearing goggles to view its flight. But the operator can still take manual command of the aircraft at any time."

"I still don't understand why you are calling it a drone now when you were calling it a remote-control toy before," I said.

"From your description, the quadcopter that buzzed you probably cost its owner between four and five thousand dollars. The item that really converts it to drone-like status is the after-market programmable module. I know because we make them too. You can attach these artificial intelligence modules to an unsophisticated quadcopter and it's immediately programmable."

"I read the batteries on these things are extremely limited," I said, trying to impress him with the research I had done before our little get together. "How long would you think this thing could fly? I mean, it seemed to cover a couple of miles downtown."

"Whoever is flying this thing, probably added a two-power Lipo battery upgrade. It would give the copter a twenty-minute fly time. It would be better to have a two-pack battery to ensure at least half an hour. We just came out with a five-power Lipo which will last forty minutes to an hour depending on the aircraft's weight.

"I just sold one to a young woman last month. She was buying it for her niece, who apparently is a huge aviation nerd. The lady and I were supposed to have dinner at the Portland City Grill, but she stood me up. She was on a business trip so I thought maybe she got called out of town suddenly. I guess I was protecting my ego."

"I sure wouldn't have stood you up." I smiled at him and I'm sure there was a twinkle in my eye. "In fact, why don't you let me treat you to dinner for all your help?"

The drone returned and made a majestically short landing on the small runway before either of us had a chance to speak.

"Why don't you let me treat," he said. "I've always felt bad for ignoring you at the wedding a few years ago. I wanted to come over and say hi, but my date was kind of clingy."

"If I remember correctly, you didn't seem to mind too much at the time."

He blushed. "I was a cad. Let me make it up to you."

"I'd like that," I said, in a musical tone that really didn't sound like it came from Billie Bly, the tough P.I.

Senator John Stanton sat in a chair with his feet on a coffee table in a Miami, Florida Ramada Inn suite. He had just finished a grueling five-city campaign tour in the state. His campaign manager handed him a can of Fresca, his go-to drink after a hard day.

Stanton was a recovering alcoholic, a label which could hurt him in his presidential bid. But he used it as another example of how he related to the working man. He wasn't perfect, he told his supporters, but he would do the best he could for his voters.

"We're going to have a visit from The General," his advisor, Greg Graham, said. Graham was a short, pleasant-faced man, with brown hair, in his early forties. He wore black-rimmed glasses and chewed gum at a frenetic pace, resulting in snapping sounds when he became anxious, as he was now.

"I just got a call from his assistant. He just left his suite at the Four Seasons a few minutes ago. He should be here soon."

"Cripes," Stanton said. "What does he want now?"

"The same thing he wanted the last four times you met with him," Graham said. "He's going to ask you to switch from the Independent ticket to the Republican ticket."

"The first time the Independent Party has a real chance to make a difference in this country and both Democrats and Republicans want to interfere," Stanton said.

"They're scared," Graham said. "Your polling numbers are strong."

"Not strong enough to win the office." Stanton took a swig of Fresca and wiped his mouth with the back of his hand.

"But maybe strong enough to steal important votes from both candidates."

"I want to do more," Stanton said. "I want to win the damn thing."

"The presidential election is eight months away," Graham said. "If your numbers continue to improve, you might have a real shot."

Stanton crumpled the empty soda can in his fist and tossed it across the room. It banked off the wall and toppled into a garbage receptacle.

"Two points." He raised two fingers.

In his youth, he played high school basketball and went out for college ball at Stanford as a walk-on. At six-foot-six he had a decent shot and could hit an open man with a pin-point cross-court pass before an opponent could recover. But Stanford had used its quota of scholarships for a couple of potential NBA-bound players who were a bit better and a few inches taller.

He sighed at what might have been. He had maintained his basketball fitness, but he hadn't played a pickup game during the last six months because of his rigorous campaign schedule.

A knock resounded on the hotel door before he could sink too deeply into melancholy. Graham opened the door and retired General William A. Pace marched into the suite in regal fashion. Stanton thought all he needed was the stereotypical riding crop and tried to stifle a grin.

"Senator," he said, and offered his hand in a rigid gesture.

"Hello, General." Stanton's drawl revealed his tiredness and agitation.

"I'm sorry to bother you," The General said. "I'm on my way to D.C. first thing tomorrow and I wanted to see if you had thought about my offer."

"Not really," Senator Stanton said. "It was a non-starter from the beginning."

General Pace's facial features didn't reveal any disdain at Stanton's coldness. "I know we talked about a possible Vice-Presidency if you were to switch parties, but now I think we can sweeten the pot a bit."

Stanton didn't bite, leaving General Pace standing there awkwardly.

Graham cleared his throat. "Out of morbid curiosity, how sweet would this pot be?"

General Pace continued watching Stanton. "I've been caucusing with Republican Party leaders, including the House Chairman, and I think they are ready to offer to support you for the nomination."

"Really?" Stanton could hardly help but smile. "What about Reese, McCarthy, and the other fourteen prospective candidates?"

"Oh, you would have to fight them for the nomination, but I can assure you they won't have the funds we can provide you."

"How much support is the party willing to offer?" Stanton walked across the room and fished out another Fresca from the mini fridge. He popped the top and took a healthy gulp.

"I can guarantee you $30 million seed money to get you started, with a guarantee to match any money the other candidates may raise. Of course, once you win the nomination, you will have all the resources of the Republican Party and Super PACs, which raised over half a billion dollars in the last election."

"And if I lose my bid for the nomination?" Stanton asked.

"Anything is possible," General Pace said. "But you won't lose with our support."

"It is a very generous offer," Stanton said. "But I like my chances on the Independent ticket."

Furrows grew deep above General Pace's brow. "Alone, your chances are slim and none. You may get the Independent Party's nomination but any hayseed could. Once the national elections get underway, you'll be trampled in the dust."

"It's a risk I'm willing to take."

"Why?" he asked.

"Because I've already given my word to quite a few people promising I'd represent them and not the special interests. With your party, as well as with the Democrats, I'd have donors standing in line afterward with their hands out, asking for some form of repayment."

"You're a fool," General Pace said. "You can't win a campaign without special interest groups or PACs. It's built into the system."

"Not my system," Stanton said. "Oh, I'll have to take donations from some special interest groups but only the ones which will help low-income and middle-class workers."

"Ha, you're an idealist!"

"Damn right, and I'm proud of it. My staff is screening our donations and anyone donating money with the idea of enriching themselves down the line is refused. Eighty percent of my donations, so far, have come from individuals planning to vote for me."

"Bah. You can start out as an idealist. Scores of losers before you have had that notion too. In the end, they all wind up taking money any way they can get it. I can give you what you want. A presidency and a chance to make some of the changes you want. All you have to do is change parties."

Graham had been quiet during the discussion and finally offered an opinion. "There is another reason Senator Stanton won't switch Parties."

General Pace whirled around and sneered at him. "I'd like to hear it!"

"He can't," Graham said.

"What the hell do you mean, he can't?"

"I can't renege on my pledge to the Independent Party," Stanton said. "It promised to support me and I promised to do right by the party. I also promised the people I would stand by them. If I were to switch horses now, my supporters would abandon me."

General Pace kicked the waste bin Stanton had scored on earlier and several Fresca cans tumbled out. His face reddened and he spit his words with rapid-fire tenacity. "You are going to be fucking sorry, mister. I'm going to fucking dedicate myself to making your fucking life fucking miserable."

Graham and Stanton chuckled as he stomped out of the suite.

Chapter 8

Ping Lau adjusted the scuba tank on Dave Lambert's back and checked his dive computer. "Everything looks good," she told him. "We should be able to get two hours in, no problem."

"I'll grab my camera from the truck." Lambert was tall and lean. His wavy blond hair blew in the early spring wind. He looked back at his beautiful Asian date and couldn't believe his luck. His worries about her being interested in him because of his money were not a concern. She had no idea of his wealth or station in life. They had met two days before at a fundraiser to save the marine life in Puget Sound.

Now they were entering his glorious sanctum, and he was about to open a whole new world to her. She had never swum in the Puget Sound, despite her years of diving experience. Indeed, this was her first trip to Seattle and what were the chances he would hook up with his potential life partner in the short time she was attending a business convention?

Things had heated up last night. They made love for hours before he finally passed out. In the morning she greeted him in bed with coffee and they went at it again. He was thankful they had planned this excursion because she was wearing him out.

He had pointed his underwater camera at her and faked taking her picture. She posed seductively and smiled at him. Yes, sir, he was one lucky guy. She might even be a soulmate. They seemed to share an abundance of similar interests, the chief one being their politics.

She was definitely a Republican, as judged by their brief sojourn into politics over lunch yesterday. He hadn't told her he was a chief money raiser for the Republican Party's presidential campaign. He didn't want to disclose his skills around money lest it aroused a prurient interest in him. He liked her but he had to be sure she wasn't just after his money.

As it later turned out, she wasn't.

"Follow me and stay close, I wouldn't want you to miss anything," Lambert said. "The water is generally crystal clear this time of year, so once a GPO spots us it will likely cover-up by emitting a cloud of black ink."

"GPO?" Ping Lau said.

"Its local lingo for Giant Pacific Octopus," Lambert said. The Sound is home to the world's largest octopus. The biggest GPO ever recorded weighed in at six hundred pounds and its tentacles stretched over thirty feet."

"I wouldn't want to run into him," Ping Lau said, as they entered the water.

"Don't worry. They are usually gentle, very intelligent, and generally harmless."

Ping Lau took Lambert's hand along the rocky shore and stumbled briefly before succumbing to the water. She plunged underwater behind him and followed his fins kicking in front of her. They swam out a short distance and he suddenly began descending.

She had expected to go further, guessing they were only a few hundred feet from shore. But it *was* deep. In another few minutes, they leveled off. Her wrist dive computer indicated they were at forty-five feet.

Green and purple colored large-leaf vegetation dotted the sandy bottom giving the impression of a royal carpet of colors. White mushroom-shaped fauna, attached to large rocks, swayed gently with the current and small pale-green fish darted around them.

An eight-foot-long grey wolf eel snaked its way toward them. Lambert took something from a side pouch and extended sea urchin treats in his hand. The wolf eel swam lazily toward him, bared razor-sharp teeth, and sucked the meal from his hand. He turned and gestured to her to give it a try. She shook her head and waved them to continue onward.

In the next 30 minutes, they spotted a painted greenling with white convict-suit-like stripes across a muted purple body, a series of various rockfish, and a long-fin sculpin with brilliant reddish hues. Lambert snapped away with his underwater camera as Ping Lau checked her diver watch for the umpteenth time.

He turned toward her and waved his arms wildly. He joined his fingers and took them to his mouth, a diver signal indicating he was out of oxygen and needed some from her. She played dumb and gave him the Okay sign. He placed his palm down and made a cutting motion across his neck. He wanted her to give him her spare regulator or share her air with him.

Fat chance, she thought. This was going to be an accidental drowning with a little help from her. She had tampered with his dive equipment after he fell asleep last night. She emptied half of his air tank and hacked into his wrist dive computer to make it show a false full reading.

Lambert continued with emergency gestures, swimming frantically toward her. She swam away from him, staying out of his reach. He began thrashing toward the surface still about ninety-feet above. She pounced on him and held him back. He tried to grab her air regulator, but she pinned his arms behind his back. He thrashed and tried to spin out of her grasp. He almost escaped with one last frantic adrenaline-fueled spin. But Ping Lau held tight until he quit struggling.

His last air bubbles streamed toward the surface. She let go of his lifeless body and let it sink to the bottom. Below them, stirred an orange giant with an oversized head and tentacles stretching twenty-five-feet across.

The Giant Pacific Octopus didn't release the inky black cloud Lambert had mentioned. She only stared at Ping Lau as if comprehending what she had done.

She tried to pace her return to the surface to avoid decompression, but she was tempted to cheat because she had to be back in Portland by four o'clock. However, she was forced to do a safety stop at the forty-five-foot mark for three minutes.

She ascended another ten feet and rested three minutes. She continued her safety rest stops at ten-foot intervals until she reached the fifteen-foot mark under the surface. Her chest felt heavy so she stayed at that depth for five minutes.

She broke the surface quietly, looking for potential witnesses. By her calculations, she had a fifteen-minute surface swim to her rental car, which was parked half-a-mile south on the beach. She would have to leave David's truck on the beach for the authorities to find. She made sure no one had known about their scuba dive so it would look like he had gone alone and suffered an equipment failure.

Her muscles ached from the combination of the underwater struggle and the day's activities. She day-dreamed of the money she would earn for this job to help fight fatigue during the swim to her car. The demise of the Republican Party's chief money-raiser would net her a cool five million dollars. Not a bad day's work.

She finally reached shore and saw her rental car a hundred-feet up the beach where she stashed it at near an abandoned industrial site's parking lot. She staggered up a rocky incline with Lambert's heavy underwater camera in tow. She had not wanted to leave any incriminating evidence behind. She didn't realize he was only pretending to take her pictures underwater.

The rocky outcrop along the shoreline bruised her feet as the waves threw her petite body off balance. She struggled with the rocks and the waves for what seemed forever before collapsing on the sandy beach. She lay there for several minutes, trying to catch her breath.

She had not realized her escape route would prove so difficult. Her feet ached, and she was pretty sure the sharp rocks had pierced her rubber fins and her feet.

She looked over the beach, hoping no one had noticed her. Off in the distance, maybe a couple of hundred yards, she saw two men running along the beach toward her. She forced herself up and hobbled awkwardly, still toting the underwater camera, toward her car. She threw the camera in the back seat, kicked off her swim fins inside the car and tried to start it.

"Shit," she cried when it failed to start. She looked down at her bloody and bruised feet, and then over her shoulder at the two men, still about a hundred yards away.

"Why won't this fucking car start?" She turned the key again as the joggers began to close in. Her mind swam with potential scenarios, one which included pulling her nine-millimeter Glock from under the seat and killing these two good samaritans when she noticed the automatic stick shift was in drive.

She must have bumped it while she was removing her swim fins. She put it in the park position, switched on the ignition, and grabbed her Glock. Then she did a quick risk assessment. Were they too far away to distinguish she was wearing a wetsuit? If they noticed her attire, they could provide a link to the lone scuba diver's drowning death and the authorities would suspect foul play. Okay, so his death wouldn't necessarily look like an accident, but could these two runners identify her? Not unless she turned toward them now.

She squeezed the Glock and had an urgent desire to let them see her face. She forced herself to put the gun on the seat beside her and sped away as the two men shouted after her. In the rear-view mirror, she saw them, hands on knees, watching her drive away.

Great, she thought. I must be back in Portland in three-and-a-half hours to begin the second part of my plan. She wondered if she could change clothes in her car while driving a hundred-miles-an-hour and bandaging her feet.

Then she wondered if she would be able to be on her feet for six hours or even walk for that matter.

Chapter 9

Ping Lau limped from table to table waiting on customers at the Portland City Grill. She had followed up on her instinct to work here because it fit into her plan. The restaurant was on the thirtieth floor of the of the Big Pink, one stairway from the rooftop.

Ping Lau coveted the rooftop. This was her first night here and she'd already learned the employees sneak up to the roof to grab a smoke. It was better than she had hoped. Not only would it be possible to access the roof, but with remodeling in the building, workers came and went with impunity.

There was no security on the weekends and one could walk in amid long sheets of plastic draped down from the lobby ceiling and take the service elevator to the top floor. She was sure the rooftop door would be locked when the restaurant was closed, but she was adept at coaxing locked doors to open.

"Su Ling? You have guests on your station," Cindy said. "I just seated them." Cindy had told her about the open position here and she must have felt responsible for her. She was always pointing Ping Lau in the right direction, coaching her and making sure she stayed on good terms with the manager.

"Thank you. I'll get their menus." Ping Lau had decided to use another cover name while working at the restaurant. She limped over to a table stacked with menus, hobbled by the cuts she received earlier in the day along the rocky shoreline in the Sound. Without Dave Lambert to show her the best route to her car, she'd made a bee-line toward it in the water, not realizing she'd have to wade through jagged rocks.

She regretted killing Lambert. He was a decent lover and although her plan to tire him out for the swim worked well, she found she'd enjoyed their lovemaking.

She endured Happy Hour on a Friday night at the city's most popular bar. Now, she must suffer four more hours of waiting tables. She would be off but was expected back Sunday morning for their popular brunch.

She couldn't even give her feet the day off tomorrow because she planned to scout the rooftop as a potential launching point for her drone and do some practice flights on a remote strip of Delta Park near the Columbia River.

She took the menu over to table-five and turned up her smile for the couple she was serving. The blonde stared intently into the gentleman's eyes and he at her. Ping Lau didn't recognize the boyfriend right away.

"Good evening," she said in a sugary voice. Best to keep management happy if she planned to use the rooftop.

The woman looked up at her and smiled. She was attractive, her hair barely touched her shoulders. She wore nice mascara, although Ping Lau thought maybe she didn't really need it. Insurance, she thought. Her soft red lipstick over full lips balanced a milky complexion and her blue eyes sparkled in the dim light. Yes, Ping Lau thought to herself. Probably their first date, the way she fusses over him.

The man, also with blonde hair, turned toward Ping Lau and stared with his mouth open.

"Miss Wu? What are you doing here? I thought you were in New York. And why are you working here?"

Shit. It was the nerd from the drone factory. She tried to maintain a steady facade. Tried to control her surprise. "I'm sorry? "My name is Su Ling." She touched her gold name tag with the words *Su Ling* and gave him a beautiful smile which said *you must be mistaken, but I'm happy to serve you anyway*.

"You were at my factory a month ago," Wright said. "I showed you around my plant."

Ping Lau gave him a puzzled look and began speaking in a staccato of Chinese dialogue. This would be a hard sell. She had the shapely hips and buxom figure men didn't forget.

"I'm sure it was you," he said. "I have an excellent memory for faces."

"Maybe I have a twin," she said, leaning heavily on an accent.

"Are you sure, Brett?" the blonde said. "She doesn't seem to recognize you."

He cleared his throat, and Ping Lau saw a glint of embarrassment in his face. "I thought I was. Tell me, Miss, ah Ms. Ling, do you have a niece who wants to be an aeronautical engineer?"

"No nieces," Ping Lau said. "Three nephews. All want to work with computers."

"I like your ring, it's unique, with the black dragon in the center," the blonde said.

"A gift from my grandmother," Ping Lau said, fingering it. She always twisted the ring on her finger when she became nervous.

"Would you like to order, now?" she asked.

"Give us a few minutes with the menu," The blonde said.

Ping Lau nodded, glad for an avenue of escape. She hurried over to Cindy on the other side of the restaurant and tugged at her arm. "Cindy? A favor please?"

"What's the matter, dear? You look like you've seen a ghost."

"You know the couple you just seated?"

"Oh, the lovebirds."

"I think I know the man. He was sweet on a friend of mine and he wouldn't take no for an answer. He practically stalked her. It took months for her to get rid of him."

"That's terrible," she said.

"I was just over there, and he thinks he knows me. I think I convinced him he doesn't, but he may remember me from when he was after Kim. He even called me Kim."

"Don't worry," Cindy said. "Todd wants me to relieve Sally because she went home sick. You can take Sally's area and I'll cover for you."

Ping Lu nodded vigorously. "Thank you so much."

"No problem, dear."

"Please do not broach the subject with him. We don't want to encourage him. He's with the cute blonde tonight, but who knows what motivates him."

"Don't you worry a bit. I'll play dumb if he asks about you."

So, here we were, in a beautiful restaurant thirty floors high with a night view of the Willamette River and thousands of twinkling lights in the background. But *where* were we?

Brett had asked me out, but I wasn't sure if were on a date or, as he said, he was making up for a snub when we met at a wedding a few years ago. In high school, he had been one of the nerds hanging out with the other nerds.

Still, he seemed dressed for a date. He filled out a handsome suit in the shoulders and other areas. His perfectly combed blond hair, charming manners, and sexy smile had my heart doing flip-flops. I thought things were going well until the waitress appeared.

She seemed to unsettle him. Did she remind him of some other woman he lusted after? Of course, being a snoopy P.I., I had to know.

"Who was she?"

"I thought she was a lady who visited my plant a few weeks ago. She certainly is a dead ringer."

"A woman with a figure like hers would be hard to duplicate," I added, not so subtly.

He shook his head. "It has to be her. But why did she pretend it wasn't?"

"Maybe she didn't want you to know she was a waitress. Maybe she has a sister or a twin she doesn't know about."

He turned on his smile again. "Do you think there's another person walking around Portland who looks just like her?"

"It happens," I said. "Why does it seem to bother you so much."

The smile was gone. "I don't know. It seems like my life is starting to spin out of control. First, the identity theft thing and now this person isn't who I thought she was."

"Identity theft thing?"

He took a sip of water and let his eyes wander through the window into darkest parts of Portland. "Yeah. I got my credit card bill today and there were a bunch of charges I didn't make."

"What kind of charges?"

"That's the screwy thing. Some were to my company for parts we supply. I could have taken them home if I needed them. Why would I charge them on my card?"

"I don't think you would." I rested my hand over his hand to soothe him. "You said there were other charges?"

"Those could have been legitimate, except I don't recall ordering them."

"What were they?" I asked.

"Various materials we use in assembling our prototypes and some tubing and small basket materials ordered from a website in Pakistan. The parts would be used for a cradle to hold something like a camera or package. The basket would be a little too big for our needs. We use miniature cameras and wouldn't need such an elaborate structure."

"And you don't remember buying these supplies? Maybe one of the other employees ordered it for a project."

"We have a company credit card our employees can use, but they have to run things by me first."

"Brett, the ring she wore tonight. Did you notice it on the woman who visited your factory?"

"She had a ring but I think it was a gold band."

"She could have twisted it so the dragon wouldn't be noticed," I said.

"Maybe. I really can't remember." He acted like he didn't want to talk about it any further.

"Hello, I'm Cindy and I will be your waitress tonight." I looked up to see a buxom dishwater blonde woman in a short, black skirt with a matching top displaying a good portion of her cleavage.

"Have you had time to decide?"

"What happened to Miss Wu?" I said, attempting to follow up on the former waitress's denial. I was curious whether the lady was lying to us or Brett merely mixed her up with another woman.

Cindy looked genuinely perplexed. "Do you mean Su Ling? She injured her foot today so we switched. My station was more compact which will mean less walking for her."

"Oh. She looks familiar. Has she worked here long?"

"I'm sorry, dear," Cindy said. "We're not allowed to divulge employee information."

But Cindy did not look sorry. She looked satisfied. I changed the subject and we struggled for a minute over the menu. Brett ordered the twelve-ounce boneless ribeye and I went for the smaller eight-ounce center cut filet mignon. We ordered a bottle of red wine and decided on a Northwest Cioppino soup instead of salads.

The prices on the menu were rather high. Over two hundred dollars for our meal was obscene. Brett said he would pay, but I wondered if this evening would be considered a date or something else? Did he bring me here to talk about the thievery on his credit card or to get to know me?

"Brett, maybe I should share the cost of the meal. It's a little much for an apology over a slight that happened years ago."

He turned his charming smile on me. "I don't think it's too much. I've got it."

"Are you going to put it on your expense account?" I couldn't help myself. I kept prying.

"Nope. This isn't a business expense. It's our first date, isn't it?" And he leaned over and kissed me softly on the lips.

"Oh," I said and kissed him back.

Chapter 10

Dear Diary: Last night was fabulous. After the kiss, we didn't talk about credit cards or anything resembling business. We shared our most intimate thoughts and got to know each other better. I no longer need to worry about if we were dating or Brett was just trying to get some free advice. It was definitely a date!

Okay, I don't really have a diary. But last night's events made me want to go out and buy one. After dinner, we drove around and stopped at the airport, of all places, and necked feverishly for over an hour. I would also like to note, other than being a terrific kisser, he was a perfect gentleman.

He drove me home, and we made plans to get together this morning. We were going out to Delta Park to watch some hobbyists fly remote-control aircraft. He said he'd give me a flying lesson and we agreed to talk about his credit card problems and my aerial misadventures.

I had spent an hour tearing through my closet looking for the appropriate model airplane flying outfit and settled on blue jeans (yes, they were tight-fitting) and a long-sleeved grey hoodie sweater with an asymmetric hem which wrapped itself around my waist.

The long sleeves also hid bruises on my arm from my run-in with the crazy helicopter person who sent me flying onto the sidewalk with her SUV. In addition, I applied extra coverup on my cheek around my eye. Last night, the dimly lit restaurant helped me hide my bruises. Today, in the daylight, I needed the extra help. Unfortunately. the coverup made my face look a bit unbalanced. At some point, Brett would notice.

There was a knock at the door and my heart did a bit of a flutter. I've never reacted to a man like this before, even in high school.

I opened the door and Brett stood on my porch with the most beautiful smile. He wore tan chinos and a Superman T-shirt –I told you he was a nerd— under a tan lightweight bomber jacket, and he held a dozen red roses.

"Am I early? I know we said eleven o'clock, but I couldn't wait. I stopped and got these for you and I still had forty minutes to kill. I thought I'd kill them here."

"Oh, thank you," I said, practically gushing. "I just finished dressing, so your timing is perfect." I'd been mooning around the house in anticipation of his arrival for an hour, but I didn't want him to think I was easy. He, on the other hand, was an open book I planned to read at my earliest convenience.

"Come in. I'll put these in water."

He entered, and I saw him scanning the living room as I went to the kitchen. "You have a desk in here he said. And another desk inside the formal dining room. What's with the door?"

"I've converted it to my office." I put the roses in a vase left over from a Christmas bouquet and ran the water over it, spreading out the flowers in a more eye-pleasing arrangement. "The desk in the living room is Angel's."

I needn't have hollered because the next thing I knew he was behind me with his hands around my waist in a delicious hug. "Where do you eat?"

I set the roses on the kitchen counter and turned around to face him, his arms still around me. "We have a little nook over there." I pointed to a small table with four chairs. He gazed into my eyes and said something but I can't remember what.

"We'd better get going," I said. I don't know why I said it. I liked where I was.

We held hands out to his car, a 1964 orange Thunderbird, with a removable T-top, in pristine condition. "This is not the hybrid Toyota we were in last night."

He chuckled and brushed a blond curl from his forehead. "No, this is an eight-cylinder gas guzzler I usually drive in the summer. But I thought I'd push the envelope and show it off today because of the nice sunny weather."

"I would say almost May is pushing summer a bit, but at least you left the top on. It's barely sixty degrees."

He laughed and held the door open for me. Chivalry was not dead. Was that me speaking? I don't usually like people doing things for me. In my business, you have to be tough and not show any weakness. But I was behaving like a schoolgirl around Brett.

"I hope you don't mind this kind of activity on a date," he said, as he pulled away from the curb. "But since you were interested in drones, I thought we could combine a little education with some fun."

"I think it's a splendid idea." Did I say splendid? I sounded like Mary Poppins. Time to change the subject. "I've been thinking about the credit card charges you mentioned last night."

"Really? All I've been able to think about is your delicious smile and then I get weak in the knees."

"I'm trying to be serious, Brett."

"Okay, I give. What were you thinking?"

"First, you should call your credit card company and dispute the charges."

"Already done," he said.

"I can put Angel on the scent. She's pretty good at tracking down identity thieves. We have this young man who comes in and helps us occasionally with computer technology stuff."

"Is he any good?" Brett asked. "I think I have a virus on my computer, but my software programs have been unable to find anything."

"I think he's excellent. He helped me find a serial killer a while back by tracing his IP address through a maze of spoofed addresses."

"Is he available for small things like computer viruses?"

"He's been working on a hologram computer with one of my clients, but he's always available for me. Say the word and I'll have him drop by."

"First, I think it would be best to find this identity thief. I'd like to know how he's gotten my credit card information and why he's using it to buy my products? I mean, does he do this every time he wants to make an online purchase? How many other victims are out there having him use their credit card to buy things from their company? Is it some kind of a capitalistic protest?"

"This is really getting to you," I said.

He pulled the T-Bird into a parking space at the edge of a field covering several acres, turned the car off, and rested his arms on the steering wheel.

"It bothers me when things spin out of my control. I'm an engineer. My world revolves around order. When things become convoluted, it really bugs me."

He looked over the steering wheel at several planes and helicopters buzzing in the sky and he seemed to soften a bit. He noticed me watching him and smiled.

"When I play with my toys if affects me positively. You'll see." He got out of the car and hefted an aluminum shell suitcase from the T-Bird's trunk.

"The person I saw, the one who tried to kill me," I stammered. "She put her drone into a large suitcase on wheels like yours."

"Hobbyists, with complicated setups, might use something like this to make it easier for transport," Brett said. "Some enthusiasts make their own racks for transport, which fit into their car trunk."

He pointed to a homemade two-tier plastic rack in the back of a pickup. "That one would hold two aircraft, probably airplanes, one on top of the other. You see a lot of those."

"I'm sorry. I guess it kind of shocked me to see you pull out a similar suitcase. You don't own a black SUV, do you?"

He laughed. "Just my Toyota, a Mercedes, and this. I *do* own a project pickup parked back at the warehouse I use for transporting gear back and forth, but that's it."

I felt my face flush. "Sorry. When I saw you pull out that suitcase that night flew back to me. The quadcopter, the SUV, the gunshots fired at me."

"Gunshots? You never said anything about someone shooting at you."

I had brushed off Brett's inquiry about my arm in a cast the first time we met at his office. The cast was off during dinner last night, and I'd left out the part about the black SUV running me up on the sidewalk and shooting at me. I went over it with him as he set up his quadcopter.

"No wonder you seemed alarmed," he said when I had finished. "Did you really think I might have been the one who . . . ." He left the sentence unfinished.

"Maybe just for a second. It's the fight or flight thing. I think I might have post-traumatic stress disorder."

He enveloped me in a soft hug. "Was the cast you wore to my office earlier this week the result of this madman who tried to kill you?"

I nodded.

"Is it still tender?" He held my hand gingerly.

"It's better. Just a muscle strain."

"So, if I held you like this would it be okay."

"It would be great."

"And if I kissed you like this, would it be okay?"

He gave me a long soft kiss. I returned the favor as my answer. We smooched a few more times and stood there, him holding me tenderly in his arms.

"I'm sorry you had to go through the ordeal," he said. "It must have been difficult for you to face it alone."

I nodded like a sophomore in high school, and he brushed a kiss along the side of my face.

The next hour was a blur. He set up his quadcopter and gave me lessons on how to fly it. He said I did a remarkably good job for the first time. I'd have to take his word for it. I only remember I didn't crash it and he smiled a lot.

I had developed a huge crush on him, and I was busy enjoying his company, his smiles, and those kisses. I felt like a school girl instead of a hardened P.I.

He made me wear those virtual reality style goggles and I watched the ground from the sky as the quadcopter covered over a mile while he operated the controls.

The I took a turn, flying the copter over the Columbia River to the Washington side and back into Oregon. I loved it, mainly because I could lean against him and smell his aftershave.

He gave me lots of little pointers when I flew it and encouraged me to try stunts and maneuvers. I think I actually *did* do a good job, but my head was full of euphoria where the PTSD had been earlier, so I'm not really sure.

When we finished my lesson, Brett went to the car and brought back a pair of tiny chairs with only three legs and a piece of canvas to plant your butt, and we watched other hobbyists fly their planes. He also had packed a picnic basket with some locally brewed beer and sandwiches. I gave him credit for the romance factor. It had turned out to be a beautiful spring day with the sun warming us.

Some older men flew World War I airplanes measuring eighteen inches long to three feet in length with single and double wingspans. The planes did loop-de-loops and dive-bombed make-believe targets.

A Red Baron German bi-plane chased a British yellow Spitfire, as two friends took turns getting the upper-hand in pretend dogfights. I had to admit, it was a great way to spend an afternoon on a date.

Until reality intervened.

Off to my right, I spotted a quadcopter similar to Brett's in size and equipment. It had the camera and basket under the camera. The operator was on a bluff about a hundred feet high and a hundred yards away.

The quadcopter dropped something off in the distance. At first, I thought part of the copter had fallen to the ground. It circled around the fallen object about fifty feet above the ground and another object fell from the aircraft.

"Brett, that helicopter seems to be falling apart," I said, pointing.

He looked over and watched it hover. "It seems to be flying okay."

At that moment, it flitted upward about twenty feet and sped back toward the operator on the bluff. I couldn't make out the owner's face or gender, but I could see the black SUV parked at the top of the cliff.

"Brett," I cried.

"I see it," he said. "Do you think it's the same SUV which tried to run you over?"

"It's too much of a coincidence to be anyone else."

When the person on the bluff started packing things into the car, we scooped up our chairs and the picnic basket and ran to his Thunderbird. It took us at least ten minutes to find the road leading to the cliff, and when we arrived the black SUV was gone.

"Are you sure this is the same spot?" I asked, knowing the answer.

"We're too late," he said. "Whoever it was is gone."

I made him drive me back to the area where I saw the copter shedding its parts. We searched the area in earnest, but we could find nothing except a dozen or so pinecones.

Brett held one up to his eye. It was a medium-sized pinecone, about six inches tall and two inches in diameter. "What do you think this means?"

"I don't know," I said. "There aren't any trees around here."

"Why would the quadcopter drop pinecones?" he said.

"It doesn't make any sense," I said.

And it didn't at the time.

Chapter 11

I had not ventured back to Pioneer Square since I was assaulted the previous Sunday. Maybe because I didn't feel well enough or maybe I *was* suffering from PTSD and was nervous about returning to the scene of the crime.

But when I saw that Black SUV at Delta Park the previous day, and the person dropping pinecones from a quadcopter similar to one attacking me, something inside snapped. I wanted revenge on the person who tried to kill me.

What was her motive? Yes, I was sure the person driving the SUV was a woman. I also had a niggling suspicion she might be responsible for Brett's identity theft problem. I don't believe in coincidences. And when I learned the waitress at Portland City Grill might be the same person who visited Brett about the time someone stole his credit card, well, *you* do the math.

I sat in my '73 MGB GT sports car, parked on the corner of Southwest Yamhill and Broadway across the street from Pioneer Square. I'd arrived at three a.m. to make sure I didn't miss my target.

My eyes burned and I was about to head home once the sun began its ascent. Darkness gave way to glints of light turning morning clouds into wisps of orange and pink across the sky. But as I started toward Starbucks, a familiar whining echoed up Broadway. I got out of my car and squinted into the ambient light. It was the same quadcopter I'd seen a week ago, and yesterday afternoon, surfing over the sidewalk against a slight wind.

I knelt by the side of my car, so as not to be seen by the aircraft's camera. The quadcopter shot up into the shadows of dawn, and I lost sight of it momentarily until a streetlight caught it circling over Pioneer Square.

It dove hard toward the bricks, pulling up at the last minute, and soared high above The Square again. I got in my car, turned over the engine and drove to the end of the block where I made a left and another left, anticipating where it would go next. I scanned the lower elevation of the brick square looking for the copter's navigator or the black SUV.

Neither was in sight. The copter flew a block down Southwest Sixth Avenue following the same path it had taken last time and then abruptly changed course and returned to Pioneer Square. I pulled over to the curb and watched the show.

The aircraft approached the brick square from an array of angles, each time halting over the southside where layered stairs curved in an arch, giving the impression of a miniature amphitheater.

The aircraft flitted up a side street, zipped around the block, and again returned to The Square. I counted twelve different approaches into the block from as many different angles, sometimes low to the ground, sometimes from high above. Each time it stopped and hovered for a moment about forty feet above in the middle of Pioneer Square.

Before I could decipher the reasoning for the various flight paths, the quadcopter dropped and shot down Sixth Street along the route I'd followed when I was run over. I hurried back to my car and cranked the engine.

This might be the time to mention the intricacies of Betsy, my 1976 MGB. In her day, the nifty little sports car would run forever without a problem. But when you factor in her age, even with a rebuilt engine, you might expect she would have difficulty starting on a cold morning. Never mind she started right up fifteen minutes earlier. That was fifteen minutes ago, and this little car was cold again.

As I cranked on the ignition and smelled the gas flooding the carburetor, the peppy little aircraft sauntered down Sixth Street without a care in the world. I, however, had many reasons to be concerned.

By the time I finally got Betsy going again, the trail was cold. I drove over the same area I had searched a week ago, but this morning, thankfully, there was no black SUV trying to run me over and no wicked female gunman trying to kill Billie Bly.

Somehow, I didn't feel better about it. I was concerned someone was up to something nefarious, and I wanted to know what lay ahead.

Angel and Chris rose early Sunday morning hoping to finally catch Gerald Green in the act of infidelity. They had tailed him three different times during the past week but were unable to catch him with a woman. Mostly, they just cooled their heels outside his office waiting for him to leave.

Tuesday, they followed him at a distance as a caravan of realtors visited seven homes and returned to the office. There were quite a few attractive women in the group, but Gerald didn't seem to be taking advantage of the opportunities as far as they could tell.

Thursday, Angel and Chris snapped a photo of Gerald flirting with a cashier at the local New Seasons grocery. Other than learning the camera worked, there was nothing to report.

Saturday, Gerald chauffeured a smartly dressed woman in and out of homes in the trendy Irvington District. She was in her sixties and Chris said he'd have to be pretty hard up to give *her* a tumble.

Angel was feeling the pressure to get results. Mrs. Green had called twice asking for updates and they had nothing to tell her. Her reply had to do with Chris's earlier comment about having the goods on him.

"Your associate said it would be 'a cinch,'" she said. "He also guaranteed video. So far, I'm out fifteen hundred-dollars with nothing to show for it."

Gerald Green exited his real estate office this Sunday afternoon with a shapely blonde and, for a moment, things began to look up. The blonde walked alongside Gerald to a blue Toyota Prius. She planted a wet kiss on Gerald and handed him a set of car keys.

Chris leaned out the window with his telephoto lens and zoomed in on them, but the blonde blew Gerald a kiss and returned to the office.

"That must be Veronica," Angel said. "She looks like the photo of his receptionist given to us by Mrs. Green."

"But she's going back inside and I didn't get a picture," Chris said.

Gerald ducked his head while entering the Prius and slumped in behind the steering wheel. Angel could see him adjusting the front seat and the mirrors. A minute later, the Prius lurched out of the parking spot and stopped.

"He's borrowing her car," Angel said. "Something's up."

They followed him being careful not to get too close. Fifteen minutes later, he pulled alongside a curb at a corner about half a block from his home.

"What is he doing?" Chris asked.

They waited for about ten minutes before Angel replied. "I think he's doing the same thing we are."

Chris focused his camera and took a few shots of him watching his home. About then, the garage door opened and Andrea Green, driving a silver Mercedes sedan, backed out. She drove off and the blue Prius followed her at a discreet distance.

"Son of a bitch," Chris said. "He's following her. He's staking her out."

Angel took a phantom puff of a cigarette that was no longer between her fingers. "I don't get it. We're following him and he's following his wife. It's like we're in a damn parade."

Andrea was a safe driver. She plodded down the street at a robust twenty-miles-per-hour. Gerald, apparently aware of his wife's habits, plodded along at the same speed. He hit his brakes several times to keep from catching up to her.

Angel, a nervous wreck by now, once slammed on the brakes so hard Chris did a faceplant into the dashboard.

"Cripes, you're going to get us killed," he said. "Why don't you just stop at each block, count to ten, and move on? They're not going to lose us anytime soon."

Twenty minutes later, Andrea pulled into the Monarch Hotel across from Clackamas Town Center. Her husband followed behind at a safe distance and turned into an auxiliary parking lot. Angel, now up to three packs a day if she was still smoking, gave a two-finger salute as she phantom puffed her way toward Andrea who still hadn't vacated her car.

"This is awkward," Chris said. "What if she sees us? How do we explain why we're following her?"

"I'm more worried about her husband seeing us," Angel said. "At that point, we're pretty much *made* and out of a job."

They sank down in their seats, Angel peeking over the steering wheel, and Chris gazed back over his seat at Gerald.

"She's got a shoulder bag," Angel said. "Now she's going into the hotel lobby. What is she up to?"

"I don't get it, either." Chris popped up and took several pictures with his telephoto lens.

"Now she's talking with a man just inside the door," Angel said. "Holy Crap. They're kissing."

Chris, who had turned his camera on Gerald, twisted back toward the hotel lobby. "Man, her husband is getting quite a show."

"This sucks," Angel said. "He's got more on her than we have on him."

They sat in silence weighing the actions of Gerald and Andrea Green. A minute later Gerald walked briskly past their car. He glanced into their window and Angel grabbed Chris around the neck, pulled him into her, and kissed him.

"This isn't the time to make out," Chris said.

"Shush. Green just walked by and he saw us. Shit. We're the worst private investigators ever. Our client is screwed and so are we. He stared right at me and frowned. He must suspect we're tailing him."

"Maybe not," Chris said. "Maybe he'll think we're following her too. He might think it's her boyfriend's wife who hired us to follow him because she suspected him of cheating."

"I guess it's a possibility," Angel said.

"You bet. And I'm tired of being a step behind in this investigation." He opened the car door and got out with his camera.

"What are you doing?" Angel said.

"I'm going to get a better look."

"Chris wait!" Angel sighed and absentmindedly raised two fingers to her lips.

She almost caught up to him as Green stepped into an elevator, but Chris bolted to the stairs and disappeared. She went to the lobby desk and waited as a short-haired brunette in a black uniform dress typed something into a computer.

"Can I help you?" she said after she finished.

"I'd like a room," Angel said.

"Sure," the clerk said.

"Has an Andrea Green checked in yet? We're supposed to meet here."

She tapped at the computer. "I don't have a Ms. Green."

"Green is her pen name. She's a writer. I'm afraid I don't know her real name. She's in her mid-forties, tall, with raven hair and steely blue eyes."

"Oh, she just checked in with her husband a few minutes ago. Let's see. John Howard."

"Is he tall, with blond hair, and athletic looking?" Angel asked.

"Exactly," the clerk said. "You don't know his name?"

"Never met him, but Andrea said her husband might be with her. Could I get a room near hers?"

"Surely. She's in three-fifteen. How about three-twenty. It's right across the hall."

"That's fine." She handed the lady her credit card.

"Do you have luggage?"

"It's in the car," Angel said. "I'll get it later."

Angel took her room key and tapped the button on the elevator.

When she got off on three, she spotted Chris lurking just inside the stairwell door with his camera aimed at Gerald, who was lurking outside room three-fifteen with his ear against the door. She went over to the stairway, opened the door and twisted Chris's arm behind his back.

"This way, dear." Gerald now appeared to be typing something on his cell phone and trying to look inconspicuous."

She swiped her key card in the door of three-twenty and pushed Chris through the open door. "Would you mind telling me what you were trying to accomplish?"

"He was trying to take a picture through the peephole in the door with his camera phone," Chris said. "I got a picture of him doing it. That's got to be against the law, right? Invasion of privacy or something."

"Like what we're doing to him?" Angel said.

"Oh, yeah. I guess I screwed up. I just got frustrated because we're getting nowhere. I thought maybe I could trip him up on a technicality."

"I rented this room so he wouldn't be suspicious if he saw you," Angel said. "I also learned the name of the guy Mrs. Green is with. It's John Howard unless he's using an alias."

"Yeah, but we aren't supposed to be investigating him," Chris said. "We must be doing something wrong."

"Oh, we're doing everything wrong," Angel said. "Maybe Billie is right. Maybe we shouldn't be doing domestic cases. They're trickier than I thought."

She picked up the room phone and dialed the main desk. "Yes, this is Ms. Lemon, in room three-twenty. There's a man walking up and down the hallway leering into peepholes up here."

She described Gerald Green to the clerk. "Will you make sure he leaves the premises? I'm afraid to go outside with him around."

She turned to Chris and smiled. "That should take care of the snoopy Mr. Green."

She dialed room three-fifteen. "Mrs. Green? This is Angel. I'm afraid I have some bad news for you."

"You haven't nailed him yet?" she answered.

"Worse. Your husband is in the Monarch Hotel."

"Oh my God. What is he doing here? I mean there."

"I'm afraid he followed you, dear. He's just outside your door trying to peep through the keyhole."

"Oh no. Gerald's here." She was briefing her friend in the room across the hall.

"Angel, what am I going to do? He can't find me here."

"I've taken care of it. Hotel security will be ushering him off the premises soon. Wait half an hour and leave very discretely. Watch out for a blue Prius with a *Ronnie* vanity plate."

"Well, we've got this room," Chris said when Angel hung up. "Might as well take advantage of it."

"Oh, we're going to take advantage of it," Angel said. "*You* are going to glue your eyeball to the peephole on our door and tell me when Mrs. Green leaves."

"This isn't what I had in mind," Chris whined. "What are you going to do?"

"I'm going to take a nap."

Chapter 12

"Is Dan Bly available? This is his sister, Billie."

It was Monday morning and I had gotten quite a shock. I was catching up on my newspaper reading online via Oregonlive and came across a Saturday story about a drone sighted outside a Chase Bank window on Friday directly across the street from Pioneer Square.

According to the story, the drone zipped from window to window on the upper floors of the building. A witness said it appeared to be taking pictures or filming. The rest of the story gave the background of other incidents where people flew drones too close to buildings, of Realtors using them to film properties, and one instance of a drone flying around the Space Needle restaurant in Seattle, Washington.

"Dan, about this drone flying around the Chase Bank at Pioneer Square."

"I knew you would call," he said. "I looked into it earlier. The investigating officer said there wasn't much to it. The thing was gone when he got there."

"What happened?" I said.

Dan cleared his throat. "Three or four employees said a helicopter flew in front of their office window. It happened a few days earlier too, but it was kind of a novelty thing for those involved so nobody reported it.

"But last Friday, one of the vice-president's noticed a camera mounted on it. There is sensitive information in his office, and he was afraid someone might be spying on his financial records."

"Can I have his name?" I asked.

"Why? The way he was worried about spies, he's not going to talk with you. You don't even have a case related to it."

"Let me worry about getting him to talk," I said. "It's personal with me. Maybe *it is* with him too. Those damn drones, suddenly invading your life, can rattle you."

I heard a long sigh through the phone. The kind I've heard from him many times over the years. Dan raised me after my parents died and has put up with my stubbornness since I was a teenager.

"His name is Benjamin Knowles," Dan said. "His position with Chase Bank is kind of vague. He has something to do with investments. Don't tell him we sent you to him. I don't need any more complaints about you down here."

I might have neglected to mention my unpleasant history with the Portland Police Bureau. It started with my days as a uniformed cop. I had several complaints about being too rough with some of the perps I arrested.

Once, a man arrested for domestic abuse tried to grab my gun when I went to cuff him so I head-butted him, breaking his nose. He fell backward and hit his head on the sidewalk and filed a complaint against me hoping to use it as part of his defense.

A few years ago, I had a run-in with a dumb thief who tried to steal my purse when I was off-duty and shopping for Christmas gifts. He was also the reason the police bureau used to dismiss me. I had slammed his head in a revolving department store door for his efforts.

Internal affairs asked me why I had to slam his head in the door so many times—five or six by my guess. *What else could I have done?* My gun was buried in my purse and even if I had found it in time, he'd likely have bit a bullet. So, in my eyes, he got off with a warning. I mean, stealing a woman's purse is the lowest. Forget the credit cards and money. Do you know how much cash I have tied up in makeup?

Unfortunately, he sued me and the city for police brutality. If I would have shot the crook, there would have been no complaints, or lawsuits and the creep would have been out of my life for good.

Ironically, maybe as penance, the thief later became Angel's boyfriend, Chris. Somehow, he turned out to be not such a bad guy. He refused to collect on a court-ordered settlement he won and, for some reason, thinks I saved his life once.

To avoid the stress of fighting to keep my job, I quit and became a P.I. But it didn't stop my butting heads with the Police Bureau. The second year as a P.I., I found a killer who turned out to be a cop, which didn't settle well with some of my former comrades.

"You're not going to cause any problems for me, right?" Dan said.

"I shall not divulge my sources or my clients," I said.

"Are you raising your right hand as you say this?" he asked.

I looked over at my raised hand. "Of course, I am. I'm a smart ass."

"I know. Please be careful. I know I can't stop you, but if you get into trouble, please let me help."

"When have I not asked for help when I needed it?" I said. "I'm asking for help now, aren't I?"

He sighed and hung up on me.

It was a little after two o'clock in the afternoon when I was ushered into Benjamin Knowles' private office.

"Hello. Miss Bly," he said. "Billie Bly. I must say your name sounds familiar. I've been wondering where I've heard it. Have we met before?"

"I don't think so, Mr. Knowles. I think I would remember you if we had."

"Well, please *do* sit down, so we can get to know each other."

Knowles was a youthful fifty-year-old with a classically shaped face. He wore a conservative blue suit with a black and grey-striped tie. His blue eyes hid behind gold, wire-rimmed glasses. The tailored suit fit his body nicely, and I guessed he probably ran marathons in his free time. Translation: *Woof!* I'd go out with him if it weren't for Brett.

I noticed he took a long look at my strapless Wonderbra-enhanced ample bosom, my short red-dress, and my legs. I didn't know if my little ruse would work, because I don't usually like to show off whatever assets I may have. I was kind of a tomboy growing up and don't like wearing dresses or flirting with men.

But my dates with Brett had me seeing things differently. Perhaps showing my soft side has some advantages, the chief one being finding a good man. So, why not use it to help me get what I need? In this case, getting some information from a conservative banker.

"Thank you, Mr. Knowles. I really appreciate you taking the time to see me."

"Please call me, Ben. I don't normally handle investments directly, but I do try to keep in touch with our clients." Translation: *my secretary told me you were one hot number in a red dress.*

I sat and crossed my legs for him. "Thank you, Ben. I do appreciate your time." Translation, *I might have implied I had a lot of money to invest, and I would only talk to Benjamin Knowles.*

"So, how can I help you, today."

Okay, I was in his office, we were on a first name basis, and he was smiling and staring a bit. It was time for me to be honest. The worst thing that could happen was he could throw me out of his office, and I'd been thrown out of better places than this.

"Ben, I may have led you on about why I'm here today."

"How so?" His face changed little. Then he gave me a bemused smile, which might have said *I doubt you could mislead me.*

"I'm not here to invest any money, but I do need your help."

It didn't seem to faze him. He put his elbows on his desk and made a steeple with his fingers. "I will help you if I can, but if you're selling something . . ."

"Oh, I assure you I'm not," I said.

He smiled broadly. "You didn't let me finish. I was going to say, I might be buying."

I felt my face flush. He was flirting with me. This dressing like a slut and flirting was working. Why had I avoided it all my life?

I told him my real reason for the meeting. The drone nearly decapitating me that first early morning, the woman I spotted flying it, and the black SUV barreling down on me the next morning when I tried to follow her. I didn't mention the shooting. I didn't want to scare him.

He sat quietly, listening, not asking any questions. When he did speak, it was with a measured cadence, choosing his words carefully.

"Miss Bly, I can appreciate your position. You being a private investigator and someone trying to kill you because of something you've seen. I would imagine you are a naturally curious person by profession and maybe you would like to know more about this potentially dangerous person."

"You aren't wrong there," I said.

"I too, have had some curious things going on in my life. If I speak frankly, can I have your assurance of confidentiality?"

"Why?" I said.

"I am in a position where if certain facts become known, my clients could be harmed too."

I decided to take a flyer and accepted his request. "You have my word, as long if what you share is lawful."

He offered the briefest of smiles. "It's like this. I am not associated with this bank, I merely rent an office here. I am the West Coast Regional fundraiser for the Democratic Party. I am currently raising money for the presidential campaign.

"A week ago, Dave Lambert, the chief fundraiser for a Republican Super PAC, was found drowned in Puget Sound. The police said it appeared to be an accident. The oxygen in his air tank was depleted. It will be a serious blow to the eventual Republican nominee for president with elections in November.

"I don't like the explanation," Knowles said. "I knew Dave. He was an expert diver and wouldn't make a mistake of this sort. He kept a summer home in Seattle, so he could dive in the Sound. He knew the area and would never dive alone. It's not conceivable he wouldn't double check his air supply."

"Where you are going here?" I said.

"The police said witnesses came forward reporting they saw a scuba diver emerge from the water, climb in a car and drive away quickly the same day he died. They think it was a woman."

"I see," I said. "A woman might have gone scuba diving with Lambert."

"And you ran into a woman flying a remote-control helicopter, who tried to kill you. Then there are sightings of drones circling the building. I wasn't here, but my secretary saw it hovering outside my window the day I reported it to the police. You see, it could have been looking for me."

"Do you think the fact you and Lambert are both fundraisers for political parties might be a tie-in?" I asked.

"It had occurred to me," Knowles said.

Ping Lau opened the door easily after taping the door latch snugly with scotch tape the night before. She removed the tape now, allowing the latch to engage again and rolled her suitcase behind her onto the roof of the Big Pink.

It took her 10 minutes to remove the two drones, set them up, and check the battery capacities to make sure they had enough flight time. She dropped a grenade into a custom-made basket under the belly of each drone. The grenade activation pins were attached to an automated switch which would pull the pins when she triggered the release switch.

She hoped she might finally catch Benjamin Knowles in his office today. Her previous attempts to find him by flying around the office windows had proven fruitless. His office had been empty except the time when she spotted his secretary.

She programmed both drones on a route taking them high enough no one would notice them flying until they zoomed down for a bird's eye view of Knowles' office, where they would hover waiting for her commands.

She activated the remotes and each helicopter took off in turn. The larger drone, Healy, took the lead with an elegant ascent.

She watched through goggles as Healy sped over downtown Portland, maneuvering around the taller buildings. Little Healy zipped alongside, as programmed, so Little Healy and Ping Lau could keep an eye on the results if things ran smoothly.

Healy was twenty-four inches in diameter and its sibling was twelve inches. Both had 1080p cameras and although Healy had a limited 30-minute flight time, Little Healy could stay airborne for forty-five minutes.

She became dizzy as the quadcopters zoomed side to side, occasionally up and down as wind drafts caught them. Finally, she spotted Pioneer Square ahead. The drones didn't fly low over The Square, which was filled with employees sitting on the curved brick stairs with their lunches as others passed through on route to Starbucks and other locations.

They were programmed to circle the roof of the Chase building and gradually descend the side of the skyscraper, as a window washer might gradually motor down. She watched as the drones floated down floor-by-floor until they reached Benjamin Knowles' office on the fifth floor.

Her heart skipped a beat when she saw a man and woman sitting on each side of a desk. Healy hovered about fifteen-feet from the window, as she zoomed the camera lens to give her a closer look. She was seeing their side profiles and the woman was foremost in the picture.

She stared in awe. Sitting in a chair with her legs crossed in a very low-cut red dress, was the woman she had seen with Brett Wright at

Portland City Grill. What the hell was she doing here? A thought occurred to her. It flashed in her brain the way her headlights had borne down on the woman on the bicycle the night she had tried to eliminate a persistent witness.

Was it the same woman? It had to be. Who was she and why was she always popping up at the wrong time? It didn't matter. If the man in the office was Benjamin Knowles, she would be eliminated once and for all.

Ping Lau guided Healy closer to the right of the window and aimed the camera lens at Knowles. She had researched him for several days and it was an easy identification. All systems were go. She backed Healy away from the window to get a running start. She didn't expect it to crash through the glass. She would trigger that grenade before charging the window and let it explode upon impact.

She saw the woman stand and point out the window at Healy now and Knowles then approached the front of the window. Perfect targets. She released the grenade pin, counted off the appropriate seconds, and propelled Healy toward its targets. She switched to goggles linked to Little Healy to catch the moment of impact.

The woman in the red dress dove to the side of the window as Knowles backed away, his face eerily contorted, just before fire and glass made shambles of his office. Smoke oozed from the shattered window and debris of glass and parts of Healy cascaded to the sidewalk. Little Healy hovered for a full minute outside, as she watched for survivors.

After the flames died down, the small quadcopter entered the charred office through the shattered window and hovered in the middle of the room. She sighted the camera on Knowles in a lifeless heap on the floor. He was covered with smoke and ash.

Remembering the blonde woman, Ping Lau, spun the drone around to where she lay. She too appeared lifeless. Ping Lau considered exploding the second grenade aboard Little Healy as insurance but decided against it. They were obviously dead. The smaller drone had been armed as a backup in case something went wrong with Healy. Its primary use was as evidence of the kill. Something she could show The General if necessary.

The smaller quadcopter turned and panned in for a closeup of Knowles charred face. It appeared to take the full force of the blast. His head was riddled with shards of glass and he appeared lifeless.

Little Healy turned for one last look at the blonde. Ping Lau could spot no visible marks on the woman, but she wasn't moving.

She sighed and summoned Little Healy to return to the Big Pink. It might be a day or two before she knew the results of her attack. As she began packing the gear and putting it away, she wondered about the blonde.

She must have been the one who followed Ping Lau downtown the night after a successful drone flight. Then, she and Brett Wright appeared at the Portland City Grill inside the Big Pink building, from where she would eventually fly her drones. Such a coincidence was hard to fathom. But being with Knowles at the exact minute she killed him? What were the odds?

Ping Lau decided she must find out who this woman was. If she had somehow stumbled upon her planned assassinations, someone else could be working with her.

Chapter 13

"Hey, Gerry, are we still on for the little tour we had planned this afternoon?" Veronica Sloane bent over and hiked her black nylons up under her very short blue skirt. She stood and combed her fingers through her shoulder length blonde hair. Her green eyes sparkled, as she scrunched her small turned-up nose at him.

Gerald looked up from a stack of real estate papers and smiled. "You bet. I only have one house we can view. I need some pictures for the listing. Do you have your camera with you?"

"Right here." She picked up a compact digital camera from a nearby desk. They were going out under the premise that Veronica was taking the real estate test to become a broker. Gerald had taken the former office receptionist under his wing, and she was doing most of the listing and marketing work allowed by non-licensed personnel.

"Today, we're going to the Henderson home over on Southeast Fifty-Fifth Avenue," he said, for the benefit of any interested ears in the office. Everybody probably knew they were *getting it on*, yet Gerald felt he had to put on a show lest his wife might find out. He planned to divorce her and had quietly been salting away his assets in secret accounts.

They left the building and drove a short distance to the Henderson abode. It was a two-story salt block home built in the 1940's, newly painted and completely remodeled with hardwood flooring, granite kitchen counters, and freshly painted interiors.

Gerald planned to put it up for $620,000 with a seven-percent commission. Normally the commissions were split between the buyer's agent and the selling agent, but Gerald had three good leads from some of his buyer prospects. If he brought the buyer, he kept the whole commission, $43,400. To ensure he received the whole commission, he talked the seller into a thirty-day exclusive listing, in which case it wouldn't hit the market for a month, plenty of time for him to find a buyer.

He reached over and fondled Veronica's left breast as they pulled into the circular driveway.

"Gerry! Can't you wait until we get inside?"

"No. You have that effect on me."

"Where are we going today?" she asked.

"I'm not feeling too kinky today. I thought we could use the homeowners' bed. It's a king-size."

"Not very exciting," Veronica said, as they exited the car.

"Ronnie, dear. This house has a series of wireless cameras. I offer these little perks to entice people to list with me. The Hendersons are on vacation this week and they jumped at the idea of having security cameras."

Veronica grabbed Gerald's suit lapels with both hands on the front porch and pulled him against her well-endowed breast and pouted. "How does that get me off?"

"One of the cameras is in their bedroom. It's pointed at Mrs. Henderson's jewelry cabinet at the moment, but I'm going to point it at us when we get in their bed."

"Oooh. You mean we're going to let the security office monitor us as we have sex?"

"No, you nitwit. The video feeds all go to my mobile phone. Of course, they're on my online storage account too."

"Home movies!" she squealed.

"That's the plan. We can watch ourselves later on my phone or cast it on your big screen television."

He unlocked the front door and was rewarded with a big wet kiss. He patted her behind as she scooted through the door and looked wistfully toward the finely manicured front lawn.

"I love being a Realtor."

"Did you get it?" Angel asked from behind a large elm tree.

"I got the kiss and the butt groping," he said.

"Well, it's a start. Maybe our luck is changing."

They waited about ten minutes before approaching the house from the side. They would be difficult to see from the street because of a five-foot fence on one side of the house and several large rhododendrons on the other side.

"I'll bet the master bedroom is up here," Chris pointed to a window on the back corner of the house.

"How would you know?" Angel said. "It could be one of the kids' rooms."

"You forget. I have experience casing homes. After you burgle a couple hundred houses, you learn the tendencies of floor plans."

"How did you pass the background check to qualify for a P.I.'s license?" Angel asked.

"Never caught."

"Never is a big word."

"Okay, the only time they ever convicted me of a crime was when I tried to steal your boss's purse. And when I sued the city for police brutality my lawyer got the conviction expunged."

She rolled her eyes and shook her head.

"Hey, I had a good lawyer, okay? I'm going to see if the ladder on the side of the house is tall enough for a peep inside the master bedroom window."

"Do you think it's a good idea?" Angel said. "It's pretty high up."

"Once again," Chris said, pointing at himself, "master criminal."

"I can't watch. I'm going around the front and see if I can find them doing it on the couch or something. I noticed the window blinds are all open. "I can use the camera on my phone if I get lucky."

Chris watched, as she disappeared around the corner, and gazed up at the bedroom window. "It *is* awfully high and the ladder doesn't look very sturdy."

He walked to the back porch and withdrew a credit card from his wallet. "I hope this door doesn't have a deadbolt." He was inside in an instant. "Got to love these old houses with their original locks," he murmured.

He tiptoed through a mudroom and slid quietly into the kitchen after peeping though the door. It was quiet and it assured him their quarry was upstairs. Just the same, he stealthily negotiated the area until he approached the living room window.

Angel stood just outside the window with a look of panic. He smiled at her and did a finger wave. She mouthed a curse word. Chris smiled, did another finger wave and headed for the stairs. He heard a rattling from the window behind him but thought it best not to look back.

This time he was going to *get the baddie*. He took the camera from the strap around his neck and checked to be sure the lens cap was off. He checked the battery and light settings and made sure it was in film mode. There was another disturbance from behind him followed by Angel swearing. It wasn't clear enough for him to understand, probably because of the triple-pane insulation.

Again, Chris thought it best to ignore her. He figured if Gerald and Veronica were going at it hot and heavy upstairs, they probably wouldn't notice him. He tiptoed to the top of the stairs and stopped short when he heard a woman moaning. He inched up to the doorway and heard the sounds clearly.

The door was closed so he would have to risk opening it a crack. It opened with a lingering creak. The moaning and other sounds of ecstasy didn't soften. He peeked around the corner and was thrilled with the results.

They were going at it like rabbits. He began filming, checking every few seconds to make sure the camera was running. It was only after a few minutes he realized he was aiming from behind, and he couldn't clearly identify his victims.

He thought about pushing the door open more and sliding along the wall for a better shot. He was about to do so when a vice-like hand pinched the tendons on his shoulder and yanked him out of the bedroom.

"What do you think you're doing?" Angel whispered.

"I'm just about done. I just need the coup de grace," Chris said.

"If they catch you, you can forget being a P. I.," she said. "We'll both go to jail."

"But I don't have the clincher," Chris said.

"If you don't leave right now, no sex ever again." Angel grabbed his free arm and bent it behind his back. Chris grimaced at the pain and realized she was serious.

"Okay, let's go."

"Did you hear something," Veronica said, from the bedroom.

"I did," Gerald said. "I better check."

Angel sized up the distance to the front door. No way they would make it in time. She pushed Chris toward another hallway door, opened it and dragged him into another bedroom, and closed the door softly.

They heard Gerald in the hallway and after a few minutes, the bedroom door opened. "Did you find anything?" Veronica said.

"I thought I heard something in here," he said. He picked up a baseball bat and signaled Veronica. She stood to the side of a closet and turned the door. Gerald cocked the bat, ready to swing it. But he didn't.

Angel saw only bare legs from under a queen-size bed. Chris lay next to her, holding his breath. Angel also held her breath as Gerald and Veronica stepped back into the hall.

"Let's check the other bedroom," Veronica said. "I'm sure I heard someone whispering out here."

"Wishful thinking," Gerald said, but we'll check.

A minute later Angel heard them in the hallway again. "Wouldn't it have been a hoot if the Hendersons came home early from their vacation."

"What would you do?" she said.

"I'd probably have to move to another real estate firm."

"Would you lose your license," she asked.

"Nah. Maybe a slap on the hands. It's practically impossible to lose your license. I know a Realtor and mortgage broker who sold homes to straw buyers and left the banks holding the bag. The Realtor just started his own firm. The mortgage broker got a suspended sentence."

Angel listened as their voices gradually disappeared. She and Chris scrambled from under the bed and Angel put her finger to her lips. He pointed to the door and she shook her head.

"They might be downstairs," she whispered.

"What do we do?" he whispered back.

She shrugged. "Wait until they leave, I guess."

She sat down on the bed. Chris watched out the window for them to leave. A few minutes later, he joined her on the bed. *This is not the way to be a private investigator,* Angel thought. She also was having second thoughts about Chris applying for his license.

How would she break it to him?

After Gerald and Veronica tired themselves out, they watched themselves on his phone. It was quite fun for them. They pointed out sequences where they felt they could have done better, laughed when they were obviously having fun, and high-fived at the climax.

"Can you check and see if anyone *did* enter the house while we were going at it?" Veronica asked as they were getting dressed.

"Maybe," Gerald said, tugging on his loafers. "I haven't spent too much time learning how to search the various cameras, and I had the alerts turned off," Gerald said.

"Alerts?" Veronica intoned.

"Yes. You can set the system up to send you an alert each time the camera catches movement. It's kind of a hassle because they mostly go off when the mail is delivered, or someone is walking down the sidewalk. It was fun to watch at first, but it was alerting me too many times a day for wind blowing or someone driving by on the street."

"Can you go back and check for alerts?" she asked, buttoning her blouse.

Gerald grabbed his phone from a nightstand and started pushing buttons. His face took on various contortions as he attempted to search the various cameras around the house. Most of them revealed nothing except a man walking by on the sidewalk and a car pulling alongside the sidewalk.

"Wait!" he cried. "Let's go back a bit here." He sat on the bed open-mouthed while a petite woman with blue hair put her face up to the living room window.

"Let me see," Veronica said. Gerald rewound the fifteen-second clip. They sat, mesmerized, as the woman peered through the front window. "Who is she?" Veronica asked.

"I don't know." Oh my God. Look at this guy. He's in the living room, and he's heading for the stairs."

"He's carrying a camera," she said. "Look at the time stamp. Isn't that about when we thought we heard someone?"

Gerald nodded. He was engrossed in going through various film clips. "Here the lady comes through the living room and goes upstairs too."

"They were spying on us," Veronica said.

"Yeah but . . ."

"What do you see?" she said.

"It's what I don't see. I see them coming, but there's nothing here showing them leaving. Not even going downstairs."

"You mean they're still up here somewhere?" She hugged her naked self and shivered.

"We never looked under the bed." Gerald pulled on his trousers and shirt, picked up the baseball bat again, and went back to the child's bedroom he had checked on earlier.

"Oh, that's such a cliché," Veronica said, following behind him.

"Maybe, but they didn't leave the house so they must be up here somewhere."

He opened the bedroom door, raised the bat with one hand, and stepped into the bedroom with Veronica remaining behind the door in the hallway.

"Be careful," she said.

Chapter 14

The first thing I remembered after the blast was an EMT shining a penlight into my eyes. I felt groggy and someone kept asking me what day it was. I didn't know.

Gradually, I remembered some answers to their questions. As I did so, my cognitive processes slowly rounded into shape and I began to remember things more clearly. Like the white and grey drone hovering outside the window.

I remembered how I marveled at the novelty. Here we were several stories above the ground and this remote controlled eight-bladed helicopter sauntered up to the window and tapped at it like a woodpecker.

Then I remembered what was in a little white plastic basket nesting between the drone's landing gear. A grenade. The starkness of the situation struck me dumb. A grenade. Me trying to warn Knowles. My evasive action toward the floor in the corner of his office away from the window.

"Knowles," I cried automatically. "Is he okay?"

It was then I noticed two men in navy blue pants and light blue dress shirts squatting over me. "Is he okay?" I asked.

The two men looked at each other. One of them glanced over his shoulder at two men in black T-shirts with *Portland Fire* lettering on their backs. They were in Knowles office. I had been dragged out into the main office area.

The EMT looked back at me and shook his head. "Do you have any pain?"

"Speak up," I said. "My ears are still ringing."

"Do you have any other pain," he yelled. People around me stopped and looked our way.

"No." I tried to get up, but the medical guys made me stay down while they checked my vitals. The blurred figures around me came into focus. My brother, Dan stood a few feet away watching me carefully.

Over in the corner, I spotted my former cop partner and former boyfriend, Lieutenant Steve Thomas, chatting with the Chief of Police. Chief Samuel Hardy was a fifty-eight-year-old white-haired drill sergeant type, attired in the dress-blue police uniform, decorated with gold and brass medals commensurate with his experience.

Hardy was saying something about assignments. Steve appeared to be ignoring him in favor of watching me. I tried to smile at him, but it must have come off wrong because he frowned.

I caught bits and pieces as my hearing cleared up. The word *terrorism* was bandied about. Chief Hardy was yelling about *the damned FBI*, and someone said *the poor guy never had a chance.*

Then the EMT's started rechecking all of my vital signs and asking me questions about the day of the week, my birthday, and asking if I knew where I was? When they seemed satisfied, they put a stretcher on the floor next to me and rolled me onto it.

"I don't want to go," I said. "Really, I'm okay. Just let me stand up."

"We can't do that Miss. You have to go to the hospital and get checked out for possible internal injuries."

I looked up at the guy's nametag. "Really, Randy, I'll absolve you from any responsibility."

They elevated the stretcher and wrapped a sheet around me. It was then, I noticed I had been strapped to the stretcher. "Damn. I mean it. Let me go right now. I've got work to do here. I'm a primary witness."

"Don't let her give you any sass," Chief Hardy said. "She's nothing but trouble. You get her to the hospital and make sure they book a room for her. Dan, you go with your sister and get a complete statement if she's feeling so good."

My brother stepped over to me and held my hand. "It will be okay, Billie. I'll take good care of you."

"Will you fill me in on everything happening after I blacked out?" We were rolling toward an elevator now. He didn't commit. "At least tell me about Knowles. Is he all right?"

Dan waited until we were out of Chief Hardy's earshot. "He didn't make it. Glass and shrapnel did a number on him."

I started crying. "I saw it coming. I tried to warn him, but there wasn't time. I dove away from the window into the corner of the room."

Dan asked the EMT's to give us a few minutes before loading me on the elevator.

"Your instincts were good," he said. "The explosion occurred on the other side of the office window. Apparently, the explosion area was limited to straight ahead inside the office and the rest of the blast zone was outside the building. The explosion couldn't reach you."

"I wish I could have helped him."

"It sounds like there wasn't time. If you tried to save him, you would be dead too."

I thought about it for a minute. He probably was right. I barely got the words out of my mouth. Knowles didn't have time to decipher what I'd said, let alone act. Then something else occurred to me.

"Why did Chief Hardy usher me out of the crime scene? The protocol is to get a witness statement while their memory is still fresh."

"There are two answers to that question," Dan said. "First, he's pissed you are involved in any of this. Something about how you always manage to come back and bite him in the ass."

"He deserves it. He is an ass."

Dan managed a smile. "Do you remember this morning when I said you were skating on thin ice with the bureau and not to do anything to make it worse?"

"Yeah. I kind of broke through the ice, didn't I? But it wasn't my fault. Things seem to happen to me. I can't help it if some mad bomber attacks at the exact moment I'm on the scene, can I?"

"I don't think Hardy sees it your way. He wants to know why in the heck you're investigating an act of terrorism before it happened instead of telling us."

"When he cools down, remind Hardy I to tried tell someone. You were there when the lunatic lady tried to run me over and she emptied her gun at me. There was even a police report, and I really didn't know anything other than having a few suspicions."

"I know, but I think it's better at the moment not to mention it to the Chief."

"Okay. What was the other reason he wants me gone?"

"The FBI is in the building. He would prefer them not to interview you. He doesn't want them trying to take over jurisdiction."

"They can't do that, can they."

"No. It's our case unless we ask for help, and Hardy would rather ask for the Oregon State Police to help than any federal agency."

"I still don't understand why he doesn't want me to stick around."

"He's also afraid you might say or do something to jeopardize the investigation. He wants to take over the investigation and be a hero."

I sighed. "It sounds just like him." I looked down the stretcher. "Do you have my purse."

"Right here," he said. "What do you need?"

"I'd need to call Angel again. She'll be frantic if she hears about this on the news. She knows I was seeing Knowles today."

Randy unstrapped me and I took my phone and dialed, but there was no answer. I left a message and sent a long text message explaining what happened, and I was all right. By the time the EMT's had loaded me into an ambulance, I hadn't heard back.

"That's unusual for her," I said. "She usually responds right away. Oh, well. She must be busy."

Ping Lau hung around with a crowd of people on the far side of Pioneer Square, a block away from the blast. She wore a pair of raggedy jeans, dirty tennis shoes, an oversized coat too warm for a 66-degree day, and a baseball cap she bought from a street person for five dollars. She looked like one of the many street people you might find panhandling in downtown Portland.

She stood up on the high end of the block which enabled her to look down on the lobby door of the Chase Bank building. Police had the area roped off with yellow police tape, and she stood at the forefront of the mob. She knew the police might be filming the crowd in case whoever bombed the place might come back and watch.

A smart bomber would never do such a thing, but she had to know. Did either of the victims survive? Her homeless outfit helped her hide among the rubberneckers and made it hard for an identification.

She knew the crime scene wouldn't be disturbed for several hours if they were dead, but they might be taken to the hospital if they survived. It had been an hour and she was beginning to think it might be time to move on when it happened.

Two EMT's wheeled a woman out on a stretcher. A blonde woman. "Shit!" she said under her breath. She back-peddled through the crowd and began walking to her car parked four blocks away.

"The woman leaves a charmed life." She took off the hat and smelly coat and crammed them into a garbage receptacle on a street corner. "I have to find out who she is."

She climbed into her black Ford Explorer, fastened her seat belt, and nearly sideswiped a BMW as she accelerated from the curb in a fit of anger.

"It's personal now, you bitch. I'm going to find you and kill you."

Chapter 15

Angel shimmied down a gutter's drain pipe on the side of the two-story home. She first had to crawl backward on her hands and knees on a small, slanted roof over the front porch to reach the gutter. This desperate move had been precipitated by the exclamations they had heard from the neighboring bedroom from Gerald Green and his little tart.

Chris watched from the rooftop, abruptly looking over his shoulder to the window. Had he closed it behind him or left it open for Gerald to discover? She couldn't see from her angle, which was just as good anyway, as her fingers and knees dug into the aluminum downspout at least fifteen feet above the ground.

"Come on, girl, concentrate," she told herself. She moved her hands slowly below each other, clenching the pipe in a death grip. Her knees ached as she dug them in to drain pipe in an attempt to fight gravity.

"Just slide down the pipe," Chris whispered from above.

"I can't. I'll kill myself."

He leaned over the ledge. "No, you won't. At the worst, you burn your hands a bit."

A window slid open behind him and Chris ignored it. He dropped flat on the roof and smiled at Angel. "You can do it. Take it nice and slow and release your death hold a bit and slide down like you used to do in grade school."

The window shifted again and he heard a grunt behind him. *Oh shit*, he thought. *I wonder if he has a gun.*

He didn't wait to find out. He dangled a foot over the edge, followed by both hands frantically gripping for the gutter because the other foot had followed the first foot without his approval. He was in a panic free-fall when three fingers managed to ratchet themselves onto the edge of the gutter.

He swung like a pendulum at the mercy of the orbiting earth and the aforementioned gravity, which pulled at him like a flushing toilet. "Eeek," he squeaked.

He tried to reach the gutter with his free hand, but his left arm was below his body center. He couldn't risk it with the precarious grip he had, without wrenching his fingers from their death-grip.

"Quit monkeying around up there," Angel whispered. "I need your help down here."

"Who's out there," a gruff voice echoed from above.

"Oh shit," Angel muttered.

"Oh Shit," Chris bellowed.

"I've got a gun," said the voice at the window. "Show yourself."

One of Chris's fingers slipped from the edge of the gutters. He took a deep breath and reached mightily for the gutter with his left hand just as he lost his two-finger grip with his right hand. What happened next was eerily transcendental. He hung in mid-air for what seemed an eternity but realistically was only a split second, while he philosophically pondered his life and the choices he had made. In that split-second, he came to an abrupt realization. He wanted to continue in this life.

Almost magically his left hand found the gutter, which he knew shouldn't have happened because he was completely air-born with neither hand clinging to anything but hope. Yet, somehow, he had miraculously hovered in the same spot while contemplating his life and then managed to reach up and grab the gutter.

"Quit goofing around," Angel said. "I need help getting down."

Chris realized he was only in a slightly better situation than before. He had four fingers gripping the gutter. He looked below and spotted the drainpipe.

"There you are, gotcha." He hooked his knees around it. Green loomed above him, displaying a satisfied toothy grin followed by a pompous sneer.

"Hi," Chris said. "We were doing a gutter inspection for the owner and the ladder got away from us. Could you get it? It's on the back side of the house."

While Green momentarily contemplated this pitiful lie, Chris grabbed onto the drain pipe with his free hand, clung to it with his knees, let go of the gutter and slid down the spout. He made it about seven feet before colliding with Angel. She had such a death-grip on the pipe he cascaded over her and hit the hard ground with a thud, knocking the wind from him.

When Angel saw him lying there helplessly and realized she was about eight feet from terra firma, she sighed and slid down the pipe. Green, meanwhile, cursed from the roof and threw the bat, which missed them by a good fifteen feet. The momentum from his wild swing carried him over the edge, and his free-fall landed him on top of a rhododendron bush, which had grown halfway up the front of the house.

"What should we do?" Chris huffed. He sat up, hands flat on the earth, gasping for air.

"We can't just leave him there," Angel said. "I'll go get the ladder."

"I'll sit here and watch him," Chris said.

Angel went around the back of the house looking to get the ladder they had seen earlier and a shapely blonde came onto the front porch, clad in only black-lace panties and a matching bra, which did little to hide her endowments.

"Is he dead?" she asked. She scurried to edge of the wooden porch and looked toward the ground in the general vicinity of where she thought Green fell.

"Where is he?"

Chris pointed up to the top of the gigantic bush.

"Oh, my. How did he get up there?"

Chris didn't answer. It occurred to him he could get a picture of both her and Gerald if he backed away far enough. Her in her scanty bra and panties and him without shoes and socks and his unbuttoned shirt. It would be the money shot. He looked around for his camera and found it behind him.

"Oh no!" he cried. The camera lens was bent and the little slot holding the SD card, or film, was gone. He scurried about the grass, spreading its blades apart with his fingers, hunting for the micro-SD card.

"Who are you guys?" The blonde stood over him as he expanded his search radius in larger circles.

Chris ignored her until she pushed herself in front of him and bent over into his eye line. He caught himself staring at her breasts about the time Angel came around the corner of the house dragging a ladder.

"I said, who are you guys?" The blonde was still bent over with Chris still staring when Angel gave him a dope slap sending him reeling into the next county.

"I can't leave you alone for a minute," she said.

"I think he's hurt," the blonde said. "He can't talk. He just stares."

"Go in the house and put some clothes on, slut." Angel gave her a push, which didn't send her as far as the dope slap but propelled her well on her way toward the front door.

"Don't." Chris moaned, from about fifty feet away.

"I'll take care of you later," she said, and started back toward the ladder.

"Get her picture," Chris blurted. "She's half-naked. Get her picture."

Angel turned back toward the blonde, but she had disappeared inside the front door.

"Crap. I was so mad at you, I didn't realize. Why didn't you get her picture instead of gawking at her?"

He walked toward her, displaying the camera with a bent lens. "I was looking for the camera's SD card. It popped out of the camera in the fall. She poked her boobs in my face while I was hunting."

Angel stared at the camera, then back at the front door and finally to the top of the rhododendron, where Gerald was wobbling on the branches and trying not to fall into the center of the bush.

"You could have used your phone camera on her," Chris said.

"Uh, I think I left it upstairs. It probably fell out of my back pocket when we were under the bed. What a friggin mess. Keep looking for the film while I help this horny moron off the bush."

Chapter 16

A Portland Fire Department EMT transferred me to a white and blue ambulance with the emergency red-and-yellow stripes on the back end.

"I'll meet you at the hospital," Dan said and left.

"Can you take me to the hospital against my will?"

The attendant, Zack looked around and shrugged. The earnest-looking young man checked my restraint as if he thought I might flee.

I might have if I got the chance. He ignored me, so I asked again.

"You don't have any right to transport me if I don't want to go, do you?" It was more of a statement than a question.

Zack appeared startled. "Ron? This lady says she doesn't want us to take her."

An older man working on an impressive beer belly appeared from the side of the ambulance. "She doesn't, does she? Too bad. The cops want her transported."

"They aren't paying the bill," I said. "Besides, Chief Hardy is only trying to get rid of me because he doesn't like me."

Ron seemed to consider this. "I never liked him much, either. He's full of himself. I especially didn't appreciate the way he handled the homeless sweep last month. He made us haul away campers who wouldn't leave because he said they had health problems. They weren't any sicker than you or me. The cops just didn't want to be bothered. They loaded them on our stretchers and told us to dump 'em somewhere."

"Yeah," Zack said. "What goes on downtown is criminal. They move the homeless from one area and a month later they move them again from a different campsite."

"Well, he wants me out of here because he's afraid I'll talk to the Feds about this bombing," I said. "I gave them information they disregarded a week ago and it blew up in their faces today. Hardy is afraid I'll make him look bad."

"Tell you what," Ron said. "We'll take you a few blocks from here and drop you off if you promise not to tell anyone."

"I promise," I said, trying to raise my restrained hand in a judicial swearing-in gesture.

"And you can't come back here," Zack said. "We might get in trouble."

"I've got something else in mind," I said.

They lifted me into the back of the ambulance and shut the door. "Ron has to radio in and notify dispatch you've refused transport," Zack explained.

"I wonder if I could ask one more favor?" I said.

A few minutes later they unstrapped me and helped me out of the ambulance. I looked across the street at the Big Pink. I wanted to be here to see if that Asian waitress was working today. If she was, my working theory would have to be reworked.

"Thanks for the lift, boys. I appreciate it."

"Now, I know who you are," Ron said. "I've been going over it in my mind. It just came to me. You're Billie Bly, the P.I. who caught the Facebook Killer."

"She is?" Ron said. "Wow."

"I had some help," I said, somewhat embarrassed.

"Your picture was all over the newspaper and T.V. for a week," Ron said. "I knew you were somebody. I would have recognized you sooner if you didn't have all that soot on your face."

"What? Have you got a mirror?"

Sure enough, I had black smudges all over my face and no one thought to mention it to me. I took off the police jacket my brother had lent me and did another shriek.

My legs were covered in soot and I could see where the EMT's had cleaned and put Band-Aids over superficial glass cuts. Smoke-stains pocked my modest little red dress and my black lace Wonder Bra glared over the top of my dress's low-cut cleavage.

I adjusted the girls. "I can't go out looking like this."

But I had to. I was able to clean my face and adjust my makeup inside the ambulance. My hair didn't want to cooperate, so I doused it with hairspray and set out to find the Chinese bitch who likely had tried to kill me only a few blocks from here.

"Thanks, again, guys. I appreciate your help." I looked back and caught them in what I thought might have been mid-ogle. I smiled to myself. If I could still attract men's attention looking as bad as I did today, then I must have something going for myself.

It was five p.m. as I entered the elevator. I hit the button for the thirtieth floor and began wondering what I would do if Miss Su Ling, or Kim Wu, or whatever she's calling herself today, was working.

Maybe I was wrong. Maybe I should turn around and get out of here until I think things through. I could be letting her know I was onto her. Maybe I was too damn mad about being blown up to care, and besides, maybe she already knows I'm onto her.

The memory of the blown-up part took over my brain, and I marched out of the elevator directly into the lounge. I spotted the same blonde, who had waited on Brett and me, talking to the bartender and walked right up to her.

"Is Miss Ling here?" I demanded.

Cindy gave me a puzzled look. Her freckles seemed to join her frown in a downward motion as she looked me over. "What on earth happened to you, dear?"

I wanted to say her friend almost blew me up, but, at the last moment, I bit my tongue. "I've had a bad day. Now about Su Ling . . ."

Recognition bloomed in her eyes, and I realized she remembered me from my date with Brett.

"I'm sorry, Su Ling worked the weekend. She's off today. Can I help you with something?"

I could tell I wouldn't get anything from her. "No. Just took a chance I might catch her here."

I turned and walked back toward the lobby elevators. While waiting, I noticed two waitresses entering the stairwell through a side door. I continued waiting for the elevator, occasionally glancing toward the stairwell.

Where were they going? Certainly not taking the stairs down. Only one floor up, and that would be? The roof? The elevator pinged and the doors opened. I ignored them and went for the stairwell door.

It turned out it was two floors to the roof. When I opened the door, sunlight blinded me temporarily and I tried to shield it with my hand.

"Bright out today, huh?"

"Uh, Yeah."

The two waitresses both wore black skirts, almost up to their butts, and matching black tops fitted to maximize their other assets. They leaned against the wall with cigarettes in their hands.

"Got a cigarette?" I asked casually. "Left mine at home and I'm dying for a drag." In truth, I haven't smoked since high school when I was in my rebellion phase. I couldn't stand the taste or the awful smell on my clothes.

The short redhead in killer heels offered me one. "I'm Karen. I haven't seen you up here before."

I took the cigarette, slipped it into my mouth, leaned over for a light, and coughed at the first inhalation.

"I'm trying to give them up."

The slim, bordering on anorexic woman, with mousy brown hair and no bust to speak of, nodded. "Aren't we all? I'm Jessie."

"I'm Kelli with an *I*," I said. "I'm a temp on twenty-eight."

"I see you found the only place you can smoke on the premises," Karen said.

I took another drag on the cigarette and tried not to gag. "I was up here the other day. I met another one of your co-workers. Su Ling, I believe was her name."

"Oh," they said in unison, and I wondered about the odd emphasis they placed on the word.

"Something wrong with her?" I asked.

"Not to speak ill of her . . ." Karen began.

"But she's a royal bitch," Jessie said.

"And she's never waitressed in her life," Karen said.

We stood there, all of us taking another drag, in contemplative thought.

"I didn't think she was so bad," I said.

It remained quiet among the formerly gossipy waitresses.

"Of course, what do I know? You really think she's never been a waitress? How did she get a job at Portland City Grill?"

"Exactly!" Jessie flicked an ash into a makeshift coffee can ashtray. "Cindy vouched for her for some reason."

Karen snorted. "She said Su Ling knew some people high-up in government. Apparently, Su Ling told her she could bring in more high-profile government types and some other celebrities."

"How long has she worked here?" I asked.

"Three hellacious days," Jessie said. "Three days of her being too good to bus tables or really do much of anything except flirt with the men."

"She can't even get the orders right," Karen said.

"And she's dropped plates half-a-dozen times, already," Jessie said.

"Why do they keep her?" I asked.

"She brown-noses Cindy," Jessie said. "From day one. It's like they were long, lost sisters. Who knows? Maybe she has something on the boss."

"Probably those tits. She throws them around enough," Karen said. And they both burst into laughter.

"Oops. Break time is over," Karen said. "Happy hour is upon us."

Jessie stubbed out her cigarette in the coffee can. "Nice meeting you."

I deposited my mostly unsmoked cigarette in the can and surveyed the roof. Not much here, I thought. Several huge air conditioning units, what looked like a storage shed, and a lot of pigeon crap on the ledges. Who would think pigeons could even fly this high?

I looked around for any sign someone might have launched a drone from the roof but came up empty. No discarded helicopter parts, no obscure footprints, nothing to indicate anyone visited this roof except to smoke.

I didn't ask them if Su Ling had joined them on the roof for a smoke. I was the one who said she was there. For all I knew, she had never been up here. But this would be a perfect place to launch a drone strike. Unless a smoker stumbled upon her. How would she handle that?

I went to the door and noticed the door had a little metal ring attached to it. A similar ring stuck out from the door frame. With the door closed, the metal rings lined up. I searched further and found a crowbar stuck down a vent pipe, the curved part hanging on the edge of the pipe.

I removed the crowbar and fitted it onto the rings, likely meant for a padlock, but the crowbar barely slipped through. Perfect, I thought. This is where she did it.

Unfortunately, I had no proof. It was all speculation and neither the cops or Feds would believe me. There was no evidence linking this Su Ling or Kim Wu to the bombing other than the fact they were both Chinese, and the very odd coincidence Brett thought she resembled a woman who bought a drone from him.

But I don't believe in coincidences.

Chapter 17

Angel flushed through the front door with an arm full of Gladiolas and laid the flowers on her desk. "You look business-like this morning."

I brushed lint from my conservative black dress with a brush. "What are you going to do with all the flowers?"

"I thought they'd *brighten up* the office. I know how you like Glad's."

"They *are* very pretty. Are we expecting someone special? I don't remember anything on my calendar this morning."

"No. I just wanted to *brighten* your day a bit."

That's the second time you used that adjective," I said. "I *do* appreciate your trying to make me feel better after the horrific time I had yesterday, but I feel like bad news is coming."

"Oh?" Angel fidgeted with her fingers, trying to interlock them at her waist and finally succumbed to her vile anxious habit of lifting the damn phantom cigarette to her lips. "Did you have a bad day yesterday?"

I stopped brushing the lint from my dress and winced. "Not really. Aside from being blown up by a drone bomb and watching someone die in front of my eyes. No, I'd say it wasn't a bad day. I've had worse. Like the time I nearly got stabbed in the throat by a serial killer."

"Oh my God," Angel said. "I saw that report last night on the news. Were you involved?" She shook her head, and I noticed her orange and pink hair color had some green streaks in it today.

"And speaking of yesterday, where in the hell were you? I tried texting and calling you several times."

"I uh, left my phone someplace." She picked at her hair and a blade of grass drifted to the floor.

She watched it glide and met my eyes. "I, uh, didn't have time to wash my hair this morning."

I did an eye-roll, imagining her and Chris sewing their oats in a field. "Maybe the grass is a clue to where you left your phone. Never mind. I have to go."

"I was hoping we could talk for a minute," she said. "I have something I need to discuss."

"It will have to wait. I have an appointment in half an hour with Chief Hardy, Mayor Jackson, and the goddamn FBI."

"About the bombing?" Angel said.

"No. We're going to plan a little celebration parade for the individual who blew up half the Chase Bank building."

I grabbed my purse and bolted out the front door, slamming it so hard I cracked its lead-glass window. I swore when I realized what I had done. I was so damn mad at Angel I couldn't stand myself.

"Hello, General? Ping Lau here. Have you heard the news?"

"It has been broadcast on the national news outlets all morning," The General said. The law enforcement agencies have been tight-lipped with the media. Have you any further news in Portland?"

"No, but I happened to be downtown a few blocks away when it happened. The noise was deafening. I went to see what happened. It looked like only a small part of the building was blown up, maybe an office or two from what I could see."

The two were being coy over the phone in case anyone might be listening.

"They said there was one other victim, an unidentified woman."

"I saw them load her into an ambulance. I believe she's been released, according to local news this morning."

"Well, the whole thing is unfortunate. How is everything going at your end?"

"Perfect, sir. All the pieces are falling into place for us."

"Good. I was calling about the update you promised me on the election polls."

"Yes, General. As you know, Oregon law allows major parties to decide whether to hold 'open' or 'closed' primaries. In this year's May Primary, both the Democratic and Republican parties will hold 'closed' primaries – meaning a voter must be registered with those parties to cast a vote in their primary election. The Independent Party of Oregon primary will be 'open' to all non-affiliated voters in the state, as well those voters registered as members of the Independent Party."

"I understand," The General said.

"There's a bit of an anomaly here. It seems the Republican numbers are down about ten percent and the Democratic registered voters are down fourteen percent in the last few months."

"What about the Independent registration?"

"It's up over 600 percent," Ping Lau said.

"Impressive. Why?"

"Democratic registrations rolls have lost 133,860 voters and the GOP numbers have fallen by 62,700 voters. The Independent Party has picked up most of their voters.

"How many unaffiliated voters are there?" The General asked.

"Eight-hundred-and-twenty-thousand," Ping Lau said.

"Whew, if Stanton's numbers hold up with unaffiliated voters. . . well, he could score a major upset in Oregon. I checked and he's gaining ground in almost every state, but this would be the first time an Independent candidate has mounted a major challenge in the primaries, let alone a national election.

"He could be the first candidate to win more than one state in a national election since George Wallace ran on the American Independent Party ticket in 1968. The only Independent Party presidential winner was George Washington in 1788."

"Stanton isn't likely to be the second Independent Party President," Ping Lau said.

"You never know. Sometimes, if the planets line up just right in their orbit, anything can happen."

Ping Lau was taken aback at his musing. She knew he wanted Stanton gone, but it sounded like he was admiring the Senator's achievements. She would never understand politicians.

"I'll wait for your next report," The General said. I suppose you will be taking some time off now for a few weeks."

"A month, actually," Ping Lau said. "I have some time coming and I thought I would use it during the lull. You won't need me again for a while, will you?" This was all for the ears of any government wiretaps. They both knew she would be back within a month to take care of Senator Stanton.

"I'm not sure. It all depends on the cooperation I get on my end. I'll let you know in a few weeks."

There he goes again, Ping Lau mused. This last line was entirely off-script. He was known to be ultra-secretive and a bit paranoid. Maybe he was playing for a supposed wiretap. It made her nervous. If there were a wiretap, she shouldn't be on the phone with him.

Yet, there was an issue she had to discuss on the phone and it had to be done right now. "General, there is one issue I'd like to resolve."

"Oh, a problem?"

"Sort of. I've run into a situation with someone I've been forced to work with at my end. She's becoming rather a problem, always sticking her nose in my business."

"Is this the woman you told me about last time?"

"Yes, sir, only she's getting worse. I'm afraid she's going to sabotage my hard work."

"I see. What would your solution be?"

"I think she should be terminated before she becomes a problem."

"Things have been running smoothly so far, but I'm concerned too much disruption at this juncture might bring unnecessary attention to our project. Why don't you give her a little time and see if she doesn't turn around? I'm assuming you will still be supervising our project during you little, ah, sabbatical."

"I *am* a bit of a control freak," Ping Lau said. "I'll give her a chance to prove herself."

"I'll leave it to your discretion," The General said. "You are on the scene and probably a better judge than me here in Washington. But do give it a chance."

When she disconnected, Ping Lau was not happy. She had planned to be at the opposite end of the country after the Feds arrested her dupe, but now this Billie Bly had become an unexpected thorn in her side. One she needed to rid herself of immediately.

But The General wanted her to wait because he was afraid her sudden death could draw unwanted attention to the terrorist investigation and Senator Stanton might cancel his Portland appearance.

The Oregon Primary was scheduled for May 15, and Senator Stanton would arrive in Portland the week before. Today was April 8, which left little time to prepare for the assassination and also kill Billie Bly.

I was nervous about my meeting this morning with the Feds, the Mayor, and Chief Hardy, none of whom I'm sure would want to listen to my ideas of our little drone flyer.

Portland City Hall takes up an entire block between Southwest Fourth and Fifth Avenues and is just North of the bombing site by about a block. I entered the 1895-built four-story Italian Renaissance style building on the Fourth Avenue side through the rotunda entrance.

I was met by a token security guard, signed in, and walked fourteen steps across a black and white checkerboard marble tile floor to a circular oak stairway, which took me to the second floor. From above I could look down and see the first floor from a railing.

The walls were solid walnut and the receptionist desk featured a forty-two-inch matching walnut fence, with a little gate opening to the Mayor's office. While I waited for the missing receptionist to return and admit me, I gazed around the lobby at various copper and bronze plaques honoring previous city dignitaries.

A low rumble of voices emitted from somewhere behind the security gate. I wandered over to the locked entrance and cocked an ear in the direction of the mumbling.

I jiggled the gate, concerned something important may be happening beyond it. There had to be an electronic release at the receptionist's desk but it was out of my reach.

Now, this wouldn't be the first time I've broken into city hall. Actually, by my count, it would be the third time. I glanced around the empty office, backed to the gate, placed my hands backwards on the gate, hopped my fanny on top and tried a graceful spin move designed to aid me in slipping over to the other side.

Tactlessly, my heels caught on a post sticking six inches higher than the gate, and I fell inelegantly in a heap on the other side. Now, this isn't the first time I've taken a fall at city hall. Once before, I fell from a second-floor window into a heap of bushes while escaping in the dead of night. Still, this one stung a bit.

I looked up at the stout face of Chief Hardy snickering at me. "Did you break anything? If you did, you could be charged with breaking and entering." He chuckled and bent over to offer me a hand.

"Thanks, Chief." He had ditched his police dress uniform today for a navy colored power suit accessorized with a speckled light blue tie.

He caught me sizing him up. "Got to look better than the Fed types inside."

Inside consisted of a conference room with a gigantic maplewood oval conference table where no one was seated. Mayor Jackson, a tall, thick, younger man, wearing a more casual earth-tone suit, spoke to Detective Steve Thomas in one corner. In another corner of the room, three men in their forties, wearing blue suits, were in an animated discussion.

"Ah, it appears our guest of honor has arrived," Mayor Jackson said.

Jackson has called me a lot of things, but I doubt *guest of honor* ever entered into any of the adjectives he used. I did a little sarcastic curtesy.

"Thank you, Mayor. It is an honor to be here." Jackson's face reddened. I'm not sure if it was embarrassment or rage. Maybe a bit of both.

"If everyone will be seated, we will begin," he said.

I chose the chair closest to the door for a quick exit. You know, like in case of threatened arrest, or someone throwing something at me.

"Billie Bly, this is FBI Senior Agent Thom Miller, next to him is Assistant Director of Homeland Security, George Nelson, and at the end of the table is Special Agent Lou Sanchez, of the Bureau of Alcohol, Tobacco, Firearms, and Explosives.

I looked down the table as each introduction was made and nodded. Miller had black hair, a full square face, and a trim mustache. He didn't smile at all. Nelson was serious-minded too. His hair was brown and thin, his body was fit, and he wore brown-framed glasses.

Sanchez was the only one of them who smiled. His face was small and weathered like he'd spent too much time in the field. His hair was short and neatly groomed and he had no facial hair.

"Agent Miller will lead with the questioning," Mayor Jackson said. "I understand you've already been interviewed by Detective Thomas?"

Steve had remained standing, but he slid into a chair next to me upon hearing his name mentioned. "Yes," he said. "We talked at length last evening after she evaded her police escort."

It was a little dig at me for not meeting my brother, Dan, at the hospital. "We got our signals crossed," I said.

"I gave a full report to the Chief Hardy last night," Steve said. "I understand he forwarded a copy to everyone here, including the Mayor."

Hardy nodded.

I raised my hand. "I didn't get a copy."

"I didn't think you needed one," Hardy said. "You know what you told us."

"But I don't know if the report is accurate," I said. "I'm sorry, Steve."

"She's correct," Mayor Jackson said. "We need to be sure there are no errors. You can have my copy, Billie."

I took a minute to read it. It was rather long for something happening in such a short time period. I re-read it to make sure I hadn't neglected anything. On the third reread, the natives started to get grumpy.

"Can we get on with this?" It was Senior FBI agent Miller.

"Let's start with your conversation around Benjamin Knowles and Dave Lambert," Miller said. "You said Knowles knew Lambert and had some concerns about his death?"

"He said Lambert was an expert scuba diver, and he couldn't believe he would dive alone. He told me witnesses identified a woman walking on the beach a few hundred yards from where Lambert drowned during the same time period."

"It *is* strange," Miller said. "Lambert chaired a Republican Super PAC fundraising effort and Knowles raised money for the Democrats. Two people with the same job description dying within a week of each other."

"It's just a coincidence," Special Agent Sanchez said. "The first death was a drowning. This one was done by a remote-control helicopter with a grenade. The MO's are completely different. We're here to deal with this specific incident. The explosion."

"You're both wrong." Nelson lowered his glasses and peered over them. "This is a terrorist attack. The two killings fit perfectly in a scenario of a terrorist group trying to circumvent an election. We could be talking about two different cells operating independently of each other."

"*Excuse me.*" I raised my voice to be heard over their diatribe. "*I'm talking here.* You wanted me to come in and tell you what I know. How are you going to learn anything if you aren't willing to listen?"

The three startled federal agents stared mutely at me. I noticed a sly smile from Chief Hardy and Mayor Jackson beamed at me.

Billie Bly, the troublemaker, had just stopped the Feds momentarily and brought things back to the local level. I might have made a few allies.

Chapter 18

"Billie is right," Mayor Jackson said. "She's here to tell her story about the bomber. It is not the time to argue over jurisdictional theories which can be settled later. Please continue, Billie."

I went over the report written by Steve again. My discussion with Benjamin Knowles, including our joint concern over his colleagues in Seattle. This interested the FBI considerably. Miller asked pointed questions, insisting Knowles must have said something, anything, I may have forgotten.

"There was one thing. It's may be nothing."

"Anything might be important," Miller said.

"It's just a hunch, you know, but he was a very nice person. I think he was going to ask me out."

Miller sat there with his mouth open. A ripple of chuckles erupted around the table. He slammed his fist on the conference table. "Damn it, this is serious."

"Can you elaborate a bit more on what brought you to Mr. Knowles office?" Chief Hardy asked.

I told them about my encounters with the mysterious woman flying a remote-control helicopter in Pioneer Square, the fateful morning when I went on an early run, and about the following morning when I decided to find this woman who nearly took my head off with her helicopter. I gave them the blow-by-blow description of my chasing her, losing her, and almost being run over and shot at by the woman in the black Sport Utility Vehicle.

"I filed a report with the police, but she seemed to avoid the downtown area afterward," I said.

"Do you think this woman with the drone is our assassin?" Sanchez asked.

"I do now," I said. "I didn't know what to think before she killed Knowles other than she must be crazy."

"Why did you go to see Knowles in the first place?" Sanchez asked.

"There was a story in the newspaper about a drone being spotted outside one of the offices at the Chase Bank building. I did a little snooping and found out it was Knowles' office. I made an appointment with him because it seemed likely there was a connection between the drone almost taking my head off and the one spying on him. You know, both occurred in the same exact area."

"Billie is a former police officer with the Portland Police Bureau," Mayor Jackson said. "She has three brothers that are with the Bureau too."

"And a former boyfriend," Chief Hardy said, looking at Steve. "Meaning, she can get information not always available to the public."

"Such as whose office the drone was circling?" The Homeland Security representative, George Nelson, had been quiet up to this point. "It sounds like Ms. Bly has done more legwork on this than the police. Are you working with anyone in the department Ms. Bly?"

"I'm kind of a loner," I said. "I might ask for a favor here or there, but I tend to keep things to myself unless I have something significant I think the police should know."

"Do you have anything significant on this investigation you haven't shared with us?"

I could feel the adrenaline surge through me. *Of course*, I had facts I didn't share with them. How did he know?

I told them about how the mysterious Chinese woman, Kim Wu or Su Ling or whatever her name was, visited Brett's business and bought a drone from him. I admitted I met what appeared to be the same woman when Brett and I ate at Portland City Grill, and how she claimed she didn't know him.

I didn't tell them about the unexplained items on Brett's credit card. He claimed he didn't make the charges and I tended to believe him.

If this woman was linked to Brett, it might not be a good idea to bring it up at the moment. I needed to do some investigative work. I thought about my young tech friend, Eric Williams, who helped me with a recent case involving a Facebook killer. I would call him and ask him to hack into the whole stolen credit card issue. For now, I would stay as mum as the September flower.

"Is this information in your report to Detective Thomas?" Nelson said. "I don't see it anywhere here."

"No, it's just another coincidence, right now," I said. "But I don't like coincidences."

"Neither do I." Agent Miller glared at me. "We'll check into it further."

I would have to be on my guard with the Feds. They would be hunting for any potential clue, and I knew they could pull me in for intensive questioning if they thought I was holding out on them.

"Senator, did you hear about the bombing in Portland yesterday," Greg Graham asked.

John Stanton looked up from a proposed legislative bill he had been speedreading at his desk. "The one with the little remote-control helicopter? Lord, what is this world coming to?"

"It happened practically on the spot you are to give your speech next month."

"I'm aware. It flew into a building and killed Benjamin Knowles. What a loss. He was a great person. It will be a huge loss for the Democratic Party."

"Do you think maybe we should cancel the date?" Graham said. "The police haven't found the perpetrator and it could be dangerous for you."

Stanton took his bifocals from his nose and rubbed his eyes. "It's a bit premature to cancel. Let's wait and see if they find the culprit and maybe we'll find the motive behind his death."

"It could be political," Graham said. "He was one of the Dem's top money raisers."

"Could be. But I don't see how his death could be related to my speech. Besides, I don't want to miss the Portland date. Every venue, every voter, is important to me."

"Christ, it could be risky," Graham said. "It happened directly across the street from the downtown Pioneer Square. If you had been there yesterday more people could have been hurt. Hell, you could have been the target."

"I hardly think I'm important enough, for somebody to want to kill me," Stanton said.

"Are you kidding? You've been surging in the polls every month. Your candidacy has both the Democrats and the GOP on edge. At the rate voters are defecting from both Party's to register as Independents, you could become a favorite by November."

"So, I need to go to Portland. They have almost 900,000 unaffiliated voters who are free to vote for me as an Independent candidate. I think the May primary will be a good indicator for the presidential elections in November."

"Oregon has only seven electoral votes," Graham said. "It's not worth putting your life in jeopardy, and the government is not going to give you the same security as the major candidates. You can bet on it."

"If it will make you feel any better, why don't you contact Reggie Jones over at the FBI. Find out what they know and ask him to keep us informed, as a personal favor to me."

Graham sighed. "It's actually a good idea. Not as good as canceling your rally, but it's a start. If Jones suggests it's too dangerous, will you reconsider canceling?"

"Let's just wait and see how this thing unfolds," Stanton said.

"I'm glad you're safe," Brett said. We sat together on my red leather sofa in the living room.

"I'm a bit shakier this morning than yesterday," I said.

"You should have let me come over last night."

"What would you have done? Held my hand?"

"It might have helped." He took my hand in his. "Sometimes just knowing you're not alone can make a difference."

I had to admit, it felt pretty good right now. "I appreciate your concern. I'm not used to asking for help or accepting it."

"If we're going to continue this relationship, we should be able to help other."

"Is this a relationship?" I asked.

"I would like it to be. I think you're wonderful."

"I kind of like you, too," I said.

He brushed my cheeks with his fingers and held me steadily in his cupped hands. He looked into my eyes and there was something in his, something sensitive. I could feel him looking into my soul. Our bodies aligned and we held each other. He caressed my face with his fingers, nudged it with his nose, his cheek, and slowly brushed his lips across mine.

He covered my lips with his, and I could feel the shape of them messaging mine. His kiss held me in a pulsating embrace, and I responded with several soft short wet kisses over different angles on his lips.

Whatever problems I incurred, whatever stress I had experienced, whatever physical injuries I suffered during the past week: all were gone. Replaced with a warm glow and the knowledge *here* was a man who was in tune with me. Who wanted to be with me, to share himself with me.

In my relationship with Steve, he abandoned me emotionally. We never connected except during sex. Steve didn't know how to be intimate and I believed I couldn't be either.

But there was something about Brett giving me hope I could be intimate with him. Maybe it wasn't me. Here was a man with whom I wanted to share my feelings. At least, I certainly was willing to learn.

He kissed me again, softly yet passionately, and I felt an electric pulse resonate through me. The night of our first date, I had held back during the *good night* kiss. I thought I held back because I still wasn't sure he liked me, but now I realized I had held back because I didn't want to be hurt again.

I tensed up at this sudden realization and Brett stopped. "Is something wrong?" he asked.

Before I could answer, the front door opened and Angel entered. "Sorry, I'm late. I had to stop and get some office supplies."

She stopped short, seeing us in an embrace. "Oh, am I interrupting something?"

"No, we were . . ." Was I embarrassed?

"I am interrupting. I'll just go into the kitchen and unpack some of this stuff. I can put it away later."

I swear that woman's timing is awful.

"Do you want me to go?" Brett said. "Maybe you have work to do."

"No," I said. "I want you to stay here and keep me company for a while if you can."

"Of course, I can." A broad smile crossed his face.

I realized I had a firm grip on both of his hands. "If we could talk for a while, I think it would be a good idea to share what happened to me yesterday."

"If it would help, I'm here."

So, I told him about Knowles and how I liked him as a person. I told him about the drone hovering in front of his window, and I explained how I reacted too late when I saw the grenade in a container under the drone.

"I wasn't able to do anything to help him," I said. "It happened so fast. Before I knew it. I tried to push him away, and then I jumped to the other side of the window. The explosion was so loud my head ached for hours."

"Instead of trying to save him, I saved myself." Tears streamed down my face. "I chickened out. It's my fault he's dead. I sacrificed his life for mine."

Brett held me in his arms and listened until I finished. "It wasn't your fault. Your reaction to save yourself is natural. Anyone would have done it. I know I would have."

"I feel so guilty," I sniffled.

"It shows you cared about him. Your compassion is one of the things which first attracted me to you."

Angel carried a ream of computer paper to her desk, which is situated just north of the front door.

"I was wondering if we could talk for a minute," she said. "I have this problem. I mean, Chris and I have this problem."

I wiped my eyes with a tissue from my purse. "I'm not in a problem-solving mindset right now. Could it wait until later? Brett and I need to talk some more."

"I guess," she said. "Is it okay if I come to my desk now? I have to work on a report for a case of ours."

"Sure. Give us a couple of minutes," I said.

I wasn't really listening. If I were, I might have asked her which case? It was only later, I learned her case of *ours* was not one of mine.

"Brett dear, I really like you," I said. "But if I seem a little standoffish at times, it's because my last relationship didn't end well."

"Oh," Brett said.

"I would like to take things slow and get to know each other better."

"I think it's a good idea, too."

"Really? You might have to be strong enough for both of us because if Angel hadn't come in earlier, we wouldn't have taken it slow at all."

"Really? I must have missed some important cues," he said.

"I have a feeling we'll get there."

"Let's make sure Angel isn't around if we do," he said.

"I'll send her on a *fool's errand*."

Chapter 19

Veronica came into Gerald's office and stood behind him as he sat at his desk at Crowe Realty, sifting through video files on his computer.

She had worn a provocative red dress showing just enough cleavage to be suggestive, but not amoral by office standards. It was a difficult balance because seventy percent of the Realtors in her office were women, many of whom already thought she was a slut.

"Have you learned anything?" she said, massaging his shoulders with both hands.

"The guy has a digital camera and entered through the back door. I got him on the camera on the back porch and in the kitchen and living room. There aren't any camera's in the hallway but there are cameras in all of the bedrooms in case of break-ins. I'll remove them when the Henderson's return from vacation.

"Look at this." He clicked on a time-stamped file and a video showed the bedroom door lurch open, a man and woman rush in, and the woman closing the door softly. She hesitated, with her ear to the door, and signaled the man by pointing to the floor. In the next instant, they were both under the bed.

"Oh my God," Veronica said. "We didn't think to look under the bed. They were there all the time. Those bastards probably spied on us during our lovemaking."

"They did more than spy. They had a camera and filmed us."

"Oh!" Veronica gasped. "Your wife. She must have hired them."

"Oh, she hired them all right. I wasn't as clever at deceiving her as I thought."

"But Gerry, what if she finds out you are planning to divorce her and marry me?"

"It doesn't look good, babe. But it may not be as bad as we think. After I saw the bedroom scene with them under the bed, I decided to go back and see if they left any clues. I wanted to know who they were."

"Did you find anything?" Veronica asked.

Gerald opened his left desk drawer and picked up an iPhone, laid it on his desk, and tapped it with his finger.

"What?" Veronica asked.

"I found it under the bed. I've noticed a lot of women slip their phones into a rear pocket when they aren't carrying their purse. It must be what happened here. It dislodged from her pants pocket while they were under the bed."

"Uh, huh," she said, not sure what this meant.

"It wasn't password locked. I know who she is."

He turned the phone on and scrolled through her messages. "See, here's her name. *Angel*. And she has a long list of texts to some guy named Chris and some woman named Billie. Just a minute, here are some pictures."

Veronica gazed at the photos with him. A woman with orange hair standing next to a blonde. A woman with blue hair and orange streaks standing next to the same woman. A woman with cherry-died red hair with a skinny halfway good-looking guy with shifty eyes.

"This is the same woman with different colored hair," she said. "She doesn't look much like an Angel. She looks like she's trouble."

"Well obviously," Gerald said. "She works at a P.I. agency in Northwest Portland with the blonde. Her name is Billie Bly. As far as I can tell, this Angel broad doesn't have a last name. At least I can't find it on her phone."

Veronica clapped her hand to her mouth and gasped.

"What is it, honey?"

"Billy Bly," she said. "I know her. She was in the newspaper today."

She ran out of the office and returned a minute later with a newspaper in her hand. "Look, just look!" She slapped the newspaper with each mention of the word *look*.

"What the. . . *a bomb*? Someone used a drone to kill this guy? I didn't hear about this." He read through the article, shaking his head. "Man, this is nuts."

"Read this part." Veronica pointed out a paragraph.

"Billie Bly, who owns a private investigations agency in Northwest Portland, also was injured in the explosion. She suffered

minor abrasions and was sent to a local hospital and apparently released. There is no record of her being treated at any of the Portland area hospitals.

"She was meeting with Mr. Knowles as a client at the time of the incident, according to Elaine Spinner, a receptionist at Chase Bank. Miss Bly has not responded to repeated attempts to contact her."

"So what? She was in the wrong place at the wrong time," Gerald said. "What are you all worked up about?"

Veronica put her hands on her hips and looked at Gerald defiantly. "She has a history of being at the wrong place at the right time. She's the one that caught that Facebook serial killer last year. She's also the one who found a serial killer inside city hall the year before that.

"She's frigging famous, Gerry, and she's coming after you."

"We'll see about that. I have an idea of how to put her in her place, starting with her two undercover operatives."

"Let me understand," Andrea Green said. "You have proof my husband is cheating on me, but you don't have proof?"

Angel tried to maintain calm, as she stirred her latte while sitting at a table in Starbucks. "We saw him inside a house with Veronica and they were going at it in a bedroom."

"But I lost the flash card with the proof," Chris said.

Angel gave Chris a dirty look. "What Chris meant to say is we were only able to film the event from the rear. There were no faces. It could have been any two people going at it and so we have no proof other than ourselves as witnesses."

Andrea Green's face became contorted. "I still don't understand how someone could lose a film card. We might have been able to isolate a frame and blow it up. Maybe from an angled shot. How in the hell did you lose the digital film anyway?"

"On the way down the roof." Chris raised both palms up in a *shit happens* gesture. "I sort of fell and landed on my camera. When I got up and looked, the camera slot was open and the flash card was gone."

"The roof?" Andrea said. "Were you filming from the roof?"

"No, we were in the doorway, but your husband must have heard us because they stopped their, uh, lovemaking, and he came out to investigate."

"We had to hide under the bed," Chris said.

Angel shushed Chris.

"I'm beginning to wonder whom I hired," Andrea said. "You two are either the best detectives around, or you're the worst to ever put on a badge."

"Oh, we don't wear badges," Chris said.

"Chris, please be quiet," Angel said, in as a civil a tone as she could muster. "Mrs. Green, you wanted us to get video of your husband's infidelity. You must realize it is very difficult, especially when his romances take place on the second floor in bedrooms of the homes he is selling."

Andrea scrunched up her nose. "I suppose you're right."

"It means we have to take chances," Angel said. "In this case, we put ourselves in a very precarious position. A position so precarious, we may not have come out unscathed."

"What do you mean?"

"I mean, your husband saw us as we exited the house." Angel waited a minute to let it sink in. "Also, he may have film of us entering the house."

"Film of you? How?"

"He had security cameras inside the house," Angel said.

"And outside too," Chris said. "I should have noticed them, me being a former burglar and all, but I guess I was too excited about getting pictures and all."

Angel kicked Chris in the shin as hard as she could. She wished she had worn steel-toed boots instead of Vans tennis shoes.

"What?" Andrea cried. "You were a burglar?"

"He's just kidding," Angel said.

She gave Chris a stern look. "Tell Mrs. Green you were kidding, Chris."

Chris appeared puzzled. "Oh, yeah. I sometimes joke around when I get nervous."

"Andrea, the crux of the matter is, well, you might be hearing from your husband about this. I mean, he'll probably figure out you're having him tailed. He might confront you."

"He hasn't said a word so far," she said. "I suppose it was inevitable he would find out sooner or later. I guess him seeing you will make it harder for you to do your job."

"We'll manage," Angel said. "We still have a few cards up our sleeves. The main thing is your safety. If you feel threatened, get away from him. Have you a safe place you can go where he can't find you?"

"Let him try anything," she said. "I can take care of myself. Besides, he can't risk his precious reputation. How would it look to his colleagues or his clients if I charged him with wife-beating?"

After they finished their coffee, Chris and Angel left Starbucks and walked in silence for a block. Chris rushed to open Angel's car door and she slid behind the steering wheel without a word.

"Are we okay?" Chris knew he was in trouble, but he was unsure exactly why.

Angel sat with both hands on the steering wheel and looked straight ahead. "If we are going to work together, you are going to have to keep quiet when we are talking to a client."

"I can do that. Did I say something wrong?"

"She didn't need to know we were chased out of the house and had to jump off the roof. She certainly didn't need to know we lost the digital film."

"Oh," he said. "I thought it might have been about me mentioning I used to be a burglar. That's when you kicked me, anyway."

Angel turned toward Chris and tried not to smile. "Yes, it certainly would not instill confidence for a client who suddenly discovered she'd hired a burglar, would it?"

Chris chuckled. "Probably not. Unless they wanted something stolen."

"Chris, dear, do you know what Billie calls us?"

"I'd hate to think," he said.

"She refers to us as *Bonnie and Clyde*. Do you think she's ever going to allow us to work with her as P.I.s if she has such a low opinion of us?"

"No?" he asked.

"We have to change her mindset and the best way we can do it is by not screwing up and certainly by not getting caught screwing up."

"Like we just did," he said.

"Exactly," she said.

"What did Billie say when you told her?" Chris said.

"I tried." Angel pecked him on the cheek and managed a half-hearted smile. "But this whole bombing thing has her all messed up. First, she's mad at me for not knowing what happened to her and today she's all shook up and playing kissy-face with the Brett Wright character."

"Isn't it nice that she has someone in her life she can turn to?" Chris said.

"Wow. You were very insightful, Chris. How unlike you."

"I guess hanging around with you has changed my perspective some. I mean, I kind of rely on you to show me how to be different from my days as a con artist and burglar."

"I have a hard time believing you could ever con anybody, dear. No offense, but you aren't the sharpest tool in the woodshop."

"I may not be sharp, but I know the names of the tools and how to use them."

"No doubt, you learned from your prison buddies."

"I've never been in prison. Okay, I was in the county lockup for a few months, awaiting trial, until my lawyer got me out. But not long enough to learn a new trade. I have a natural ability to steal things and not get caught."

"Until you ran into Billie," Angel said.

"Yeah. She's kind of special, which is why I think it's good she found someone. She's been moping around here for the last year after breaking up with Detective Steve."

"I know," Angel said. "I should be happy for her, but there's something about this Brett guy that rubs me the wrong way. I can't put my finger on why, but I'm worried he'll hurt her again."

"Shouldn't we get going if we're going to shadow Gerald Green?"

"No hurry, I put a tracker on his car," Angel started the car, looked in her side mirror and pulled away with a sigh. She tapped at a video device on the console and a navigational map illuminated.

"I *have to* get me one of these," Chris said.

A red blip moved along Southeast Seventeenth Avenue in the Sellwood neighborhood. "He's on the move," Angel said. "Give me directions so I can keep my eyes on the road."

Chapter 20

Ping Lau watched through military grade binoculars from a nearby hillside as Brett Wright stood inside the gondola of a rainbow-colored hot air balloon on the back lot of his manufacturing site.

She could see the burst of fire from the balloon's portable burner wafting heat into the nylon envelope, gradually raising the balloon to its forty-foot height.

Billie Bly stood aside gazing up at the majestic sight, clapping her hands together like an excited schoolgirl. She wore a black leather jacket over a red-and-black plaid long-sleeve shirt and blue jeans.

Ping Lau knew they were on the front end of their date. She had used a sophisticated radio receiver to intercept Bly's phone transmissions the day before and learned she and her new boyfriend, the person Ping Lau had framed for the bombing of Knowles' office, were meeting for an early morning balloon ride.

He planned to take her to a tour of a winery in nearby McMinnville where they would stay at a bed and breakfast overnight and return by air the next morning. This gave Ping Lau plenty of time to survey the area and pick the correct location for the murder of Billie Bly.

Because of a spurt of unseasonably warm weather in April, Brett had suggested a hot-air balloon ride to McMinnville. We would tour the downtown area of shops and microbreweries and later check out a winery outside of town.

I was excited, not because of the itinerary, but because Brett had taken the time to plan the perfect getaway for us. He was so thoughtful and I liked him so much for it. He said I needed to get away from the whole bombing incident and relax, although I wasn't sure how relaxing it would be to fly above the ground several hundred feet.

"Are you ready?" he said, motioning me toward the basket or gondola, as he called it.

"Ready as I'm ever going to be," I said. He helped me aboard while the balloon hovered a foot off the ground. He fired the propane burner again, wearing heat protective gloves to avoid burning his hands, and we began ascending.

A sudden wind caught us and we lurched violently upward for a second. "I think I left my stomach back on the ground," I said.

"It will be much smoother once we're fully aloft," he said.

I looked around the gondola. "How do you steer this thing?"

"I can't steer it," Brett said. "We just go where the wind takes us."

"I think I want to go back to the ground."

"It's okay," he said. "I can raise and lower the balloon and the wind direction is different at various heights. I've studied the wind charts and know where and when to raise and lower the balloon to catch the right wind direction."

"I'll take your word for it." I gazed downward. We already were several hundred feet from the ground, and I felt queasy.

"Don't look down until you get used to it," Brett said. "Watch the horizon."

I looked where he pointed as we crested a stand of Douglas firs wrapped along the Willamette River. We floated above the treetops and followed the river. The sun glowed a golden aura against the top of majestic pine trees, which ironically cast elongated early morning shadows across a patchwork quilt of farmland.

There wasn't a cloud in the sky but the frosty morning air chilled me. I had been smart to dress in layers and wear a leather coat. Still, the briskness in the air was invigorating. I could feel a surge in adrenalin as my body responded to the cold and danger of being higher than most birds and totally out of control.

"We'll be able to return in the balloon tomorrow if my wind calculations hold." Brett turned up the fire and a series of whooshes lit up the balloon as we climbed higher, changing direction slightly in the process.

"We're sailing on a wind from the east today. Tomorrow we'll have a south-westerly wind. You've got to love the Pacific Northwest. The weather changes daily and sometimes from minute-to-minute."

We spent about forty more glorious minutes in the air before descending. It was the most fascinating experience in my life if you don't count people trying to kill me.

"I can see our chase crew below," Brett said.

I examined the highway below and spotted a tiny flatbed truck and further back I saw a black SUV and a red pickup truck. They looked like matchbook cars. Jack and Mary, Brett's employees, were following us in the flatbed in case they had to rescue us and haul the balloon back to Brett's warehouse or to simply help us land.

I noticed the black SUV. Was it following us or did it just happen to be behind Jack and Mary? *Sigh.* Even up here I can't escape my fears. I decided there were hundreds of thousands of black SUVs and I wasn't going to let this one ruin my day.

Brett used a walkie-talkie to radio his crew. "I'm going to set down in the field behind the Victorian House Bed and Breakfast." He opened a vent, letting hot air escape from the balloon's envelope and we smoothly descended,

Below, I saw the flatbed pull into a field and Jack and Mary hopped out and ran toward us on our downward path. The balloon glided softly until we came closer to the ground when a gust of wind caught us and the gondola skipped across the rugged terrain. Jack and Mary tugged at the ropes trying to secure the balloon, but they seemed to be just along for the ride.

Eventually, the balloon settled and our chase crew, now I know how they got the name, tethered us to the ground. Brett climbed out of the basket first and offered his hand. I jumped from the two-foot-high hovering basket into his arms and kissed him hard.

"Are you okay?" he asked.

I kissed him again.

"I take it you want to fly back tomorrow morning," he said.

"Yes. I loved it. I don't have a care in the world up there."

Almost, anyways.

After a full day of surveillance, Ping Lau drove her black SUV up a winding dirt road and pulled off into a small meadow. She had charted wind directions the previous evening and, if her predictions held up, Wright's hot air balloon would pass over this hill on their way back to Wilsonville.

If her forecasts were wrong, she would have to eliminate the chase crew, follow the balloon on its path and hope to get close enough for a shot. If this failed, she'd simply have to try something else.

Although The General suggested waiting a few days before disposing of Bly, Ping Lau had come up with a better idea. Why not terminate both Bly and Brett Wright? Dead, Wright wouldn't be around to deny his involvement and somehow wriggle out of the charges. He would be presumed guilty after the fact and any fears Senator John Stanton might have would also evaporate.

The key to her plan had been to launch her attack on Knowles during a time Wright had no alibi. He had been home sick the day Ping Lau had blown up Knowles. She knew because she bugged his office. She also put a tracker on his car and later broken into his home and bugged it. She left nothing to chance.

When he was dead or arrested, she would collect her equipment to make sure there was no trace of her handiwork. She smiled to herself at her cleverness as she stared out the window of her car toward the panoramic view of McMinnville.

The smile vanished, replaced by an anxious moment.

She was remembering earlier in the day when she stood casually outside the Golden Valley Brewery and Restaurant and gazed through a window. Billie Bly and Brett Wright were sampling various micro-brew beers at a heavily varnished oak bar with an equally impressive oak backdrop housing bottled micro-brews.

They seemed to be laughing and having a good time. It made her irritable. He was handsome and apparently good company. Was she jealous? After all, she could have dated him if she didn't want to set him up for the fall.

No, she decided. It was Billie Bly who had gotten under her skin. It perturbed her to know the woman who somehow tumbled onto her plans was enjoying herself at Ping Lau's expense.

But something about the way Bly carried herself also intrigued Ping Lau. The woman she had run up against was stubborn, resilient, and difficult to kill. Yet the version she had seen at the Portland City Grill and around town today seemed soft and feminine. A stark contrast in character, Ping Lau thought.

She's in love with him, Ping Lau decided, and wondered to herself what it must be like to be in love. She had never let those feelings get in the way of her career. Now, she wondered if she'd missed out on something.

Ping Lau huffed a sigh at missed opportunities. It won't make any difference. Tomorrow she would end their romance for good.

I tripped on the wooden circular steps leading to our room. "Oops. I took a wrong turn."

"I know the feeling." Brett grabbed me by my elbow and guided me. "I tried not to drink too much tonight, but I definitely have a small buzz going."

"A small buzz is okay," I said. "As long as it doesn't interfere with your driving tonight."

"But I'm not going anywhere."

"Oh, yes you are." I giggled because I too had had a little too much to drink. First, the microbrews at lunch followed by the evening wine tasting at The Eyrie Vineyards. I tried not to partake too much of the wines because I wanted to enjoy my date with Brett to the fullest.

We already determined we wouldn't be using the separate bedroom, Brett, the perfect gentleman, booked for me. Halfway up the staircase, I stopped, turned, and kissed him. He kissed me back and we continued the sweet missives until I forced myself to scurry up the stairs.

I grabbed a red negligee from my bag and ran into the bathroom as he entered the bedroom. "I'll be out in a minute. Make yourself comfortable."

Now, I have to admit, I'm not one of those flirty women. I don't often wear dresses and I don't giggle at men's jokes, and I never do the *touchy* thing with men's arms or the *hair flip* thing followed by laughter.

As a young girl, I was a tomboy who now has matured into a tom-woman if there is such a thing. In my business, I can't afford to show weakness. It either costs me money or it causes me pain.

But for Brett, I'm willing to make an exception. In fact, I've long thought I needed to work on my femininity but I haven't known how. However, Brett makes it easy. I just want to make him as happy as he's made me.

I adjusted my negligee in the mirror and didn't cringe. I looked pretty good. Heck, I might even have looked hot. I did a curtsy to myself in the mirror and entered the bedroom.

Brett lay under the covers in the queen-sized bed. His awkward smile told me he was as nervous as me and now I began worrying about my performance. It's always a little embarrassing the first time I'm with a man. The one exception was when my former boyfriend, Steve, and I hit the sheets. We had a sexual desire which undercut any feelings.

But Brett was different. He freely expresses his feelings and as a result, I've managed to open up more about myself. I wanted our lovemaking to be wonderful, but I wanted our relationship to be strong too.

"Are you as nervous as I am?" he asked.

"Maybe." I stood at the foot of the bed smiling.

He sat up, revealing an eight-pack I had only seen before on those bodice-ripper book covers. Okay, he wasn't necessarily herculean but I was thoroughly impressed. And lucky.

"Do you want to talk first?" he patted to bed next to him.

"I think I'd prefer to talk after."

"Too bad," he said. "I was going to tell you how beautiful you are right now."

"You look nice too." Nice? I blushed.

He reached out to me and I took his hand and followed it into bed. I laid next to him as he caressed my cheek with the strong hands I wouldn't have expected from a nerd. Obviously, he worked out now.

He kissed me softly on my neck and brushed my ears with his lips. I caressed his chest and then his thighs with soft finger touches. We nibbled at each other and whispered sweet tidbits back and forth.

He held me in his arms and I felt a sense of belonging and being protected. It was a sense of security and well-being I had never experienced before. He told me he had never felt this way about a woman and scored points for being on my wavelength.

He helped me out of my negligee and I noticed he was already naked. I became aroused and a little embarrassed but, of course, he couldn't tell.

He fondled me and I caressed him and our foreplay heightened until we were one. We matched intensity levels in a rhythmic ebb and flow which launched the bed into a fit of creaking and swaying.

In the end, our bodies writhed with the joy that only can be found in new love. We held each other and continued light kisses on the lips, ears, necks and other places too private to mention.

We talked about our dreams, our realities, and our desire to be with each other. He held me in his arms and I pecked at his chest. Eventually, the small talk transitioned into more sex talk, and I pushed him over and straddled him for round two.

We rocked each other in a steady rhythm, him cupping my breasts and me holding on for dear life. Eventually, our love erupted again and I fell off him into the tangled sheets.

"That was nice," Brett said.

"My thoughts exactly."

I blew a breath of air upward toward my sweaty brow, took his hand in mine, and fell asleep.

Chapter 21

Jack and Mary were in the process of setting up the balloon when Brett and I arrived the next morning. We were an hour late, according to Brett.

He said the wind closer to the ground is usually stagnant in the morning, allowing for a smoother takeoff and landing. By eleven o'clock it is more difficult for a hot air balloon pilot to control his or her craft.

"Morning," Mary said. "You're running about an hour late. Must have been a late night."

"We made the most of it," I said.

"I hope you brought us some coffee, Brett. It's cold out here."

Mary O'Reilly was a small woman with short-clipped red hair. She had pale skin and green eyes, typical of Irish descent. She wore a long-sleeve blue windbreaker and blue jeans.

Brett told me she and Jack Wallace had been engaged to be married for three years but apparently weren't in any hurry to tie the knot. They seemed happy enough when together and Brett told me Mary liked her independence.

Jack was in the gondola setting up the propane burner. He too was on the smallish side and he wore an identical blue windbreaker. He darted around like a hummingbird flitting from flower to flower. His long brown hair matched his ferocious motions, bouncing off his cheeks as he swooped to-and-fro.

I watched, fascinated, as a cool-air fan filled the balloon-like one of those bouncy castles and it quickly took shape. Once it stood upright, Jack pumped hot air into the envelope, giving it buoyancy. It already had been set up when I first saw it yesterday and I missed seeing this. It grew into what seemed to be a living, breathing monstrous creature, before my eyes.

When it had reached its total height, Jack stepped out of the basket and joined Mary, who wrapped her arms around him in a hug. "Nice job, hon, and in record time."

"Couldn't have done it without you," he said. "You have a knack for setting things up just right." He kissed her and it made me blush and look away."

"Hey, where's *my* kiss?" Brett asked.

I obliged him and sensed maybe it was Jack and Mary's turn to blush and look away. But when we finished, I noticed they were watching us with smiles.

"Did you two have a wonderous time?" Mary asked.

"We made the most of it," Brett said. "We did more walking around downtown McMinnville than I've done in a month."

"You both seem to have enlightened spirits," Mary said. "I can almost see a glow."

We both blushed now and Jack laughed out loud. "Now Mary, I think you may have embarrassed our boss and his lovely companion."

"Ignore them," Brett said. "They've been after me for a long time to get into the dating scene again and now they're apparently satisfied with themselves.

I looked at my man. He bought himself a brown bomber jacket yesterday to match mine. What is it about couples dressing alike when they first begin dating? Still, I liked it and I wore my leather jacket again. I had picked up a chic stocking hat during our shopping excursion because it had been cold yesterday morning so high up in the air.

"There are coffee and donuts on the picnic bench," Brett said, pointing.

When Mary and Jack went to get their coffee and donuts, Brett nuzzled his nose against mine. "I hope they didn't embarrass you. They mean well, but when they get together they can be incredibly mischievous."

"I know the type," I said. "My assistant, Angel, and her boyfriend, Chris, cause me no end of trouble. Angel is a darling, but when she is with Chris, she's nothing but trouble."

"I can't wait to meet them."

"Let's postpone it until you are madly infatuated with me," I said. "I don't want to chance them scaring you away."

"Nothing's going to keep me away." He took me in his arms and kissed me.

"You two lovebirds better get going," Mary said. "You're already behind schedule and the balloon isn't going to hold its shape much longer without you at the throttle."

Brett climbed into the gondola and helped me aboard. It wasn't difficult for me to climb into on the ground, but the constant motion of the balloon and gondola jarred by the ground wind made it a precarious leap

Brett held me tight as the balloon took an unexpected lurch, and I looked into his gorgeous blue eyes. I realized we both had blonde hair and blue eyes. We didn't have to dress alike during our courting phase, we already matched.

I gave him a peck on the cheek for luck and Jack and Mary loosened our lifelines, chasing us across the field as we bounced a few times along the ground before a short burst of flames sent us skyward.

I watched them waving to us, arm-in-arm. It felt good to be a couple, I thought. I had spent too much time alone in my life. I deserved to have someone like Brett by my side. I hoped dearly, it would be permanent.

An image of Brett and I standing before a minister flashed in my mind, and I smiled.

"What's so funny?" Brett asked.

"Nothing. Just a happy thought."

Ping Lau sat inside her SUV pointed toward the horizon. In the distance, she spotted the rainbow striped hot air balloon. She guessed it was about three-hundred-feet aloft. It would have to climb another couple hundred feet to clear this small clump of mountains.

"Oh no," she cried. "It's going too far north." She sighed at the inevitable and began mentally preparing for the chase. She got out of the SUV and put the pair of high-powered binoculars to her eyes. They were about a half-mile from her and she could see the balloon was ascending.

She knew from her abbreviated studies Wright would adjust the craft's altitude to catch a more favorable wind. Maybe one going in the direction toward Wilsonville. She went to the back of the SUV, opened the trunk door, and picked up the gun she planned to use.

It was already loaded in preparation. But would she be able to use it? The balloon continued to rise and she realized she'd been holding her breath. The balloon suddenly caught a wind gust and started a circular motion toward her.

"Yes!" she shouted. "It's coming."

She slung an ammunition pouch over her shoulder and raced for the open meadow. It would be exposed enough to get a shot off, but shadows from nearby trees shielded her from view.

The balloon drifted toward her on a slow amiable course. She could feel her adrenaline raging. She had had adrenaline highs before, but nothing like this. The revenge factor had her almost overdosing on her own adrenaline.

She waited impatiently. "Come to me, Billie. Come to me."

And the balloon seemed to respond, changing direction just enough to be in Ping Lau's line of fire.

"That was quite a ride," I said.

"The winds are unpredictable this morning," Brett said. "I'm going to have to experiment until I find the right combination."

I was suddenly cold and I wanted to be in his arms, but he had those oversized protective gloves on his hands to protect him from the roaring fire emitted by the burner.

"We should be okay for a while," he said. "We're heading in a southeasterly direction. I can probably get us within half-a-mile of my offices if this wind holds up."

I was daydreaming about our day together, the micro-brew tasting, the wine tasting, the dinner, and the . . . dessert. Oh, my. Yes, the dessert was heavenly.

A white stream of smoke screamed to the left of the balloon. "What was that?" I asked.

"Not sure," Brett said.

"Whatever it was, it just missed us," I said.

"It might have been a rocket. Maybe some hobbyist is firing his model rocket and didn't see us."

All kinds of warning alarms signaled inside me. I looked down and followed the smoke to its origin.

"It came from that hillside," I said. "And here comes another one. Someone is shooting at us."

A red-hot streaming streak of white struck the side of the gondola, not two feet from me. Flames blew over the side toward us.

"There's a fire extinguisher over there." Brett goosed the balloon with a burst of fire and we lurched up roughly.

I grabbed at the extinguisher, grappled with the safety tab, and sprayed the flames, gradually battling them back against the wind enough to spray the side of the basket.

Ping Lau grinned when the flare struck the wicker basket. She loaded another flare into her flare gun and aimed it toward the balloon. It had started to rise but it was still within the range of her white smoke flares, with a range of four-hundred-feet.

She preferred the white smoke flares because they were less conspicuous. The other set of flares would soar up to a thousand feet, but they were a brilliant orange color, and more likely to be noticed by the general public and reported.

She aimed high, guessing where the rapidly rising balloon would be when the flare arrived. They were only a couple-hundred-feet above her on the mountaintop, so she would still have a few more opportunities. The balloon was too big and they were too close to miss.

Ping Lau raised the flare gun above her head with two hands, aimed, and fired. It sounded like a cap gun when the pin struck the flare cylinder and a beautiful white streak of smoke rallied high and struck the balloon just above the gondola.

The flames erupted inside the balloon and then they were gone. She grabbed her binoculars. It was that damned Billie Bly. She held a fire extinguisher in her hands and sprayed it onto the balloon fabric.

"I'll get you yet. I'll aim for the middle where she can't reach it with the extinguisher."

She reloaded her flare gun and lifted it to sight the aircraft. Something was wrong. It was changing direction. She tried to anticipate where to aim, but the balloon seemed to be rotating in a circle.

She aimed ahead of the aircraft and launched a flare but it missed. The balloon speed had changed making it difficult for her to correctly calculate a shot. It was heading off to her right. She would have only one more chance before her sight line was cut off by a stand of trees.

She aimed, squeezed the trigger, and watched the stream of smoke cruise toward its target. It seemed to linger and, for a minute, she wasn't sure it would reach. It must have been an optical illusion, however, because the flare which emanated heat of over a thousand degrees, struck the balloon in its mid-section—a real money shot.

"Got you," Ping Lau shouted.

She watched as the crippled aircraft in flames, began a slow descent, drifting quickly north. Remarkably, it held its shape while plunging toward a forested area. Without warning, the bag collapsed into itself and plunged in a spiral between some trees. Ping Lau could not see where it crashed, but it was still at least a hundred feet above the ground when she had last seen it.

"No one could survive such a fall," she murmured.

Overnight, she had removed the bugs she placed in Wright's office and car. Now she would go to his home and retrieve the last bugs before the FBI showed up. It felt good to be going forward again.

Portland Police Chief Samuel Hardy stood before a large whiteboard and taped a piece of evidence to it. He had to admit the resources of the FBI, Homeland Security, and ATF were productive and superior to those of the Portland Police Bureau.

His team might have gotten to the point the federal agencies achieved this morning in maybe another month. Now, each section head was preparing to report his findings to his own selected team of detectives, forensic specialists, and SWAT team department heads. Hell, even one of the dogs and his handler from the K-9 unit was here. He had done his best to bring his best and brightest employees to the table.

"Agent Miller will update you regarding what the FBI has come up with on the bombing," Chief Harding said.

Mayor Jackson, sitting on the sidelines, gave Hardy a thumbs up gesture.

Miller strode to the whiteboard and fastened a photo of a mass of scorched plastic and other bits and pieces obviously found nearby and added to the debris. His square face was firm. He was all business.

"I sent this debris to our Terrorist Explosive Device Analytical Center in Huntsville, Alabama," Miller said. "They have the most extensive library of IED devices and bombs in the world.

"We've known it's only a matter of time before a terrorist organization adopted a hobby drone to carry an explosive payload. The FBI has been watching and waiting and now it appears it's happened. For several years now, Islamic State fighters in Iraq and Syria, have been using off-the-shelf remote-control aircraft modified to drop grenades. This tactic has been a real hindrance to U.S. Special Operations forces.

"Drones are cheap, easy to acquire and operate, and difficult to disrupt or monitor. Our team of forensic scientists has not only determined the make and model of this remote-controlled helicopter, they have pinpointed where it originated."

"It was manufactured right here in Wilsonville," Chief Hardy said.

Miller frowned. "That's correct. This company, *Flying Circus Aeronautics*, is working on an Artificial Intelligence module, which can be added to almost any sophisticated remote control flying device. According to our investigation, the owner, one Brett Wright, hopes to sell it to a few major delivery firms."

"Like Amazon for delivery of packages," Chief Hardy said.

"Yes," Miller said. "The company has sent out several prototypes to delivery firms in hopes of landing a major contract."

"The company has done a poor job of maintaining control of the product," Chief Hardy said. "They've already started selling some of these AI modules to the public."

"Agent Miller? If I may?" A slender man with thinning brown hair and glasses stood up.

Miller nodded. "For those of you who are new to this assignment, this is Assistant Director of Homeland Security, George Nelson. Yes, Nelson?"

Nelson nodded to Miller. "We've done a quick search of all known terrorist cells in the Northwest and come up with the only one which has shown interest in flying these smaller drones. In fact, some of them have visited this factory during a monthly tour."

"Really? Please continue," Chief Hardy said.

"Well, that's it. The cell has been dubbed Abu Sayyaf, also known as the Islamic State of Iraq. It has half-a-dozen members and is situated in Renton, outside of Seattle. They appear to be a splinter group of a branch in the Philippines.

"But we have no record of them buying anything from Flying Circus Aeronautics," Nelson said. "Just the one visit. One of our informants says their leader, Mohammad Abadi, met with the owner, Brett Wright about two months ago."

Lou Sanchez, of the ATF, spoke up: "Do you have any proof Abu Sayyaf purchased anything from Flying Circus?"

"Nothing, Lou," Nelson said. "We're still searching for paper trails,"

"But we have enough for a search warrant of *The Flying Circus* and Brett Wright's home," Chief Hardy said. "Team one will be led by me and FBI Special Agent Miller. We'll take the business site. Agents Nelson and Sanchez will lead team two in the search of Brett Wright's home in West Linn. SWAT will break into two teams and front both efforts."

Agent Miller looked at his Apple watch. "It's oh-eight-thirty. We'll reconvene at our target destinations in forty-five minutes. The plan is to hit both sites simultaneously. Let's make this a clean search. Separate any workers and home residents from the search area."

As the police and federal agents filtered out of the crowded room, Mayor Jackson ambled over to Hardy and shook his hand.

"Excellent job, Sam. We must continue to control this investigation. I want to stay ahead of the news so we can take credit."

"You can count on me," Hardy said. "I am a little nervous about the terrorist angle. It's a thing the Feds will jump on. Why can't it just be a little case of some wacko flying a remote-control helicopter into a building?"

"With a grenade?" Jackson said.

"Yeah, a wacko with a helicopter who just happens to have a grenade."

"We'll see," Jackson said. "You'd better get going."

"Yeah," Hardy said. I'm looking forward to serving this warrant on Wright. He's never going to know what hit him."

Chapter 22

"Crouch down and keep low," Brett said.

"What happened?" I yelled. "Are we hit again?"

"No, I've caught a higher wind layer and it's forcing us right, but we're caught in a minor thermal, which is making us go in a circle. I'm trying to use what little evasive action a slow-moving balloon might offer."

The ride was like hitting turbulence in an airplane but without a seatbelt. I crouched as told and said a quick prayer. The basket lurched again and we began descending.

"We have to go down before the thermal shakes us to bits," Brett said.

"Look out," I hollered. A blast of white smoke shot past the balloon, missing it by maybe ten feet. "If I ever get a hold of that crazy bitch . . ."

There was only one person who would devise a way to shoot down a hot air balloon, and I knew who because she'd already tried to kill me once.

Our descent speed was marginal because the thermal fought to lift us. I grabbed the fire extinguisher and stayed below the top of the basket, not wanting to be cast over.

"Can you find a place to land?" I asked.

"Too many trees," Brett said. "It's going to be a rough landing no matter what."

I thought of several things in the next instant. My infatuation with Brett, my best friend, Angel, and how I shouldn't be irritated with her, and I even gave the benefit of the doubt to Chris. I'd taken them for granted, as I had my three brothers. I would change all of it if we survived this predicament.

A hissing sound roared above us, like a tire with a nail in it going flat. I looked up and my heart sank. A stream of smoke spewed from somewhere in the middle of the envelope and I could see a hole growing larger.

The balloon material seemed to be melting from the inside. I stood and shot the extinguisher toward the flame, but the white powder spray couldn't make the distance.

"It's no good," Brett said. "Listen carefully. I'm going to try to find a nice soft tree branch, but it's going to be a rough landing. You need to stay low and brace yourself. Find something to hang onto and don't let go."

"Are we going to die?" I asked, stupidly.

"No. This gondola is made of strong wicker and can withstand a crash landing. If we can stay inside, we have a good chance of walking away."

I knew he was lying to me, but I stood up and kissed him one last time. Before he could say 'get down' we plunged so violently I nearly threw up. We dropped together, still in each other's arms, but snug against the basket using our feet against a supply box to steady ourselves.

It felt like we were diving seventy-miles-an-hour when something snatched us up.

"We caught a tree limb," Brett said. "Hang on."

I hugged him tighter. Something snapped and we tumbled toward terra-firm again, falling sideways now. It happened so fast, I didn't have time to scream. We must have snagged another tree branch because the gondola jolted upright,

We were dislodged from each other and free-fell fifty feet, hitting the ground with such a jarring thud, I was sure we were dead.

I never blacked out, but the wind gushed from my lungs and I sat stunned, trying to get my lungs to work. Inhale, rest, exhale. After a minute of this, I determined my lungs worked just fine. I felt my arms and legs and found no broken bones. I was about to laugh out loud when I realized Brett wasn't with me.

I struggled to pull myself up to the level of the gondola basket. Everything about me ached. I scanned the area consisting mostly of pine needles and branches. A ray of sunlight filtered through the canopy, but it was dark down here.

"Brett!" I cried. "Brett, where are you?"

The pain in my body was gone. I scaled the gondola like a high hurdler and landed on my hands and knees in the pine needles. I couldn't see him anywhere. I looked above into the tree limbs where a portion of the balloon's envelope hung smoldering. No Brett.

"Brett! Please be alive! Where are you?"

I lit out running through the forest, hoping for the best, but expecting the worst. I was about to give up and give in to the pain when I heard someone."

"Billie? Where are you?" It sounded like Mary. Of course. She and Jack had been following the balloon.

"Over here. I'm over here." A few seconds later, Mary trudged through some brush and found me. I was never so glad to see anybody in my life.

"I can't find Brett," I said, hugging her and crying.

"Jack is searching over by the basket," she said. "How did you get so far from the balloon?"

"I landed in the basket and when I couldn't find Brett, I started searching on my own."

"You're lucky to be alive. If you survived there's a chance Brett did too."

"But he wasn't in the basket with me. He must have fallen out."

"Mary, I found him," a voice crackled.

Mary retrieved a walkie-talkie from her waistband. "I found her and she's okay. How is Brett?"

Static permeated her walkie-talkie. "He's . . . We're seventy feet west of the . . . I called the Sheriff's office."

"Okay," Mary said. "How is Brett." More static. Mary turned the walkie-over and opened the back. "I think my battery's dead. We'd better get back and see."

It took less than five minutes to get to the crash site. It was the longest five minutes of my life. When we finally arrived, the air was sucked from me again.

Brett was leaning over the gondola, his feet on the ground. He stood up and grinned. "I hope you won't let this little incident deter you from flying with me again."

I ran over and slugged him on the arm. "How dare you disappear like that. I was worried sick."

He took me in his arms and kissed me. "Apparently, I got bumped out of the basket. Somehow, I wound up on top of a portion of the envelope, which hadn't burned and it softened my landing."

"I found him tangled up in shreds of the envelope not too far from here," Jack said. "He was mad at me because I couldn't tell him if you were all right."

"You should have rescued her first," Brett said, with a sheepish smile.

It took an hour to sort through everything. Washington County dispatched two patrol cars, a fire truck, and three ambulances after several people called in while witnessing our calamity. Brett had to report the crash to Federal Aviation Administration and surprisingly, a forensic team was on the scene in less than thirty minutes.

We were interviewed by the two jurisdictions while being poked and prodded by the EMTs for forty minutes before the everyone was satisfied. The FAA would remain and sketch out the crash site to see if it matched our verbal account. We were told there would be follow up interviews and the possibility of a citation loomed if Brett were somehow at fault.

The Sheriff's department sent a squad car to search the hill where I said the rockets were launched and would get back to us with the results. I didn't expect them to find anything, but I made a mental note to conduct my own investigation there later.

We were sore and weary and we were on our way to *Flying Circus Aeronautics* to unload the gondola and get my car when the call came. At the other end of the phone call, I heard a shrill, panicked voice Brett identified as Jessica Nelson, an engineer at his plant.

"What?" Brett said. "Please slow down. I can't understand you." We were on the back of the flatbed truck hunkered down behind the cab and the road noise made it difficult to carry on a conversation. Mary and Jack were inside.

"She says there are about forty police cars at Flying Circus. What? What is the FBI doing there? What is going on?"

Brett lowered the mobile phone to his side and his face was ashen. "Jessica says we've been served with a search warrant. Something about the drone that killed Benjamin Knowles."

I took the phone from Brett. "Jessica, this is Billie Bly, Brett's friend. What does the search warrant say? Did you read it?"

"It says something about just cause to search the premises based on debris found at the crime scene at six-hundred-block of Southwest Sixth Avenue."

"The Chase Bank building, Benjamin Knowles office," I said. "Can you tell what they are looking for, specifically?"

"No. They're being tight-lipped about it and they made all of the employees leave the building. We're all huddled on the flight pad we use for launching our test drones."

"We'll be there soon," I said. "We're on our way."

"I don't understand." Brett's face had regained some color. "What are they looking for and why are they looking in my business offices?"

We didn't have long to wonder. Five minutes later, Jack plodded up the driveway and we were met by a horde of police cars representing Portland, Wilsonville, Multnomah County and Washington County. There were also a half-dozen black sedans, three white vans, a bunch of men running around in white forensic outfits carrying boxes and computers, and a damn Partridge in a Pear Tree.

Son of a bitch," I said.

"I can't believe this," Brett said.

A man in a blue FBI windbreaker stopped us a hundred feet from the scene. "You can't be here. You will have to turn around."

Brett jumped off the back of the flatbed. "I'm the owner here. What in the hell is going on?"

"I'm not at liberty to say. You need to talk to FBI Senior Agent Thom Miller, the gentleman with the black hair and mustache standing by the front door.

I left Brett arguing with the FBI agent, marched up the driveway, and inserted myself between Miller and another FBI agent. "What the hell are you doing here, Miller?"

"I might ask you the same thing, Miss Bly. You have no cause to be involved in our investigation."

"I'm with Brett. He's a friend of mine."

"Is that so? Interesting. Is it a coincidence you are involved with a person of interest in this investigation?"

"Only because you don't know what the hell you're doing. I told you the best suspect is the Asian woman who flies drones, visited Brett's drone factory, and denied her identity when Brett met her later."

"Ah, yes. The mysterious Chinese woman. We talked to the manager at the Portland City Grill, Cindy Brown. She said the employee you referred to, worked less than a week and hadn't finished providing proof of her identity. No social security number, no driver's license or work permit."

"Well, she wouldn't want to leave a trail, would she?" I asked.

"We're following up on it and plenty of other leads," Miller said. "Plus, we may have to take another look at your report, now as we've learned you may be prejudiced toward Brett Wright. What did you say your relationship is with him? A friend?"

I could feel my face reddening. "Good friends. We've known each other since high school and there is no way he could be involved in this bombing. As a matter of fact, we were both shot down in his air balloon this morning. We're lucky to be alive."

Miller's face didn't show any emotion. "Really? Did you file a report with the FAA?"

"The FAA and the Washington County Sheriff's office," I said. "It was that crazy Chinese lady, I know it. When I get my hands on her . . ."

"Yes, we'll definitely have to explore these new developments," Miller said and walked away.

I knew he wasn't going to share any of the developments leading him to Brett. I would have to go to Steve or my brother, Dan, to learn the origins of their search warrant. I found Brett nearby, engaging in a heated discussion with George Nelson, of Homeland Security.

"He wants me to go downtown for questioning," Brett said.

"Do you have a warrant?" I asked.

He was still scrutinizing me. "You're the Bly, girl, aren't you?"

"I'm the Bly, woman, yes."

"What in the world are you doing here?"

"She's a dear friend of mine," Brett said. "She was with me in the hot air balloon this morning."

Oh, yes. Say, you two are lucky to be alive, Ms. Bly."

"Do you have a warrant for his arrest?"

"Not at this time. An interview at this point would be simply to fill in some missing blanks."

"Such as?" I asked.

"Oh, what type of aircraft he manufactures here, to whom he may have sold some of his drone models, maybe get a list of his customers. Those types of things, you know."

"Is he a suspect in the bombing a few days ago?"

"Oh, no. But he may have information tied to the bombing. This is what we are trying to determine right now."

"Why do you think Brett is involved?" I asked.

"It's not whether we think he's involved. Can I share a little secret with you? Promise not to tell?"

I nodded. Agent Nelson was playing the role of good cop. I trusted him less than Miller. Still, if he was willing to give some information, I would play along.

"The model of the helicopter is similar to some of the models Mr. Wright builds in his factory. I'm sure other manufacturers build similar models, but since his factory is within twenty-five miles of the bombing . . ."

"He was asking me about my artificial intelligence module," Brett said. "There aren't half-a-dozen manufacturers who have such a product."

"So, what do you say, Mr. Wright? Would you mind coming downtown and help us connect some of the dots, so to speak? You might as well. You won't be able to go home for several hours. We're searching your house too."

"You're searching my home?" Brett said. "Why would you search my home?"

"You never know what might turn up," Nelson said.

"I think I should seek the advice of counsel," Brett said.

"By all means," Nelson said. "We can have your attorney meet us downtown."

"He's not going anywhere today," I said. "And he definitely won't speak to you without a lawyer present."

Brett gave me a look somewhere between perplexed and thankful. We walked away and watched as federal agents walked out of the front door with more boxes, a few remote-control helicopters, and various pieces used to assemble the aircraft.

A thin woman, with hair too red not to have come from a bottle, approached us. She wore bottle-style, gold-rimmed glasses. Her blue jeans were tight enough to not leave anything to the imagination. Her breasts were tightly contained in a white blouse.

"Why are they doing this?"

"It's all a mistake, Jessica. Tell the employees they can go home for the rest of the day, but to report as usual tomorrow morning."

"I don't understand," Jessica said.

"Neither do I." He watched her walk toward the group of employees. "How did I ever get into this mess?"

I was wondering the same thing, only I was wondering if Brett were truly innocent or if he had been conning me all along. I'm a cynic, okay. Private investigators are supposed to be wary in these situations. Heck, I'm an ex-cop too, trained to disbelieve anything a suspect tells you.

But with love entering the picture, I didn't know what to believe, my heart or cop logic.

Chapter 23

Ping Lau looked through military-grade binoculars several hundred yards away from a hillside east of Brett Wright's property. She had been too late. The Feds swooped in earlier this morning and were ransacking Brett Wright's home. She should have retrieved the listening devices last night instead of waiting until this morning.

She had been tired and wanted to be fresh this morning when she terminated Bly and Williams so she postponed retrieving her surveillance equipment from Wright's home. But at least she had been successful in killing that damn Billie Bly.

Now, all she could hope was the FBI would not think to look for any listening devices. Why should they? They had no reason to think someone might be bugging her fall guy. They would be looking for evidence of a completely different nature.

She watched the small team of eight investigators and she noticed that they were only searching the house. No one went back to the large barn a hundred feet behind Wright's home.

Maybe their search warrant didn't include the barn. Perhaps, they weren't aware of the separate structure. Surely, they would get another warrant from a judge to check out his workshop. She had noticed it the day she planted her bugs. It was a large shop with sophisticated locks and an alarm system.

The barn gave her an idea. She had missed an opportunity there, but she might have another chance. It would all depend on whether they entered the structure today. She knew they would need to gain access eventually. If they were to come back tomorrow, she might be able to add a little something to seal the deal on Wright's frame.

She worried that The General would be upset with her in her impetuous decision to terminate Wright without consulting him. If she could convince the government officials beyond a shadow of a doubt of Wright's guilt, The General would not care about her actions this morning.

He would be expecting an update, and she needed to be able to reassure him. It had occurred to her he would likely send more work her way if things went well. Now was not the time to make him angry.

She would wait and watch until the search was over. If the shop was ignored, she would move in under the cover of darkness to retrieve her equipment and break into the workshop. The home would be empty and the alarm system and security locks would offer no challenge to her abilities.

She might even see if Wright has left some wine or beer in the refrigerator for her.

"Angel, I'm standing at your desk and *you* are not here. I need you at the office, *now*."

Her muffled voice came back at me over the phone, and I had images of her and Chris doing the nasty somewhere out in public. "Uh, I'm out on an errand. I can be there in about an hour."

"How come you're never in the office, lately? I need you here in case, heaven forbid, a potential client calls."

"All of your business calls are forwarded to my cell phone," she said.

"Why do I get the feeling you must be doing something you shouldn't?" I asked.

"Oops, losing you. Bad signal. I'll be there soon. '*Click*.'"

"Did she just say '*click*'?"

I could hear Brett and my tech specialist, Eric Williams, talking in my new conference room which used to be a bedroom off the office area. I entered and saw them engaged in an interview.

I first met Eric when I caught him in the act of a burglary. He and his friend, Jimmer, used Facebook to burgle homes of people who posted about being on vacation. I bailed him out of jail to help me track down a serial killer who also used Facebook but to troll for young women.

Eric had filled out from the skinny nineteen-year-old kid who helped me two years ago. He stood an inch taller than my five-foot-ten frame. His thick brown hair still caressed soft facial features but his brown previously worried eyes now showed confident assuredness. He wore black slacks, a white dress shirt, and a blue tie as he took notes on a legal pad.

Brett looked as if he was being grilled by the district attorney, his fingers scratching at strangled blond hair and his elbows hugging an oblong laminated table I had bought at an office liquidator store.

"How's it going," I asked.

"It's a dilly," Eric said.

"You have no idea what led them to obtain a search warrant?"

"None at all," Brett said. "Except . . ."

"The mysterious Asian lady who visited your plant over a month ago," Eric said.

"It's about the same time someone charged some *Flying Circus Aeronautics* products on my charge card."

"Billie, while you were gone we accessed Brett's credit card and found the charges for the helicopters and programming modules. I then intercepted the IP address of the bank, located a list of employees of the main branch and sent a picture of a cute kitten lying on his back to two hundred female employees' Facebook accounts.

"Viola, already three likes. My, Cheryl Denning spends an inordinate amount of time at work on Facebook. I've hacked into her account while she's looking at cat videos and now I'm using it to do some searches regarding those purchases."

"Amazing," Brett said. "How does he do it?"

"He sends her a fake Facebook link to her account. When she clicks on it she went to his phony Facebook page, where his phishing program steals her passwords. He probably used her password to access the bank's server.

"How is this going to help us?"

"Be patient," I said. "I'm betting Eric is going to try and trace the order back to the purchaser's IP address."

"It was my plan but according to the bank, the billing came from Brett's own computer."

"But I didn't do this," Brett said.

"You may have been hacked. Someone may have taken over your computer remotely to make the order. This will take longer than I thought. We're going to have to access Brett's computer to find the answer."

I sat down at the conference table and took Brett's hand. "If this is a setup, someone has gone to an awful lot of trouble to put you in the frame."

"It's like a nightmare," Brett said. "I can't believe it's happening."

"Brett, honey. Where were you at the time of the drone attack?"

"Don't you believe me?" he said.

"It's not I don't believe you. I'm looking to provide you with an alibi."

He slumped in his chair and made a sour face. "I was working at home. I had a special project I needed to finish and there are too many distractions at work."

"Can anyone verify your story?"

"Story! It's the truth. I knew it. You think I'm guilty too."

I didn't know what I thought. I wanted to believe him, but the cynical ex-cop in me thought it might be a convenient lie. It didn't help by his becoming defensive. My inner voice told me he was a good guy, and I would be defensive too if I were in his shoes.

"I'm not calling you a liar but you need to know the cops and the Feds are going to challenge you, and they are not going to be politically correct. You need to have your facts straight. I'm just trying to help you."

He sat up straighter and looked at me with those beautiful blue eyes. "I'm sorry. I was home alone. I had one call late in the evening, but I spent most of my day in my home workshop out in the barn. I didn't even see the mailman."

Eric looked up from his computer. "Wow. What are the chances? If someone framed him, they would have to be sure he didn't have an alibi."

"Are you thinking what I'm thinking?" I asked.

"Maybe someone bugged him."

"It would account for how someone knew we were going ballooning," I said. "I mean, how could someone be prepared enough to know in advance we were going to be up in a hot air balloon?"

"What are you talking about?" Eric said.

I told him about our date and how someone waited on a hillside to shoot us down with rockets. He shook his head and said *Wow* again.

"But why would someone go to all the trouble to frame him and turn around and kill him?" Eric said.

"If I were dead, I'd be guilty by default," Brett said. "Someone needs me to be guilty."

"Maybe," I said. "Or maybe someone wanted me dead. Someone named Kim Wu or Su Ling."

"The Chinese Goddess," Eric said. "Brett told me she was a real knockout."

"I thought she looked a little trampy." Okay, maybe I was a bit jealous. More likely I wanted to sucker-punch the bitch for nearly killing me—how many times? Three. Three times. The night she shot at me in the Big Pink district, two days ago when she bombed me in Benjamin Knowles office, and today in the hot air balloon crash.

"Holy crap! Maybe it's *me* she's trying to kill. Maybe Knowles was in the wrong place at the wrong time. Maybe she was after me today."

"It doesn't explain why someone is framing your boyfriend," Eric said.

I blushed. "Boyfriend?"

Eric glanced down at his computer, somewhat nervously. "Well, yeah. You two are dating, aren't you? I just assumed . . ."

"I don't know," I said. "We've been out on a handful of dates, but we haven't really talked about commitments yet."

Brett leaned toward me and kissed me on the cheek. "You must know how I feel about you. I think you're great."

It doesn't do for a rough and tough P.I. to get all syrupy sweet in front of people. As the Beach Boys once said in the song, *My Favorite Vegetables: I'm red as a beet 'cause I'm so embarrassed.*

"I, um, would rather discuss this when we're alone," I said. Then, as an afterthought, I leaned into Brett and kissed him on his cheek.

"I was right," Eric said. "You two are an item."

We looked at each other and grinned. "I guess we are," I said.

For the first time since we took off in the hot air balloon this morning, Brett smiled. "So, what do we do now?"

"We need to check your computers," Eric said.

"And look for surveillance equipment," I added.

"Good luck on the computers," Brett said. "It looked like the FBI took them this morning."

"Maybe they left your home computer," I said.

"Doesn't matter," Erick said. "If I can access his home and work IP addresses, we can get what we need."

"Let's go to my house first," Brett said. "I need a drink."

It took forty minutes to get to West Linn in Portland's rush hour traffic. When we arrived at his home I was completely blown away.

The massive T-shaped home sat on about five beautifully landscaped acres. A huge gray barn, a hundred yards away, included what looked to be separate living quarters on the second floor. Windows outlined the home so you practically had an unobscured view no matter where you were in the home.

Two padded wicker chairs sat on each side of the entry door on a covered front porch patio. When he opened the front-door I could see a beautiful canyon view through the dining room windows.

"The alarm is still engaged," Brett said. "The Feds must have notified the alarm company before they entered and had it turned on again."

The Feds also cleaned up after themselves before they left. Every pillow on the furniture remained neatly on sofas and chairs.

He took us through a quick tour of the place. It had gray wall-to-wall carpeting and wood window blinds throughout. The living room featured an oversized teak mantle bordering a large gas fireplace and built-in teak cabinets against an adjoining wall.

His den was equipped with a brown leather sofa and a blue overstuffed fabric chair. I noticed the FBI had, indeed, confiscated Brett's computer, leaving only a bunch of unplugged cables.

Next, I followed him into a man-sized bathroom, which included wall-to-wall salmon-hued marble with an oversized bath and a separate marble rain-shower.

"You're rich," I said.

"Hardly." This place is mortgaged to the hilt to subsidize my business."

"Hey, Billie, look at this." The voice belonged to Eric, somewhere in the nether-regions of the castle.

We followed his voice to an area near the granite-clad kitchen and found a teak, floor-to-ceiling, curved wine rack, about seven feet in width, with a portable air conditioner tucked above to keep the wine at the proper temperature.

I became conflicted. I knew I had to dump him because I could never live in a castle. But I could live in a wine cellar. Hmm. What to do? I decided it would be best to think it over while sampling some of his wine.

Brett suggested an unpretentious Willamette Valley Pinot and we settled in on the leather couch in the den. We sat and sipped the Pinot in silence. Finally, Eric stood from the overstuffed chair and studied the back of a computer modem. "Is Comcast your internet provider?"

Brett nodded.

"You have any paperwork from the install?"

"In the bottom drawer."

While Eric dug through the desk drawer, I took out my handy-dandy bug-detector and didn't have to go very far to hit pay dirt. I followed the signal to a clump of wires under Brett's desk and found the culprit.

"It's a surge protector," Eric said. "I bet it's got a listening device."

Brett found a screwdriver, unplugged the extension cord and took it apart to find a tiny network of wires and chips and a microphone.

"Damn. Someone's been here. How did they get in? I have a very elaborate security system."

It was true. I watched him use his thumbprint to turn the alarm off before we entered his home. "There are ways," I said. "Anything from using scotch tape to steal your thumbprint to turning off the power supply at the source."

We went room-to-room and found three more infected surge protector units and half-a-dozen wi-fi equipped light bulbs with microphones. The extension cords were in his bedroom and behind a sofa in the living room. The light bulbs were in the same rooms and in the kitchen. There was even one outside on the front porch.

Brett took them back to his den and found Eric on his laptop.

"I've connected to your internet provider," he said. "From here on in it's a lot of dull routine history searches. It could take until morning. Mind if I spend the night?"

"You can use one of the spare bedrooms," Brett said.

"Not planning on sleeping, much. The couch in here will do."

"The light bulbs probably only work if they are switched on," Eric said. "There needs to be power and I don't see a battery."

"We found eight more bugs," I said.

"Geeze," Eric said. "Someone's been busy."

"Well, this solves the question of how someone might know you wouldn't have an alibi," I said.

We left Eric in his preoccupied state of investigation and went to the kitchen where Brett prepared some sandwiches for us. I gazed through a window, taking in the enormity of the property. The sun retired behind the garage, which cast an enormous shadow over a portion of the finely trimmed green grass.

In the shadow, I thought I spotted movement. "I think someone is out by your garage."

Brett put down his knife and joined me at the window. "Where?"

"It was by the storage shed. I don't see anything now."

"Probably just the shadows. They can play tricks on you this time of day. Anyway, I have a good alarm system and solid locks on the door."

"You also had a good alarm system on the house," I reminded him.

I looked out the window again and squinted. Branches from a Japanese Maple swayed in the evening wind. Maybe I was still jittery from our near-death experience this morning.

"Let's eat," I said.

Chapter 24

Ping Lau stared toward the driveway. A silver Mercedes sat at an angle next to the home's front door. She couldn't remember if it had been there earlier in the day. There were several unmarked cars strewn about the place and Wright's could have been parked there too.

She glanced at her watch. Three a.m. The lights in the house were out. Should she enter the house tonight? What if one of his employees was house sitting? It would be safer to break into the barn and leave her little surprise for the feds. The search of the house was over so it didn't matter if she removed her listening devices right away.

Her SUV lounged at the edge of the property, just off the main road. Her backpack shifted off her shoulder and she twisted her body to catch it before it hit the ground. Her stomach reacted as if someone gut-punched her. She felt the adrenalin racing through her at the maximum rate.

Must be more careful, she thought. She slung it gingerly over her shoulder and walked the last fifty paces to the barn. She put down the delicate package and retrieved an electronic device from a pocket in the backpack.

The nifty gadget came from The General, compliments of the CIA development lab. She removed the metal housing from the keypad with a screwdriver and attached two alligator clips to red and white wires and pushed a button. Her little tool would over-ride the key-code and leave no evidence of her little break-in.

She entered the barn and left the lights turned off, relying on a small mag flashlight. The open area consisted mainly of workshop tables, tool cabinets, and miscellaneous machine parts. This is where Wright worked on his prototypes.

Ping Lau wanted a less traveled part of the barn and eventually, she found a locked tool shed way in the back. She popped the lock easily with a hammer. It didn't break and she was sure she could re-latch it. The tool cabinet measured two-by-four-feet. She spotted a small wooden crate and emptied it of some magazines.

She put the crate inside the cabinet and reached for her backpack. One-by-one she pulled four eight-inch grenades from her rucksack. They looked like little rockets with a steel hook at the tail end. She used the hook to fasten the grenades to her drones, which could then be released from above.

Ping Lau held her breath as she placed each of the four miniature rocket-like grenades in the crate.

"I hate these things," she muttered. "Give me an M-25 sniper rifle anytime."

I stood staring at the partially open barn door. My mouth opened in astonishment when the door opened wider and out stepped a svelte black-clad figure. She froze in place and her dark eyes met mine.

"You're dead," she said.

"I've come back to haunt you."

I saw the fear on her face and maybe for a moment she really thought I *was* a ghost. I slugged her in the mouth to dispel her fears.

"I'm tired of you trying to kill me, bitch."

"I'm tired of you refusing to die, you blonde bimbo."

She reached for something in her belt and I instinctively kicked her hand as she prepared to point a small caliber gun at me. The gun flew into the darkness behind her and we circled waiting for an advantage.

Hers came first as I backed up and tripped on a rock. She slugged me in the stomach before I could regain my balance, and I doubled over and grabbed her ankles. I'm proud to say she yelped when she hit the back of her head on the gravel surface.

"You're a terrible assassin and a worse streetfighter," I said. I pounced on her and unleashed a fury of fists as she lay there, but she curled into a ball blocking most of my punches. I stood up and waited for another chance.

She scurried to her feet and into some kind of a *crouching tiger* martial-arts stance. "I will kill you with my bare hands."

"Funny, I was just saying the same thing about you earlier today."

Against my better judgment, I attacked. She hit me three times in quick succession on my chest, my face, and the back of my neck.

Blue and green streaks of pain danced before my eyes, and I struggled to remain standing. My cheek ached, and I didn't have much strength left to fight. She came in for the kill and I managed to barely sidestep her and drove my knuckles into her nose.

She didn't cry out and I knew it had to hurt. I just broke her nose. She pirouetted into me, arms flailing. I crumpled in a heap on the gravel as pain hammered the side of my head and the night went silent. She cursed at me and I couldn't hear a word. I couldn't hear anything.

It was so dark I still could not see her face clearly. It was as if she were blurred, like an impressionistic painting hanging in the Louvre in Paris.

She pulled a knife from somewhere and crouched over me to strike a fatal blow. I tried to hold the knife back but she was stronger. I vaguely remembered being in this situation before when a serial killer tried to slit my throat. I was strong enough then to fight him off, but this time I felt weak.

She forced the knife closer to my throat. I tried to fight her off, but my arms felt rubbery, sapped of strength. She pushed harder and the knife tip touched my throat. A familiar thought returned again. The feeling it would be easier to give in than to live this hard life I'd been sentenced to by a God I didn't respect.

The first time I fought the suicide thoughts off. I wanted to live and I fought for my life. Tonight, my senses seemed dull, and I couldn't feel anything but fear. I wanted to live but I seemed caught up in ambivalence. She forced the knife into my throat and I screamed.

My scream woke me up in a mess of sweat.

"What happened?"

Brett's voice was slurred, in the half-awake tone you have when you've been rousted from a deep sleep. He turned on the light and I saw his reassuring face next to me in his bed. A bedside clock said it was three o'clock.

"Nothing. Just a bad dream." I gasped for breath, trying to replenish the oxygen I lost during my panicked delusional fight.

"You screamed."

"It was the nightmare from hell and it seemed so real."

Chapter 25

I awoke in the castle early in the morning. Brett and Eric awoke earlier. I slipped into the man cave's marble rain shower and let the gentle stream of water wash over me. Twenty minutes later, I sighed and turned off the shower.

I wrapped one of his man-sized Egyptian-cotton towels around me and snuggled inside the soft luxury. I had brought a business-blue dress with matching heels with me yesterday because it looked like we would be visiting Brett's lawyer.

I did the makeup thing and the hair thing, which took another forty-five minutes. Well, a girl has to look good for her man. From the window, I noticed a flurry of activity out by the barn. FBI agents scurried to and from it as others canvassed the grounds.

"What the heck?" I said, entering the kitchen.

Brett stood against the granite cooking island with a coffee cup in his hand. "Apparently, they didn't have a warrant for the outbuilding yesterday so they're back. The FBI, along with West Linn Police, and of course, the Portland cops."

"We told them about all the bugs we found, but they were not impressed," Eric said. "They seem to think we're blowing smoke at them."

"They won't find anything," Brett said. "There's nothing to discover."

We joined Eric sitting at a café-style table near the kitchen window and watched twenty federal agents running back and forth. We might have laughed at the debacle under different circumstances.

"Did you find anything last night?" I asked.

"Brett's home computer shows signs of being hacked," Eric said. "Somebody remotely took over his computer the day of the aircraft supply order. There's a problem though. Whoever did it used a series of spoofed IP addresses, so there is no way of telling who hacked it."

"Yet," I said.

"You know it. Give me some time and I'll track her down. You'd better hope she didn't use someone else's computer though."

"We found something," someone outside shouted.

We pushed our faces against the kitchen window.

"What could it be?" I asked.

"Nothing," Brett said. "There is nothing to find."

"Well they found something," Eric said.

"Oh no!" I recalled the shadow I saw the night before.

"The shadow," Brett said, reading my mind.

"What shadow?" Eric asked.

I told him how I thought I might have seen someone by the barn in the darkness and how I didn't check it out.

"What if someone planted evidence?" Brett asked.

I looked at him thoughtfully. Is this what he wanted me to think?

Half a dozen cops and FBI personnel ran out the barn's door and to safety roughly one hundred feet away. A few minutes later, a man in a white hazmat suit lowered a ramp on the side door of a cargo van and a small one-armed robot rolled down.

"They think they have a bomb?" I said.

We watched as it slowly rambled across the lawn and into the barn. My head started to ache as I came to the inevitable conclusion that my boyfriend was about to be arrested for the murder of Benjamin Knowles. The murder rap would be only the beginning. He would be labeled a terrorist and the world would be against him.

We waited for what seemed like forever. Eventually, a U.S. Army transport truck rolled up and six camouflaged soldiers exited. Three ran single file into the garage, followed by two others carrying heavy-duty pouches, and a third soldier with a wooden crate.

Fifteen minutes later, a lone soldier walked out of the barn with a sealed wooden box. Soon, the other five soldiers followed talking among themselves. I noticed the pouches in their hands appeared empty.

"What was that all about?" Eric said. "Did they find something?"

"If they did, it must be in the box," I said

A loud knock hammered at the front door of the house. I went to answer it and faced Detective Steve Thomas.

He and two Portland police officers brushed past me and the uniforms grabbed Brett, pushed him onto the floor, and cuffed his hands behind his back.

"Brett Wright, you're under arrest," Steve said.

"What for?" Brett mumbled, still kissing the floor.

The cops drug him up to face Steve. "The current charge is possession of illegal explosives," Steve said. "I'm sure the charges will be amended later."

"But I don't have any explosives," Brett said, as he was pulled toward the door. "Billie! Tell them!"

I watched, helplessly, as yet another boyfriend appeared to be history.

"What did you find?"

Steve stood there for a minute, in the disheveled brown sportscoat he always wore and avoided making eye contact with those big brown eyes of his.

"Tell me what you found!" I said.

He looked over his shoulder and, seeing we were alone, he relented. "Cripes, Billie, we found four live grenades in a storage unit in his barn. Your friend is going to spend the rest of his life designing paper airplanes in a federal prison."

"He's been framed," I said. "Last night I thought I saw someone lurking by the barn. Someone must have planted the grenades."

"These grenades looked like little rockets," he said. "I mean, they look like something he might have designed at his manufacturing plant. Helicopters, airplanes, and rockets, right?"

"I don't know if he makes rockets. Think about it, Steve. He knew you searched his house yesterday. Did he make a bee-line for the garage when we got here yesterday? No, he didn't. Don't you think he would have gotten rid of any incriminating grenades first thing after the search?"

"He might have thought he got away clean, or maybe he didn't expect us to return so soon," Steve said.

"We read the search warrant last night. It said the search was limited to his home. I even told him you'd be back this morning. Hell, when you got here, he'd been waiting for you. Did he seem alarmed when you served him another search warrant this morning?"

"Actually, he offered me coffee. I thought he appeared overly smug, and I didn't expect to find anything."

"See? He was just as surprised as anyone. He kept telling me there was nothing to find."

"Maybe," Steve said. "Or maybe he screwed up and forgot about them."

I let out an exasperated sigh. "Can I talk to him before you go?"

"Sure, but only for a minute."

I found Brett in the back seat of a Portland Police black and white SUV. A cop stood by an open back door, reading him his rights, as I approached.

"Billie, you've got to help me. I didn't do anything."

"They found four grenades in a storage cabinet in the back of the barn," I said.

His face went white. "How did they get there?"

"I don't know. Do you want me to call your lawyer?"

"If you would. His card is taped on the door of my refrigerator."

"I'll do what I can to get you out of this," I said.

"I know you will." He forced a smile.

I bent over to kiss him and the cop by the door stopped me.

"I'll try to come and see you later today if they'll let me. Keep your mouth shut until your lawyer shows up."

He nodded and the cop shut the door. Steve got into the passenger side, and the squad car rolled out with lights flashing sans siren. They were in a hurry to begin the interrogation. I turned and watched as the search team continued in earnest inside and outside of the barn. I realized another twenty searchers had shown up to help.

Eric stood at the front door shaking his head. "This is bad. Real bad."

"We've faced worse situations," I said. "Life and death situations."

"Yeah. The Facebook killer. But it doesn't look good for Brett. Did they find a bomb?"

'Grenades. They found four grenades."

He shook his head again. "This is really bad."

"You've got to find me a lead to this Chinese woman or whoever hacked into Brett's computer."

"Can I stay here for a while?"

"You can stay as long as it takes. I spotted extra housekeys hanging on a rack in the kitchen. I'll have to get the alarm code from

Brett. There has to be a numerical code in addition to his fingerprint. Meanwhile, lock up when you leave and bring the keys to my office."

I grabbed Eric by his young shoulders. "Find something for me."

"I will, he said."

I found the key to Brett's Mercedes, but before I got out the door my cell phone rang.

"Billie? It's Angel."

"Where have you been? You were supposed to be back at the office yesterday. I waited as long as I could."

"We've been sort of detained," she said.

"We?"

"Me and Chris?"

"I haven't got time for this. The police just arrested Brett. I have to get hold of his lawyer."

"Oh."

"Angel? Are you still there?"

"Yes, only . . ."

"What? *What is* your problem."

"I . . . we . . . sort of got arrested too."

"What? How did you manage to get arrested?"

"It's a long story. Could you please come and bail us out?"

"Are you okay," Eric said. "Your face is kind of purple."

"I don't know who I'm going to kill first. That Chinese slut or my assistant? Where are you, Angel?"

"Justice Center."

"You've been booked and arraigned?"

"Yes."

"How much is your bail?"

"A thousand dollars."

"A thousand dollars!?"

"Each. Chris needs to be bailed out too."

"He's got plenty of money," I said.

"He left his wallet at home, and I'm broke."

"Tell me again why the cops arrested you."

"I'd rather wait until you bail us out. I'm afraid you will leave us here if I tell you now."

Chapter 26

Ping Lau sat on the edge of her hotel bed gazing absently at her gun lodged into the flat screen television. Billie Bly and Brett Wright were alive. The car she had seen parked outside his home meant they had returned, somehow surviving the balloon crash.

It puzzled her when no news appeared yesterday after she shot the frigging balloon down. Now she realized not only had they survived but probably got the hell out of there before the cops or news media showed up.

The gun in the TV reflected her frustration and impulsiveness. It was stupid but it felt good to unleash her fury. But now the hotel would remember the crazy woman who threw something at the TV. She would tell them it was the exorbitant cost for the can of soda.

But seriously, what did it take to kill the Bly woman? She should be ecstatic. The cops arrested Wright, as planned, and she would never have to tell The General about shooting down Wright's hot air balloon.

The news of the balloon's crash was lost in the sensationalized story of Brett's arrest. Apparently, the TV news crews learned of the balloon accident, as they termed it, went to Wright's house to get an interview, and stumbled upon the cops conducting the search of the barn.

This turned out better than hoped for, too, because the cameras got a closeup of the bomb defusing robot and the army soldiers in combat uniforms. The robot was totally unnecessary because the grenades, with the safety pins engaged, were harmless if transported properly.

Ping Lau, still in her black bra and panties, draped a hotel terry cloth robe around herself and strolled into the suite's other room where she switched on the other television. She watched the looped video of the bomb detonation robot roll along the grass toward the barn as the CNN commentators described the scene.

"Senior FBI agent Thom Miller says the property here owned by Brett Wright, is the subject of a search warrant in connection with the bombing of the downtown Chase Bank office, in which the fundraising head of the Democratic Political Action Committee, Benjamin Knowles, was killed earlier this week.

She switched to a local news channel and watched as the camera panned the *Flying Circus Aeronautic* building. She turned up the volume: *"and the owner, Brett Wright, has been named a person of interest by Portland Police Bureau Chief Samuel Hardy."*

The camera zoomed into a closeup of Hardy, standing in front of City Hall. *"We are confident we have the person responsible for this horrible incident. We will hold a press conference this evening at seven o'clock and, hopefully, we'll have more information then."*

Ping Lau continued to watch, switching to MSNBC, which showed the aftermath of the bombing in front of Pioneer Square. The video showed the blown-out office window, a small clump of melted plastic on the street below, and hundreds of people milling around. She even spotted herself in her homeless clothes toward the back of the crowd.

Her mobile phone rang and she reached over and plucked it off of the small end table. She recognized the number on her caller I.D.

"Good afternoon, General. Are you having a good day?"

"Magnificent," he warbled. "I've been watching the news all day. It looks like the police already found their bombing suspect."

"They've had the help of the FBI, Homeland Security, and I believe, even the Alcohol, Tobacco, Firearms and Explosives division."

"They must believe it's some kind of terrorist plot," he said.

"I'm sure they do," Ping Lau said.

"Why don't you wait around for another day or so, to make sure things are going smoothly, and then take your little vacation."

"I'd like to, General, but I do have one little problem to take care of. The one I mentioned to you last time?"

"I don't want anything to screw this up."

"I'm afraid if I don't do something, things will be screwed up," she said. "This is becoming a serious problem."

"I don't care. You get your butt out of there, and we'll monitor the situation from a distance. You can always deal with it later if necessary."

"Whatever you wish," she said, not entirely being honest. She would honor his wishes for now, but if things started to go sideways, she would deal with it, regardless.

I didn't rush to bail Angel out of jail. My experience with her and Chris told me they likely deserved to cool their heels a little longer. I sat in the Mercedes, parked down the street from the Justice Center and in front of the Multnomah County Courthouse.

Mary and Jack already had things well in hand when I called earlier. Mary had supervised cleanup and Jack had returned with three new computers. Mary said she would take over Brett's duties until he was released.

My call to Brett's attorney had not gone as well. Michael Baker would be in court all day, every day this week. His receptionist apologized and said she would get word to him, but not to expect miracles. I asked in which courtroom his trial was scheduled and she told me, very reluctantly. I think she knew I would go after him.

I plugged the meter and crossed the street to the courthouse. I stepped through a scanning device, and my purse was searched for weapons before I was admitted. I found an elevator and it let me out three doors down from Baker's court proceedings.

I listened, as a brown-haired man in a brown suit asked leading questions of a prospective juror. He had a sincere smile and he held his glasses at his side and smiled broadly as the juror answered a question.

Since his questions sounded like something a defense attorney would ask, I decided this was Michael Baker. Also, the other attorney was a raven-haired woman, named Betty Boatwright, a deputy D.A., I'd run across before in my tenure as a cop.

I sat down in the gallery's front row directly behind Baker. When Boatwright began asking questions of the same potential juror, I tapped Baker on the shoulder and handed him a quickly-scribbled note.

He studied it for a solid minute: *Brett Wright arrested for Chase Bank bombing. Needs you now!!* He looked up at me and nodded.

When Boatwright finished her list of questions, Baker stood up. "Your honor, I've just been notified that one of my clients has been arrested in connection with the downtown bombing a few days ago. He is being questioned as we speak. I would like to request a postponement of jury selection until tomorrow so I may be with him."

A gasp erupted from approximately ten people in the audience.

The Honorable Len Stevens peered over black thick-framed glasses. "The court is not pleased. We're barely an hour into jury selection."

He glanced at the jurors and returned a stern gaze to Baker. "On the other hand, you have a duty to be there for your client in these extreme circumstances. Do you anticipate this will take the rest of the day?"

"It is likely, your honor. I will know more when I have a chance to see the charges."

"In that case, jury selection will continue tomorrow at . . ."

"Two o'clock?" Baker said.

Stevens' forehead wrinkled and he offered a forlorn frown. "We will continue tomorrow at *one o'clock*. And I will expect there will be no more interruptions."

"Yes, your honor."

Stevens banged the gavel. "Court adjourned."

Baker turned toward me. "Who are you?"

"I'm Billie Bly. I'm a P.I. and Brett and I are dating."

Baker's eyebrows lifted a notch. "Oh? Brett finally found some time for something other than building airplanes, eh?"

"Don't you think you should get over to the Justice Center?" I said. "They're probably trying to interrogate him now."

"Does he know enough to not to speak until I'm with him?"

"I told him to keep his mouth shut until you arrived."

"Good." He jammed a sheaf of paper into a brown leather satchel and zipped it. "Let's go."

We walked the few blocks together, and I filled him in as best I could in the short time frame. Inside the Justice Center, we parted company and I went up to pay Angel's bail. In a last-minute act of contrition, I coughed up the second thousand for Chris. The story was bound to be a doozy and I wanted him available when I lowered the boom.

When Angel made her appearance, she ran up and hugged me. "I'm so sorry."

"What did you do?" I asked.

"Do you remember the domestic case I told you about a few weeks ago?"

"The one I told you to forget about?"

"Because we don't do domestics," she said. "Well, Chris and I took her case. We wanted to prove ourselves as P.I.s and we needed some practical experience."

"You did what?"

Chris had just walked through the door. He did an about face when he saw me and strode back toward the jail cells.

"Don't let him get away," I said to the jailor.

The burly young man in uniform grabbed Chris by the shirt collar, turned him around, and marched him toward me.

"You're the one behind this," I said to him. "Angel would never disobey me unless you were behind her pushing,"

"I, uh, we, uh . . . We just wanted some action. I don't have a job and I get bored. I know it's supposed to be great not to have to work, but if I don't find a hobby or something, I'm afraid I'll go back to a life of crime. Angel didn't want that, so we decided to be private eyes."

"That's private investigator, dear," Angel said.

"What are the charges?" I knew by now but I wanted to hear it from their mouths.

"Trespassing, breaking and entering, and burglary," Angel said.

"The burglary charge is bogus," Chris said. "We didn't take anything."

"I don't even want to know why you entered a premise, *do I*?"

"Probably not," Angel said. "You see, we promised Mrs. Green we would get video and we weren't having any luck. We suspected Mr. Green was taking his secretary out to homes for sale and fooling around inside.

"I got kind of got carried away," Chris said. "After snooping and not seeing them, I kind of let myself in. Angel only came in later to try and get me out and we sort of had to hide under the bed."

"Don't tell me you were under the bed while they were going at it."

"No," Angel said. "We were in the other bedroom. I think we made too much noise and Mr. Green heard us."

"So, we had to climb out the bedroom window and then he saw us," Chris said.

"He saw you going through the window?" I said.

"Actually, he saw me hanging onto the gutter. Angel already climbed to the ground."

"A second-story job?" Now, I was mad as a slapped hornet but part of me wanted to laugh out loud. I suppressed this urge in the spirit of being a professional. A professional pissed-off P.I. with an image to uphold.

"Is there anything else I should know?"

"We think Mr. Green has a video of the whole thing," Chris said. "It turns out he had those wireless security cameras posted everywhere."

I put my hand to my mouth and turned away as if to scream. It was then I noticed several other people sitting in chairs, waiting for their loved ones. Their smiles ranged from subtle to idiotic.

I turned toward a bulletproof window and mouthed a message to an African American clerk. "Is it too late to return them and get my bail back?"

She just smiled and shook her head.

"Let's get out of here."

Chapter 27

Dan strolled over to my table with two coffees in his hand. My older brother is taller than me, about six-foot-three, and has the girth of a bear. But he's still shorter than my other brother, Dagwood, who has to duck under doorways at six-seven.

Dan raised me and my other brothers after our parents died, my dad in the line of duty and my mother of a broken heart six months later. He still acts like my father but fails greatly at keeping me out of trouble.

All of my brothers are cops with the Portland Police Bureau. Dan is a sergeant in Vice and he goes strictly by the book so I was surprised he agreed to meet with me.

He sat at the table and stirred his coffee glancing at me once with his penetrating blue eyes. The same look he gave me when I was a troubled teenager.

"Okay, what do you want. You know I can't tell you anything."

"You can't? We're talking about the man I love. He could be my future husband, and you can't tell me anything?" I find guilt is the best method of extracting information from him.

"You know Chief Hardy would ream my butt if it got back to him you had inside information."

"Not true. He'd go after Steve first."

Dan rolled his eyes and ran his fingers through his thinning brown hair. "Have you talked to Steve already?

"He wouldn't tell me a thing. But he did say he's the first person the chief would land on if I revealed any inside information."

"Ha, and you want me to risk *my* neck?"

"Just tell me what kind of case they've got. It looks awful thin to me."

Dan scanned the coffee shop for spies. "Steve told me to tell you to butt out."

"And?"

Dan sighed and poured more sugar and cream into his coffee.

"In addition to finding those custom-made grenades in his workshop . . . the same kind of grenades used in the bombing, by the way, the Feds traced his internet history on his home computer and found he had been studying Benjamin Knowles and his involvement with some Democratic Political Action Committee."

"Did they find anything on his business computers?" I asked.

"They're still going through the computers. There is a lot more data on them."

"In other words, they haven't found a thing," I said. "They don't have a motive, do they?"

"Maybe not a motive, but they have credit card trails showing Wright purchased some of his own equipment to do the bombing."

"Why would he buy his own equipment when he could go into the warehouse and take what he wanted? He owns the damn company for God's sake."

"No idea. It makes no sense at all."

"It does if someone is trying to frame him."

"You mean this imaginary Chinese assassin who tried to kill you with her drone? I don't think anyone in the department, the FBI, ATF, or Homeland Security believes in your conspiracy theory. Everyone thinks you are trying to protect your boyfriend."

"He's being set up. Take Brett's credit card to buy the bombing helicopter. She knows if the FBI can identify any part of the remote-control helicopter, it would lead them directly to Brett. Heck, she might have planted something in the device she knew would survive the explosion. Anyone could have bought the aircraft from his company, or from a third-party source, but this way the evidence leads straight to him."

"The guy doesn't have an alibi," Dan said.

"He works at home on special projects," I said. "We found several bugging devices in his home the police and FBI missed. Someone knew when he would be working at home and used the time for their attack. I told Steve about it, but he says those bugs could have been planted after the search of Brett's home."

"It could have happened the way you say but even if it did, I doubt the FBI would admit to missing it."

"You're saying we're screwed," I said.

"I'm saying the official position is Wright is the prime suspect. There are a few of us, however, whom would have an open mind at any ideas you might suggest."

"Like who?" I asked.

"Me for one. Steve told me he wants you to keep him updated, and he's the lead detective on the case. Your other brothers, Jason and Dagwood, are always there for you if you need help."

"Thanks, I appreciate it."

He leaned his round face across the table. "What are you going to do next?"

"I'm going to track down the little slut who set up my man, somehow. I have a few administrative things I need to take care of at home too."

"Do you have any leads on your suspect?"

"I'm working on it. I've enlisted Eric to help me track her down."

Dan's eyes widened. "He's the one who helped you in the Facebook killings, isn't he?"

"Yes." I took another sip from my coffee. "You know, I think he's even smarter than I thought. The things he can do, you wouldn't believe it."

"I'll tell Steve. He said he's not ready to bet against you and something about underestimating you in the past."

I knocked at the double-door of Andrea Green's home. The one-level white stucco ranch took up much of a large lot in one of Portland's nicer neighborhoods. A tall woman with raven hair opened the door.

"Are you Andrea Green?" She sized me up with cold steely eyes.

"I'm Mrs. Green. What can I do for you?"

"I'm Billie Bly." I pegged her for a type-A personality. All business, no pleasantries.

She offered a blank expression for a second while the gears tumbled into place. "Oh, you must be with Angel and Chris. You've come at a good time. My husband is out."

She invited me into a beautifully designed living room with modern white furniture, glass tables, and inch-thick gray carpeting. Several contemporary original art paintings hung on the walls.

"Won't you sit down? I hope you have something positive to tell me. The whole thing has been a fiasco thus far, and my husband obviously knows I'm having him followed."

"I won't be here long enough to sit. I'm only here to return your money." I took a stack of hundred-dollar bills from my purse and handed them to her. "I'll need a receipt."

She stood in front of me, open-mouthed. "Why? I don't understand."

"We don't do cheating spousal cases," I said. "Angel took it on without consulting me."

"This is outrageous," she said. "I'll talk to my lawyer."

"I'm very sorry. I am taking up disciplinary measures with Angel and Chris."

I handed her a pen and a receipt I'd already filled out. She took it and signed.

"This investigation is concluded. I would suggest you take the money and hire another firm. Here is a list of investigators who might take your case.

"This is not over." She looked at the notecard I offered and snarled. "Your associates have put me in a very precarious situation. My husband has been following me and I wouldn't be surprised if your associates somehow tipped him off.

"Good day, Mrs. Green."

I got into my little red MG and pondered my next move. This might not be the last I heard of from Mrs. Green. I started my car and headed toward Crowe Realty.

When I arrived, a bunch of men and women emptied from the office and streamed into cars. Gerald Green walked between two attractive women and they all scooted into a red Ford Escape.

A stream of cars exited the parking lot and Green backed out, stopped, and a tall, shapely redhead climbed into the back seat. No doubt about it. Green was a womanizer.

I followed them as the caravan raced up and down various streets in morning traffic, finally stopping at a split-level home with pristine curb appeal including new paint, a new roof, a manicured lawn, and hanging flower pots.

The caravan parked in the driveway and on the curb. Nicely dressed men and women burst from their cars and strolled up the driveway to the home. I watched from my car, amused. It looked like some kind of home tour.

Within ten minutes the group of Realtors streamed out of the house and back into their cars. I followed, sandwiched now somewhere in the middle of the mob. We eventually arrived at the front of an equally pristine two-story Tudor.

I exited my car and followed the Realtors inside. It was a nice home and I could tell it had been decluttered to make the inside seem larger and cleaner. No one seemed to notice me, so I followed Green upstairs. He was with the shapely redhead. I cornered them chatting in the master bedroom, as other Realtors whisked in and out muttering words of appreciation.

"Hello, Mr. Green," I said.

"Have we met?" He gave me an appraising look, checking out my legs and my cleavage. I felt like I was hanging in a meat market undergoing an FDA inspection.

"We have a friend in common. Your wife."

The shapely redhead took this as her cue to inspect elsewhere in the house. The word *wife* seemed to conjure up an urge to get back to work.

"Ah, my wife," he said in a charming manner. He no longer stared at my legs or my breasts. He looked me straight in my blue eyes and gave me a patented wide-grin.

"Are you a friend of Andrea's?"

"Not so as you'd notice. I just fired her."

A perplexed frown rolled across his face. "I don't understand. She doesn't work."

"It's a term we use in the private investigations business when we wind up with an undesirable client," I said.

"I see. You were working for her?"

"I canceled the contract. We don't do domestics. My associates took her case without my knowledge. When I found out . . ."

"When they were arrested," Gerald said, grinning.

"When I found out, I disciplined them, and I just refunded your wife's money. I'd like to assure you no evidence has been collected or referred to Mrs. Green and this matter is closed as far as we are concerned."

"I see. I'm guessing you would like me to drop the charges against your associates."

"I would appreciate it if you would."

"Well, I don't think I will. I need to teach my wife a lesson and as long as your associates are facing court time, I'm assured you won't be tempted to help her again."

"Are you sure? Is there anything I can do to change your mind?" Wrong question.

He leered at me again. "Maybe. If you would consider spying on my wife for me and maybe going out to dinner sometime in the near future."

Now, someone who knows me would think I might slap this yahoo, and they would be correct. But there is a time and a place and this wasn't the time or the place.

"I told you. I don't do domestics. I also don't go out with married men."

"Oh, I won't be married for long. The single life is much simpler and there are so many fringe benefits."

He put his hand on my arm. It was warm and it made my skin crawl. This is the time to hit him, right? Not yet. I had to get him to drop the charges against Angel and Chris first.

"Let me know if you change your mind." I left him looking at my business card and slid through his harem in the hallway.

"Come on, Gerry, everybody's leaving."

Gerald waved at me, sitting in my MG, as he drove by. I was in quite a fix. My boyfriend was in jail facing charges of murder and terrorism and my assistant and her boyfriend would have to appear in court in three weeks to face charges of their own.

I could let them face the music. It would be a minor blot on my business, but Angel is my friend and someday I could see her as a practicing P.I. She's helped me in the field before and she's saved my life a couple of times. I couldn't let her circle the drain because of her harebrained boyfriend.

If I could just figure a way to get Gerald Green to drop the charges—other than to have sex with him, I mean. There would be only one way to deal with him. Blackmail.

Chapter 28

A tired John Stanton sat at a restaurant table in Chicago after three days of on-the-go campaigning in Illinois.

Greg Graham stopped, just inside the restaurant, and gazed over the crowd. He spotted Stanton, sipping from a can of Fresca, and sauntered over to his table.

"I've got the latest on the Portland bombing." Graham, at least as tired as Stanton, chewed his bubble gum energetically. "They caught the guy responsible and there don't appear to be any other suspects."

"Then, we can go ahead with the Portland trip as planned?"

"Not exactly as planned," Graham said.

"Greg, I told you, Portland is a must. If our numbers are correct, I have the potential to be the top vote-getter in the Oregon primary. It would show the country I'm a serious presidential candidate."

Graham smiled. "We still can't go ahead as planned. Our numbers at these rallies have been way up. Twenty thousand in Cleveland, fifteen thousand in Des Moines and forty thousand here, yesterday.

"I'm getting estimates of fifty-thousand in Portland. I think we should move it to the soccer stadium."

Stanton took another sip of Fresca. "I've researched this. Pioneer Square is only a city block and it *will* be crowded. But it's hosted large crowds before. Heck, fifty-five-thousand people showed up for Hillary Clinton in 1994."

"It probably was a zoo," Graham said.

"Maybe, but it's situated in the middle of downtown Portland. Thousands of people can attend during their lunch hour and get back to work. The soccer stadium is further away and wouldn't hold fifty-five-thousand people.

"Okay, you're the boss."

"Now tell me about the suspect the police have in custody there."

"His name is Brett Wright," Graham said. "He owns a remote-control aircraft manufacturing plant. Apparently, he used one of his own creations to kill Benjamin Knowles."

"I knew Ben," Stanton said. "He was a decent person. I wonder why this Wright guy would kill him?"

"Uh, oh. He's back and who is the gorgeous woman with him?" Graham blew a bubble and popped it.

Stanton watched as the stately General William Pace strolled across the room with a short, raven-haired Chinese woman by his side. The woman wore a very short black dress exposing enough cleavage to draw stares from most of the men in the restaurant.

"Hello, boys," The General said. "May I introduce my associate to you? This is Ping Lau. I'm thinking of putting her in charge of your campaign if you decide to take me up on my offer."

She shook Stanton's hand. "I hope to be working with you, sir."

Stanton blushed as she leaned into him. The old scoundrel obviously decided to try to bribe him with this woman. He resented the implication. A happily married man for ten years, he didn't plan on throwing his marriage away for a Chinese sex-pot.

"It's nice to meet you, Miss Lau, but I don't think we will be accepting The General's offer."

She pouted and looked up at The General as if to register her disappointment.

"Are you sure? It's not too late to be a GOP candidate, but it will be after the May primaries when the primary season begins in earnest for the majority of states.

"I could still back you if you would *prefer* to stay on the Independent ticket to be true to your constituents. I can find the money to finance you, but running as an Independent candidate would make it harder for us to win."

"I have some wonderful ideas to help your campaign," Ping Lau said.

"He has a campaign manager," Graham said.

"And you will continue as such," The General said. "Ping Lau would be more of an advisor. Think of her as your assistant, Greg. She mostly would be observing the campaign and helping where she can."

"Sort of your eyes and ears on the ground?" Stanton said.

"A little bit. You can't expect me to dole out huge sums of money without some, uh, accountability."

"In which case, you might make suggestions on how we spend your campaign donations," Stanton said.

"I really don't plan to involve myself in how the advertising revenues are directed. I'll have some Super PAC money on my end to do outside advertising, independent of your campaign.

"Ping Lau will be my liaison with the campaign. She will keep me informed on how it is going if you need further assistance, etcetera."

"An interesting arrangement," Stanton said. "I don't think we need a bird dog on the campaign. I like the simple arrangement we have now. I give the orders and Greg makes sure they get carried out. We have a small but dedicated staff and thousands of volunteers across the country.

"We don't need any partners. I would suggest you might look for another candidate to back."

The General abruptly stood up from the table. "You have up until the Oregon Primary to change your mind. Afterward, I will do everything in my power to beat you down."

He watched as The General and Ping Lau strutted from the restaurant. At the door, they stopped and engaged in an animated conversation for a few minutes. The woman seemed to be making a point of some sort. The General listened intently and nodded a few times, and they both exited the restaurant.

"I don't like the way he acted when you told him *no*," Graham said. "He doesn't like to lose. We'd better watch our backs."

"My thought exactly," Stanton said.

Chapter 29

Things had not gone well during the two weeks after Brett's arrest and this morning would not be an exception.

Brett was still in jail and feeling more and more hopeless. Gerald Green would not budge in his decision not to drop the charges against Angel and Chris, and Andrea Green was making noises about suing my agency for causing irreparable harm to her marriage.

Worse, I could not find the evasive Kim Wu or Su Ling. She quit coming to work the day after I interviewed her colleagues during their smoke break on the roof. My snooping must have gotten back to her.

My only hopes rested in a meeting I finally talked my way into this morning with the FBI. My big mistake was going in alone.

When I entered their headquarters in Northeast Portland, I was greeted by *The Three Amigos*: FBI special agent, Thom Miller; Assistant Director of Homeland Security, George Nelson; and Special Agent Lou Sanchez, of the Bureau of Alcohol, Tobacco, Firearms, and Explosives. Chief Samuel Hardy and my former boyfriend, Steve, made it five-against-one.

"Thank you for coming to our little informal gathering, Billie," Hardy said. "We thought it might be a good time to touch base with you. We know the arrest of your boyfriend has strained relations."

"Oh good," I said. "Does this mean you're examining my theories about how this Chinese woman might be involved? You know, like how she buzzed me with a remote-control helicopter in Pioneer square, tried to run me over and shoot me the next night, and visited Brett's business a month before the bombing?

"And how when I got too close, she tried to kill me again, shooting rockets at us, while Brett and I were hot-air ballooning the morning you all were ransacking Brett's business and home?

"Have you followed up on how when we ran into her at Portland City Grill, she pretended she didn't know Brett and a few days later she quit her job and hasn't been seen since?"

"We've looked into your theory," Hardy said. "There is no trace of this mystery woman or proof of the events you say took place."

"You have a police report the night she ran me over and shot at me," I said.

"Another Jane Doe," Hardy said. "No proof the assailant is who you say she is. We traced the two names you claim she gave you and there are no such persons in our database."

"And you can believe we ran it through the FBI database," Miller said.

"We couldn't find either of those names on the Homeland Security watch list or no-fly list," Nelson said.

I looked at Sanchez and he shrugged. "Nothing at our end either."

"Obviously, she's using aliases," I said.

Agent Miller, who sat across from me at the conference table, shrugged. "Or you're wasting our time with some sort of smoke screen."

"Smokescreen?" I asked.

"Yeah. To protect your boyfriend."

"Everything I told you is true. You have two police reports to back it up."

"Ah, the hot air balloon incident," Miller said. "How is it your balloon crashed from four-hundred-feet and you both walked away without a scratch?"

"It's not uncommon. Brett said the wicker basket is reinforced and able to take the brunt of the impact."

"It seems uncommon to us," Sanchez said. "I had the ATF conduct an extensive search and we found no evidence of a rocket or missile launched in the area. No scorch marks on the hillside from where you reported they originated."

"You have to admit, Billie, the information you related to us is all kind of vague," Steve said.

"Vague?" I said. "It's frigging ridiculous but it's the truth."

"We understand you have some experience flying these remote-control helicopters," Miller said.

I didn't like where this line of questioning was headed. I had spent the past two weeks practicing with various remote-control devices from the aircraft pad behind Brett's business. Mary and Jack took turns coaching me on how to operate different models for a little project on which I'm working.

"Am I being followed or surveilled?" I asked.

"Not surveilled," Miller said. "But we did have reports of you flying the things out in Wilsonville."

"I'm trying to understand how those contraptions work. I thought maybe I could figure out what the real bomber is up to if I could learn how to fly them."

It was mostly the truth but I wouldn't even have believed it either if I were them.

"You wouldn't object to giving us a statement of your whereabouts of the week prior to the bombing, would you?" Miller said.

For the first time, I became cognizant of the secretary in the corner recording our meeting. I looked around the table. Chief Hardy seemed anxious, probably because he felt the investigation slipping away from him. Steve couldn't look me in the eyes. Agents Miller, Nelson and Sanchez were all business, the informal smiles were gone.

"I think I've said enough for today. I have an appointment across town in thirty minutes." A whopper to be sure but I could feel the walls closing in on me.

"Not agreeing to answer a few questions might make you look guilty," Agent Sanchez said.

"Guilty of what? Attending a Spanish Inquisition without a weapon or a lawyer?"

Sanchez stood and hovered over the table. "We can summon you to a grand jury hearing and compel you to testify."

God. Grand Juries are the worst. Your lawyer has to wait outside while you attend the hearings. The prosecution can lead the jury and cross-examine you so hard you forget when to use the Fifth Amendment.

"Go ahead. I won't say a word." This is a lie too because if a prosecutor gives me immunity I have to answer or be sentenced in contempt of court, thereby claiming my immediate reservation for a jail cell.

"We'll see," Sanchez said, smirking.

Geeze, these ATF agents are real asses. "Give me a call, when you get a court date. I look forward to it."

Steve cleared his throat. "I might remind the agents here to soften their accusations. Even though Billie offers nothing concrete in the way of proof, she has proven her abilities in the past. She told the Portland Police about her suspicions of a serial killer using Facebook to troll for his victims, and she was right.

"She also tracked down a cop killer inside City Hall, who murdered her brother and caused a mayor to resign. My point is, tread lightly, gentlemen. Billie can be a modern-day giant-killer."

"Of course," Agent Miller said. "But we do have to follow up all leads. You understand, Billie?"

Sanchez sat down in his chair and scowled. "We'll see."

Steve ushered me from the meeting and we stopped outside the FBI building.

"I'm going to be subpoenaed, aren't I?"

"Oh, yeah. Count on it."

"How soon?"

"Probably in about a week. We have some other things we need to deal with first."

"Having trouble shoring up a case against Brett?"

"A little."

"He'll be relieved to hear it."

"It's mostly circumstantial and we're lacking a strong motive. The best they can dig up is a meeting years ago with some now-defunct terrorist cell in Seattle."

"Are you supposed to be telling me this?"

He shrugged. "I feel bad for the spot you're in."

"Steve? You have feelings."

"Maybe if I showed them earlier we might have made a go of it."

I hugged him and he kissed me on the cheek.

"Will you give me a head's up when the subpoena is about to be served?"

"On one condition. Call me when you turn up something on this Chinese assassin of yours."

"When? Do you believe me?"

"Let's just say, I've learned not to bet against you. Also, we could use a win on this. The Feds are trying hard to get us to turn over jurisdiction. I think it has to do with it being the first time a hobby drone has been used in a terrorist crime. They've been waiting for it to happen and they want this case."

"Too bad," I said. "It's yours."

He kissed me again, this time on my lips, and walked back inside, leaving me somewhat breathless.

"What was that about?" I finally managed.

I drifted off into a restless sleep, a norm lately in my stressful life. I dreamed about Steve's kiss and found myself in a wedding dress standing next to a man in a tuxedo. I couldn't tell if the man was Steve or Brett because he had a shadow over his face.

I tried to peek under the shadow, attempting to lift the veil but it disintegrated in my fingers cloistering itself again over the groom's face.

In a recurring dream, the Chinese woman came at me with a knife again. She swore in words I couldn't understand and I wrestled with her for my life.

In another dream, I watched in horror as Brett sat in a dingy jail cell hunkered over a table with bread and water. Why did he need to be in jail? The FBI wanted him there. The cops wanted him there. The Chinese woman wanted him there. She framed him. Why?

My vision shifted from Brett to the woman again. She wore virtual reality style goggles and held a remote-control pad in her hands.

A helicopter circled over her head and zipped off. I saw it flying over tall buildings and hovering high over the brick flooring of Pioneer Square. A man stood there, apparently looking for someone. The drone dove at the man in slow motion. I tried to warn him but no sound came from my mouth. The man looked up just as the drone exploded into him and black-smoke and flames soared over Pioneer Square.

"Oh, my God. I know why!" I sat up in my bed in the middle of the night wide-awake.

Chapter 30

"Brett Wright is my client, and he is completely innocent of the charges the Portland Police Bureau and the FBI have brought against him," I said.

I stood on the front steps of my porch next to an oversized wooden sign, *Billie Bly, Experienced Private Investigator*. The crowd of news media nearly overwhelmed me.

After much soul-searching, and the sudden knowledge I was right about Brett being framed, I made the bold decision to go on the offensive. With my reputation at stake, I had sent out a hurried invitation to the media to meet me here for an update on the case, figuring one or two people actually would show up.

Instead, I peered over a mob of television cameras, radio station newsies holding iPhones in the air to record my words, and half-a-dozen local residents, probably wondering: *What has she got herself into this time?*

"The city and federal agencies are jumping the gun in arresting Wright," I said. "They have no motives and their evidence is all circumstantial and very weak. It consists of one of the remote-control helicopters being purchased from my client and some inaccurate sales records indicating he was the purchaser."

"Billie? Anne Cunningham, from Channel Four News. From the statement Chief Hardy gave this morning, the police seem to have a strong case. They found explosives on Mr. Wright's West Linn property."

"Brett is being framed," I said. "I have been doing a separate investigation because the police and the FBI do not want my input or any information I believe is germane to the bombing.

"It might also interest you to know two days after the bombing, Brett and I were sailing in a hot air balloon and a sniper shot us out of the air. This person, I believe, is the one who is responsible for the bombing and is also the one who framed Brett."

A half-dozen frenzied questions erupted about the balloon crash and I answered them.

"Billie?" It was a woman with black short-cropped hair. She had a hand-held recorder. "Are you and Mr. Wright romantically involved?"

"We are, uh, good friends. I went to high school with him."

"I think you *are* romantically involved," she said. "If it weren't for your reputation of catching two serial killers and revealing a murderer in city government a few years ago, I would think you're just protecting your boyfriend."

There was that word again, *boyfriend*. I was still getting used to it and now it was being bantered in the press.

"Okay, yes, he *is* my boyfriend, but it is not the only reason I'm defending him. He's innocent. I know it because this crazy person who has framed him has tried to kill me three times.

"I want to catch her before she succeeds and before the wrong person is labeled and convicted of a crime he didn't commit. And I will catch you," I said into a TV camera.

"Her?" someone said. "You think the bomber is a woman?"

"I know it for a fact and in a few days, I will prove it to you. Thank you for your time."

I stepped off the porch and back into my home and locked and barricaded the door with a chair in case someone tried to follow me in with more questions.

"You were magnificent," Angel had toned down her hair color to a respectable shade of purple today.

"It was all a bluff. I have no idea where this lady is hiding but I'm going to find her."

"I'm ready for anything." Angel adjusted a full-length lacy spring dress. "Except, the forty-five strapped on my thigh is clinging to my dress."

Angel is always ready for action. "How many guns have you got tucked away in that thing?" I asked.

"Only two today. I had to leave my Derringer home. I shot it off the other day at one of those city-raised roosters. I thought it was a rat. It came at me out of nowhere. Lucky for him I was too scared to shoot straight. Anyway, I'm out of bullets so there is no use carrying it until I buy more."

I rolled my eyes. She claims she has permits to carry but I'm amazed she's never been cited.

"You're going to go on a little business trip in Los Angeles for me this week sometime, and you will have to leave your guns home."

"I could probably get them through airport security, but I won't chance it. Heck, you can't be without a rod in LA. I'll have to borrow one from a friend when I get there."

"No guns," I said.

She didn't argue with me because she knew she was still on my bad side. I told her Chris could not come around the office until after her court case was settled. She took it okay, but Chris texted me four or five times a day asking if he could visit.

He always has a lame-brained excuse. Angel forgot her lunch, or he needed to bring flowers to celebrate the twenty-nine-month anniversary of their first date. Yesterday he claimed she forgot her car keys. I told him her car was parked out front and she got to work just fine.

There was a knock on the door and I dared to open it a crack.

"Why is the door locked," Eric asked. "Are you closed?"

"I will be soon. Did you bring what we need?"

"Right here." He jostled a small photo printer under his arm.

"Angel, we'll need your driver's license."

"What for?" She reached into her bulky purple purse, she claims matches her hair, and I spotted her three-fifty-seven magnum.

"My little press conference is going to stir things up," I said. "It's going to put pressure on the cops and the feds. With a bit of luck, it might also force our little Chinese assassin to take another whack at me.

"My first concern is the grand jury subpoena. I need to lay low before I get arrested. I think the Feds believe I'm in on it with Brett, but they have no evidence."

"Where are you going to hide?" Angel asked.

"L.A.," I said.

"We're going together?"

"No, dear. Eric is going to doctor up some fake I.D.'s for us. You are going to be me, and I'm going to be you. You're going to have to become a blonde, Angel."

She shuddered. "The last time I was blonde I got kidnapped by a killer who thought I was you."

"Exactly. You look enough like me to pass if a cop or federal agent tries to track you down. Eric will photoshop your blondeness now until you can get to your hairdresser."

"What about you?" Angel said.

"I'm going as you, complete with rainbow colored hair." I pulled a multicolored wig from a bag.

"You're cheating," Angel said. "But I kind of like it."

"I'm going to change the photos on your driver's licenses. I can delaminate your current licenses, make the changes and laminate them. Do you want me to change the height and weight?"

"It won't be necessary. Angel can wear heels and I'll slump when we go through airport security."

"I get it," Angel said "The FBI will think I'm you and will track me to Los Angeles. But what if they're watching the airport?"

"They haven't even subpoenaed me yet, and I haven't skipped any court hearings, so why would they?"

"Where are you going?" Eric asked.

"Florida, if I can catch a plane tomorrow. I figured out why Brett is being framed for Knowles' murder."

"You mentioned it on the phone," Eric said. "Can you tell us now?"

"It's because she's planning another murder. I went online early this morning and checked on upcoming events at Pioneer Square and, sure enough, we have a presidential candidate coming to town."

"Is it that dreamy John Stanton?" Angel asked.

"In the flesh. I think someone wants him assassinated."

"Why?" Eric had stopped editing a picture of Angel on his computer.

"From what I was able to learn, as an Independent candidate, he has a real chance of receiving more votes than either Democratic or Republican candidates in Oregon."

"Really?" Angel said. "I know he's a popular candidate but why would someone want to kill him?"

"I don't know but I plan to ask him in Florida. He's campaigning there for the next three days. I hope to catch him in Orlando."

"Will he see you?" Eric asked.

"He won't have a choice. I'll track him down no matter where he is."

I sat in a small sterile area in the Multnomah County Detention Center Jail facility inside the Justice Center where most inmates waiting for trial are held.

Beige walls and diamond floor tiles make up the design of the room, with three video screens mounted inside black boxes hung on the walls. The boxes have two corded phones, one on each side, for family members to talk to their incarcerated loved one.

I managed an in-person visit with Brett after filling out paperwork, getting his lawyer's permission, and generally threatening the Mayor, the Chief of Police, and FBI Senior Agent Thom Miller during the past three days.

I sat, praying they had forgotten about my appointment this afternoon, after my little PR stunt earlier today. I should have talked to the press this evening but I still had to pack for my trip to Florida.

Eventually, I found myself sitting on a fixed swivel chair peering through a bulletproof window. An African American female guard ushered Brett through a door behind the glass, and he beamed when he saw me.

He looked better than I had imagined, clad in an orange jumpsuit and blue handcuffs. He sat at a table on the other side of the glass and picked a corded telephone receiver, motioning for me to do the same.

"How are you doing?" I asked.

"Better, now that you're here," he said. "I didn't know if you still believed I'm innocent."

"I know you are and I just held a press conference today to declare it."

His eyes widened. "Really?"

"Really. I'm sure the person behind the murder of Knowles is the woman who visited your business last month. The same woman we saw waitressing at Portland City Grill."

"Have you found her yet?"

I sighed. "No, but I will."

"I've been in jail for three weeks," he said. "I've almost lost all hope."

"Hang in there, lover. I'm on the job." He put his hand on the glass and I placed mine on his.

"I'll try," he said. "They're talking about moving me to Inverness in East County until my trial date, which is at least six months from now."

I nodded. "I'm going to be out of touch for a while. There's a rumor the Feds are planning to subpoena me. I think they're hoping to jail me as a co-conspirator."

"How could they think you had anything to do with it?"

"For the same reason they arrested you. They're idiots who have found an easy target and aren't looking for other suspects."

"What are you going to do?"

"I'm going to lay low and if I do have to testify, hopefully, stay out of jail. Don't worry, if I am arrested, I'll have Angel stay in touch with your lawyer so you know what's happening."

The jailer seemed to be overly interested in our conversation so I changed the conversation toward more upbeat topics. We talked for the rest of the allowed thirty minutes about how we missed each other and things we would do when we got out of this mess.

I blew him a kiss at the end of our visit and started worrying about how to prove his innocence as I left the building. I felt bad I couldn't let Brett in on my plans to talk with Senator Stanton and avoid an upcoming grand jury subpoena, but I knew our conversation had been recorded and I didn't want the cops to find me.

How would I be able to help anyone if the Feds arrested me as a co-conspirator?

Chapter 31

The phone rang off the hook all afternoon and evening. The media had more questions and Chief Hardy screamed at me for five solid minutes. I actually put the phone down and made a sandwich, and he was still yelling when I picked up the phone again.

I got separate threatening calls from FBI Special Agent Thom Miller, George Nelson of Homeland Security, and Lou Sanchez from the ATF.

Miller actually showed some restraint. He warned me about releasing any classified information and wanted me to stay in contact with him. Nelson made a few not-so-veiled threats, saying I could be arrested for obstruction of Justice. Sanchez suddenly wanted to be my buddy. He also asked me to stay in touch if I learned anything.

I guessed they all were covering their butts in case I turned up anything, which might prove embarrassing to them.

The last call of the evening came from a phone number, which my caller ID listed as private. "Meet me for dinner?" It was Steve.

"Tonight? It's nine o'clock."

"Tomorrow," he said. "Tomorrow is the best day."

"It is?" I asked.

"Yes. Definitely tomorrow. I'll be in touch."

He hung up. I thought about it for a minute. Is tomorrow the day? What did he mean, and why didn't he set a time or place? He would be in touch?"

I gave myself a dope slap. He was trying to tell me something. Tomorrow, I would be served with the grand-jury subpoena. Shit! I had to call Angel.

"Angel, will you make coffee for me tomorrow?"

This is a phrase Angel and I use to tell each other we can't discuss something at the moment because someone is listening. I suspected at the moment the FBI had tapped my land-line and my cell phone.

What?" she said. "Chris and I are kind of busy right now."

"Forget it. Did you have a chance to change your hair color?"

"Of course. I went straight to Marge this afternoon. It's not an exact match but it's close."

"Come back to bed, honey"

"Shush, it's Billie."

"Angel, tomorrow I need you to do the other favor for me before you make the coffee. First thing in the morning."

"What's the rush?"

"I might be tied up tomorrow and I want to make sure it gets done."

"Oooh. I get it. I'll make a call tonight to get things started."

The earliest flight Angel could arrange to Orlando left at 6:45 a.m. The journey would take six-and-a half hours with a stop in Atlanta. I stood in a security line with a few hundred other sleep-deprived business flyers snaking around the stations set up to make the queue seem shorter.

My heart raced as I approached the security station. Would the FBI have me on a no-fly list? Maybe I was on the Transportation Security Administration's secret List. Yes, there is a secret list. Why do you think they ask for your ID when you take off your shoes? I know it seems crazy but conspiracy fears had taken up residence in my head.

I abruptly remembered I traveled today under Angel's name. A whole new worry occurred to me. What if the TSA agent spotted the phony driver's license?

He looked at Angel's license with my photo, stared at me and back at the photo. "Nice hair."

"I lost a bet and it sort of grew on me."

He laughed at my pun and waved me on. Apparently, they weren't looking for someone who attracted this much attention to herself.

After a tediously long flight and a two-hour nap in the Orlando Hilton, I freshened up and changed from white jeans to a slinky short black dress. I dug the matching heels from the bottom of my suitcase and put them on. I nodded at the image in the mirror. A blonde in a sexy dress and heels. Much better than the multi-colored wig I had worn on the plane.

The plan was for me to continue as Angel as far as room registrations and credit cards went. I borrowed one of her cards and promised to repay her. Angel would use her own credit cards once she arrived in L.A. and Billie would vanish.

I returned to the bathroom and touched up my mascara before taking the elevator down to the hotel restaurant for a quick dinner. I booked the Hilton because Eric had hacked into Stanton's email address and found he had a room there.

The desk said Stanton was not in his room so I planned to stake out the restaurant from five until seven with hopes he would grab a meal in the hotel. If I struck out, I would see if he returned to his room. I had photos of Stanton and his campaign manager, Greg Graham.

I ordered a club sandwich and a dark beer and nursed them both for over an hour when a very tall, black-haired man entered the restaurant with a short pleasant-faced man with brown hair and black-plastic rimmed glasses.

They sat at a table on the other end of the restaurant. The short man carried a small, canvas cooler. A waiter hurried over, made small-talk, and took their order. When he walked away, the tall man opened the cooler and brought out a can of soda.

I decided to let them have a few minutes to unwind before approaching and checked my photos to be sure I had the right man. No doubt about it. I sipped my beer and watched them. The shorter man was very animated, waving his hands and smacking gum in his mouth. Stanton sat back and listened attentively, occasionally nodding and taking sips from his soda.

I got up from my table and walked casually to theirs. "Mr. Stanton? My name is Billie Bly and I've flown five-thousand-miles from Portland today to talk with you."

Graham started to object, but Stanton stopped him.

"Portland? I'm going to be there next week. You could have saved yourself a lot of money and time."

"It couldn't wait." I gave him my card.

"I see." He ran his thumb over the embossing of my name and title and turned the card over as if it might contain a message. It didn't.

He looked up from the card at me and his blue eyes seemed alive, sparkling almost.

"What is so important to cause you to come this far to see me and can't wait?"

"I'm afraid your life may be in danger."

I went over my story while Stanton and Graham listened intently, stopping me occasionally to ask a question. When I finished, I noticed Stanton had been jotting down notes on a napkin.

"You think your boyfriend has been framed in order to take the heat off for my visit?" he said.

"It's the only logical reason," I said.

"But why would they risk showing their hand with a drone in the first place?" Graham asked.

"Test run," Stanton said.

"That would be my guess. But why kill Knowles?"

"He has some enemies," Stanton said. "You make them in his line of work."

"I don't see the link between him and you," Graham said.

"Politics, money?" I suggested.

"It seems to be a bit of a reach to me," Stanton said. "You don't really have anything which might suggest someone wants to kill me."

"Do you have any enemies?"

"Probably quite a few but I can't think of any right off-hand."

"What about The General?" Graham said.

"The General?" I leaned closer to him as the din grew in the restaurant.

"General William A. Pace but he's retired," Stanton said. "He's kind of a promoter in politics. He tries to coordinate campaign wins in exchange for a cut of the pie after a candidate wins. He wants me to switch to the GOP ticket.

"He's approached us six or seven times," Graham said. "On his last visit, he brought along a Chinese escort to entice us. We're both family men. We sent them packing."

"A Chinese woman?" I said. "What did she look like?"

"She was kind of short," Stanton said. "I noticed because she wore five-inch heels to appear taller, but I'd guess she was about five-foot-four with long black hair and a nice figure."

"What he means is her cleavage and legs were spilling out of a too-tight, too-short dress," Graham said.

191

"Did she wear a ring?" I asked.

"She had a ring with a thick gold band and black dragon embedded in the center," Stanton said. "It was one of the first things I noticed when she sat down."

"The woman Brett and I met in the Portland City Grill had a ring with a black dragon," I said. "The one who tried to kill me and the one who visited Brett at his manufacturing plant."

Stanton and Graham exchanged surprised looks.

"Did she give a name?"

"I think so," Stanton said. "It was Ping something. Greg do you still have her business card?"

"She left a business card? With a phone number?" I practically salivated over the table.

Graham unlatched a bible-sized notebook and thumbed a series of plastic pouches designed to hold business cards.

"Here it is. Oh, the phone number belongs to The General."

"Mind if I copy it down?"

"Go ahead," Graham said.

I snapped a photo of the card, which simply said Ping Lau, with Angel's phone camera. I left mine in the office and she borrowed Chris's phone. I didn't want to make it too easy for the Feds to find us.

"You must cancel your trip to Portland," I said. "I'm sure you will be a target."

"I can't," Stanton said. "Maybe we can petition Homeland Security for Secret Service protection."

"They don't normally provide protection this early in the process, but it can be done," Graham said. "I'll make some calls in the morning."

"You don't really have any proof there is a plot against me, do you?" Stanton said. "It's just a hunch, right?"

"I could be wrong but it's best to be safe, don't you think?" I asked.

"Oregon is very important to us because it could be the first state I can win outright. If I do, people will see the Independent Party and myself as a viable candidate and the momentum could carry over to future primaries.

"It's been five weeks since I last visited and I'm closing the gap on both the Democratic and Republican candidates, according to our polls. It's imperative I visit Oregon again before the primary."

"More important than your life?" I asked.

"We'll be careful," Graham said.

I left with two names and a phone number. It was time to put Eric to work.

Chapter 32

"Billie Bly is somewhere in Los Angeles," The General said. "According to my source, she fled Portland the morning they were about to serve her with a grand jury subpoena. Apparently, she didn't want to testify against her boyfriend."

Ping Lau held her cell phone away from her ear and stared at it. "How am I supposed to find her in LA?"

"You aren't. I have a reliable source inside the investigation whom will tell us when she returns or is arrested. The FBI has all of the airports covered. She will be arrested on sight."

"I'm not so sure about the efficiency of the FBI if they couldn't serve her with a simple subpoena," Ping Lau said.

"My source said they had planned to have her arrested if she refused to answer any questions at the grand jury trial."

"I'm going to find her before the FBI does," Ping Lau said.

"I want you to if she's in Portland. She's too big a risk for us to allow her to roam free. But until she returns to Portland, you need to finalize your preparations."

"Everything is ready. I assume you no longer have hopes Senator Stanton will change his mind."

"I've given him every chance but he's too damn set in his ways. I have another candidate who will work with us, but I'm not sure he can beat Stanton."

"Let me take care of your little problem," Ping Lau said. "I have the perfect solution."

"You better," he said and hung up.

Ping Lau was livid. She had finally been given the green light to kill Billie Bly but now she couldn't find the troublemaker. She had visited her home and place of business and the office was closed with nobody home.

She spent a full day outside the Justice Center hoping to catch Bly visiting Brett Wright, but she was a no-show. She even drove out to West Linn and searched Wright's residence and received more bad news. The electronic surveillance equipment she had used at his home was gone. Either the FBI or Billie Bly had found it.

But it had given her an idea. She decided to return to Bly's home and plant a few bugs. She picked dinner time, hoping she might find Bly at home. She didn't want to chance running into her at three in the morning.

Ping Lau entered the house through a back door to the basement. Bly's car sat in the garage, where it had been the day before when she first searched for the P.I. The basement door she had boosted earlier was still unlocked.

Bly did not have a security system—stupid for a person in her line of work— and Ping Lau carefully meandered through the home again. She held her new Maxim nine-millimeter pistol with an integrated suppressor or silencer. It was compact enough to holster and Ping Lau itched for a chance to use it on her nemesis.

She quietly checked each room, making sure no one inhabited the building. When she was confident the home was secure, she reached into her bag and removed two surge protector extension cords and exchanged them with one under Bly's desk and another near her assistant's workstation.

She swapped out a few light bulbs with some fitted with wireless bugs and was about to leave when she noticed a cell phone plugged into a charger on Bly's desk. She picked it up and tried to turn it on but it had password protection.

She found Bly's phone number on a stack of business cards on her assistant's desk and called her cell number from the landline. The phone on Bly's desk lit up ringing. She waited.

The phone on the desk quit ringing but the pealing continued as she listened. "Hello?"

It was Bly. She was having her calls forwarded to another number.

"Angel? Is that you?"

"Where are you?" Ping Lau asked, hoping her voice might be mistaken for her assistant's.

"Who is this?" Bly asked.

"You know who I am. Where are you hiding?"

"Ping Lau?"

This casual question sucked all of the air from Ping Lau's lungs. How had she learned her name? Well, the name she used for business purposes.

"You *have* been busy," Ping Lau said.

"Doing my best," Bly said. "I'm coming for you, Ping Lau."

"I will be waiting. I'm going to take special pleasure in killing you, Miss Bly."

"Call me Billie. I think we're on a first name basis, Ping. You'll find it hard to kill me"

Shit. Ping Lau already knew this and now Bly was taunting her.

"No comeback? I can see by my caller I.D. you're calling from my office phone. Sorry I missed you. But if you think *you*'re stalking me, you're wrong. I'm coming after you. You have no idea where I am but I know where you are and I know where you will be. I'll be waiting for you."

Ping Lau slammed the phone back into its cradle so hard the charging unit shattered.

"I have to find her and kill her before next Wednesday."

"I think I'm renting space inside her head," I muttered to myself.

I stood outside a magnificent three-story home located in the West Hills. It was one of those homes on acreage and the nearest neighbor lived a block away. Inside, Gerald Green and his secretary, Veronica were about to play house.

I had returned to Portland two days prior, after my brief visit with Senator Stanton, and secreted myself in the mother-in-law apartment above Brett Wright's barn, stashing my ride, his Mercedes, in the home's driveway where the Feds expected to see it.

Angel would be returning to Portland tomorrow after leading the FBI on a merry chase across Los Angeles, using my credit cards for bait. She had visited Disneyland, Universal Studios, and just about every other tourist attraction in Southern California. My bill would be horrendous, but not as expensive as hiring a lawyer to represent me in a grand jury interview.

I passed along The General's phone number to Eric, who was in the process of researching the gentleman with hopes of finding Ping Lau's location via calls between the two conspirators. Eric is a whiz with computers but not as proficient in cell phone technology. Still, I held hopes he might generate a lead.

I uncrated a twelve-inch helicopter, Jack and Mary loaned me, from a carrying case and installed a new battery. My hand-held control unit boasted a nine-inch video screen to let me see and record through the lens of the copter's camera.

The buzzing of the blades barely raised a decibel as it soared around the house, stopping at each window long enough to do a quick recon. I couldn't find them in any of the sleeping quarters on the second or third levels, so I brought the copter back and changed batteries, which were only good for ten to fifteen minutes.

I flew it around the first floor and struck gold in the kitchen. Through a sliding glass door, Green's bare butt faced me, or rather my camera, and two feminine legs straddled him from a kitchen island.

I maneuvered around outside the kitchen to a side window and hovered six feet above the ground. Two faces and several naked body parts writhed in ecstasy in clear view of the helicopter's 720-pixel high-resolution camera. The money shot. I let the helicopter hover and film for five full minutes before calling it home.

All the time spent with Jack and Mary learning how to fly this remote-control beauty not only paid off but would serve me well in the future when I had surveillance jobs. I called up the video on my hand-held control and watched the screen.

Green really seemed to enjoy his little getaways, and Veronica proved a very enthusiastic assistant. I would email this little gem to Green and wait for a response.

I had filmed Andrea Green enjoying some *afternoon delight* of her own yesterday. I'd followed her and a friend to a secluded spot in the Mt. Hood forest. She and a shirtless man went at it on the picnic blanket in the middle of a small meadow.

To catch them in the act, I had ditched my intrusive helicopter and relied on my Canon T3i DSLR camera with telephoto lens. I'd attached a stereo microphone and picked up their cries of ecstasy fifty-yards away. It made me blush a little to be watching their intimate moments.

Gerald and Andrea were two healthy sexually active adults ignoring each other. Why? Because it got stale? Meanwhile, my main squeeze sat locked up in a jail cell downtown and I couldn't do a thing about it.

I missed Brett and I entertained the foolish idea of visiting him. I know, stupid, huh? The minute I stepped into the Justice Center, they would book me a room and it wouldn't be with Brett.

Chapter 33

Chris rolled out of the queen-size bed and thrust open the motel curtains to reveal the cinematic view of Venice Beach.

"Come on sleepyhead, time's a wasting. I want to rent some roller blades and tour the area."

"Close those drapes," Angel said. "I have a hangover."

Angel had spent the last week living it up in Los Angeles as a red-herring for the FBI to chase, believing she was Billie Bly. The first few days were okay. She went to Disneyland and Universal Studios but quickly became lonely.

After careful consideration, or what others might call an impulse, she called Chris in Portland and invited him to join her. She knew she had agreed not to socialize with Chris until after this case was over, but the way things were going it might never be finished and the unbearable loneliness created a void she needed to be filled.

Chris certainly filled the emptiness. They returned to Disneyland and rode on every thrill ride and mingled with superheroes and movie star look-alikes at Universal Studio. Chris took her to Santa Monica Pier, where they rode the giant Ferris wheel, watched street performers, and walked along the golden sand beach.

Last night they ate and drank at every food stall in Venice. This morning she still felt bloated and a bit hungover. Maybe too much of Chris is not such a good thing, she thought. He likes to play a little more than she could handle.

"I'm not rollerblading," she said. "I want to find some shade at Muscle Beach and watch those young beefy bodies pump iron."

"Okay. I'll skate around and check out the chicks in bikinis."

"I don't care," Angel said. "I need some time to myself."

She got out of bed and changed into a light rainbow-colored summer dress she'd bought at Santa Monica Pier. The month of May in Los Angeles tended to be much warmer than Portland, although her weather app said the temperature there had been in the low-eighties this past week.

An hour later, she found a park bench in the sun overlooking Venice's famed Muscle Beach. Only three bodybuilders wrestled with weights now and the crowds were still sparse as it approached noon.

"Hey, Angel, look at me. I'm rollerblading."

"Are you sure?" she said, laughing.

He struggled awkwardly to stay on the paved path, wearing orange shorts and a Marvel Avenger print shirt. Ever so often his feet angled sideways and he adopted a bowlegged stance to keep from falling down.

"I'm getting it," he said.

"Excuse me, you're blocking my view." She had turned away from Chris to watch the weightlifters and two men in blue suits stood in her way.

"Miss Bly? I'm FBI Agent Walker and this is Agent Biel. May we have a word with you?"

Walker could give most of the weightlifters in Venice a run for their money, Angel thought. He stood at medium height but his arms fit snug in his suit coat and his barrel chest was perfectly sculpted.

"I'm not Miss Bly. My name is Angelica Lemon, but you can call me Angel." She had rehearsed what to say in the event the FBI caught up with her but her hangover dulled her senses this morning.

She had become sloppy after Chris arrived. This was to be a business trip, not one of pleasure. The plan was for her to register at one hotel with Billie's credit card and to stay at another hotel under her own credit card. But she maxed out her card seeing the sites with Chris and now relied on Billie's credit card for their lodging and expenses.

"I'm sorry, Miss Bly, we've checked your ID with the clerk at your hotel," Biel said.

Biel was thin and had shifty weasel eyes, dull brown hair and a buzz cut. His manner said he was all-business. Oh, well, she could always admire Walker's Adonis-like body.

"Uh, the clerk must be mixed up. Here's my driver's license."

Walker held it up to his face. "She's from Oregon, all right."

He handed it to Biel who eyeballed it carefully. "She looks similar to the photo we have on Bly but her height and weight are off a bit."

"People lose and gain weight," Walker said. "Maybe she wears heels when she's not at the beach."

"If you don't mind, my boyfriend just fell and needs help to get up," Angel said. She walked quickly toward Chris, who sat on the pavement. "We've got company, dear."

Walker and Biel tagged along a few yards behind, chatting among themselves.

"What gives?" Chris asked.

"We've been made," Angel whispered. "Keep your mouth shut. You know nothing of some woman named Billie Bly."

"Oh, I get it. This is why you're down here. We're trying to trick the FBI into thinking you're Billie."

"The airport security checked the ID on Bly when she flew down here," Walker said. He ran his thumb across the front of Angel's driver's license. "The hologram on this license seems one-dimensional. I think it's a fake."

"Okay, you got us," Chris said. "This is Billie Bly. Her real driver's license is in her purse." Angel, who had been holding Chris upright on the roller-blades, pushed him away from her in disgust.

"Angel, I mean Billie, help." Chris glided backward, picking up speed on a downhill slope.

"Can we see inside your purse, Miss Bly?" Biel asked.

"Don't you need a warrant?" Angel said.

"We can get one but, in the meantime, we have probable cause to take you downtown for questioning."

"*Help. I can't stop and I can't see where I'm going.*"

Angel looked over at her shoulder and watched Chris sail backward over a rail and land across three outdoor dining tables. Six diners became part of the melee which included pizza, calzones, and beer, most of which landed on the backward skater.

She sighed and opened her purse. "Have at it."

Walker took her purse and found the bogus Billie Bly Oregon Driver's license Angel had been using at hotels and other places ID might be required.

"She does have two sets of ID and credit cards," Walker said. "Probably using this other ID to throw us off."

"It would explain why we could never find her when she registered at the hotels," Biel said. "But why would she register under the Bly name at all? Why not use the Lemon credit cards exclusively?"

"Whatever her reasoning, it worked for nearly a week," Walker said. "We'll let the Portland office figure it out."

"Well, Miss Bly, I have a warrant for your arrest," Biel said.

"Of course, you do," Angel said. "Do you have to arrest Chris Johnson too?"

"Your name is the only one on the warrant."

"And if I insist I'm not Billie Bly?"

"We're not buying it," Biel said. "Let's go."

Walker handcuffed her wrists in front and they walked by a group of people screaming at the skinny guy on rollerblades trying desperately to remain standing.

"See you later, honey. I'm going back to Portland."

Chapter 34

"Are you sure she's here?" I said. I couldn't believe we had finally tracked down the elusive Ping Lau.

"Yep. I even went to the desk and asked. She's checked in under the Kim Wu name."

We sat inside Eric's copper-colored Subaru WRX, parked in a fifteen-minute zone, in front of the Benson Hotel. Eric had hacked The General's phone, using the number Billie gave him and traced all of his calls to Portland.

"The General called her number in Portland thirty times in the past month," Eric said. I also found a second number in his call log, but it must have some kind of government high-security protocol because I can't hack it."

"Ping Lau is the person we're interested in right now," I said. "Have you been able to monitor her calls?"

"Oh, I was hoping you didn't remember me saying I might be able to do that. I wanted to surprise you. I can listen in and record her phone calls, look at her texts, and even check out her billing by using a Signaling System Seven hack.

"All mobile phones have a security flaw allowing hackers to access all of this information. The SS7 software controls calls, texts, billing and even call-roaming. The intelligence agencies don't want the flaw fixed so they can listen in on the bad guys."

"I'm glad I quit using my cell phone after I learned about my being subpoenaed," I said.

"I recorded one call before you got here," Eric said. "Want to hear it?"

"Yes."

He turned on his iPad and queued up a recording.

"Hello? Any word on Bly, yet?"

"No, the FBI has four field agents looking for her. She's still in LA. The agents say she's like a ghost."

"We're running out of time. Only two days."

"You just do your job and let me worry about Bly. Have you firmed up a location?"

"I have three sites lined up. My favorite might be blown."

"Keep it to yourself. You never know who's listening in these days."

"You've got that right," Eric said.

"Shush," I said.

"You coming to Portland?"

"I wouldn't miss it."

"Okay, I need to sign off. I have a practice run scheduled this afternoon."

"Right."

Click.

"Do you have any earlier conversations?" I asked.

"I can only record them live," he said. "I have some texts but they're printed out at home."

"She was speaking about alternative locations," I said. "I believe she's talking about a base to launch the drones. Any ideas where?"

"Let me scroll through numbers she's called in the last week."

I watched as he pulled up Ping Lau's phone log. "She's called five different hotels in the past two weeks. Maybe she's changing hotels to stay out of sight."

"Or maybe she's checking out rooftops to launch her drones," I said.

"She liked hotels close to or on the river. She called the Kimpton RiverPlace Hotel three times."

"It's near the South Waterfront and Tom McCall Park," I said. "There are plenty of level places along the park to operate a drone but there would be too many witnesses to see what she's doing."

"Maybe not," Eric said. "Most people will be attending Senator Stanton's speech at Pioneer Square. The waterfront could be empty."

"I guess there are some less frequented areas further south along the river," I said. "Any other thoughts?"

"Maybe, but isn't that Ping Lau getting into the black SUV?"

I watched as a familiar Chinese woman stepped up to the curb with two aluminum suitcases and tucked them into the open trunk. An attendant closed the trunk and handed her car keys.

"Maybe she'll lead us to her launch site," I said. I thought about calling Agent Miller but I didn't really have any evidence to verify Ping Lau as a suspect yet. Besides, Miller probably wanted me arrested after eluding his grand jury subpoena for a week.

"I'll follow her," Eric said.

Ping Lau watched her rear-view mirror carefully while driving across the Morrison Bridge. The rust colored Subaru WRX, driven by a young man, slowed down when she slowed down. She could just make out a blonde woman in the passenger seat.

Could this be her lucky day? Could Billie Bly be following her? She swerved sharply left, across the middle lane and into a lane destined for the I-5 North freeway ramp. The WRX followed suit and they both barely negotiated the freeway entrance.

No doubt about, someone was following her. She dug out her cell phone from her purse and tapped the last number dialed.

"General? I'm being followed and I think it's Billie Bly. I could probably get her to follow me into a dead-end somewhere but she's with someone and I don't like last-minute situations."

"Are you sure it's the Bly, girl?" he asked.

"Ninety percent. She's not following close enough for a positive I.D."

"Where are you headed?"

"I planned to do some test flights at a field in West Delta Park in North Portland," she said.

She heard some rustling of papers in the background. "Just a moment." More rustling of papers and talking in the background.

"I found it here on my map," he said. "The FBI headquarters is about five miles from you on Marine Drive. It's a straight shot. They can be there in ten minutes after I make a call."

"Anonymously, I hope."

"Better. My contact should be there. Go through the motions and keep her there until somebody shows up to arrest her."

"Okay." She hung up and peered into the rearview, hoping she hadn't lost her tail. They hung back behind a white pickup, trying to be invisible.

"Billie, she's making another phone call." Eric held onto the steering wheel and reached to grab the computer on my lap.

"Leave it," I said. "I don't want to chance losing her."

"She's not going to lead us to her launch point," he said. "We should listen in on her call."

"Is it being recorded?" I asked.

"Yeah, I set it on automatic."

"We can listen to it later. Keep your eyes on Ping Lau."

We followed her off the Delta Park exit as she snaked around the road into West Delta Park. She obviously thought she needed more practice. I instructed Eric to take a different path and we wound up on a ridge one-hundred-yards from her.

We stood behind the Subaru and took turns watching through the binoculars I bring for any stakeout. She had her back to us so we didn't need to worry about being spotted.

"She's setting up three drones," he said.

I took the binoculars from him and watched as a drone helicopter lifted off, soared high above and circled in a tight pattern. A minute later, a second drone rose to a height about twenty-feet below the first and began circling too.

"She's flying two at a time." My stomach felt uneasy about this.

"There goes the third helicopter." Eric's hand shielded his eyes from the sun as the last bird soared in a tight formation between the other two drones.

"They remind me of vultures circling over a dead carcass in the desert," I said. "This is not good."

I could see her plan unfolding. Not one drone, but three would attack Senator Stanton in two days time. She wasn't taking any chances. I watched as she skillfully sent each helicopter into swooping motions, leveling off about fifty-feet from the grounds and hovering in place.

She went through the exercise again and again, perfecting the formations. About every twenty minutes she brought them to earth and replaced batteries before sending them into flight again.

"This is not good," I muttered. "I think we need to listen to her phone call, now."

We got back into the car and Eric opened his laptop to queue the latest phone call.

General? I'm being followed and I think it's Billie Bly . . . I listened in disgust, as Ping Lau and The General plotted against me.

"I was going to suggest we capture and hold her until after Friday but now I think we should get away from here, pronto."

Someone rapped on my window and I looked up to see a man in tan pants and a matching sports coat smiling down at me. I rolled down the window and smiled back.

"Are you a Miss Billie Bly?"

"Oh Shit."

"I'm U.S. Marshal Levan Smith," he said, unveiling a folded piece of paper from inside his jacket.

"How do you do, Marshal? I know we weren't speeding."

"I'm glad you have a sense of humor. It makes my job a bit easier. I have a warrant, here, for your arrest." He handed it through the window for me to read.

"I meant to pay those parking tickets, honest."

"If you'd just step out of the car, ma'am, we can handle this all legal-like."

"I'll go peacefully, officer, unless you call me, ma'am, again."

I got out of the car and offered my wrists. He cuffed me and walked me toward an unmarked red Mustang.

"You must be well-liked to rate a ride like this," I said.

"My day off." He opened the door and pushed my head down as I sat on the passenger side. "I guess everyone else was too busy, or I was the nearest cop around. Either way, both of our days are spoiled now."

"What do you want me to do?" Eric stood outside the Subaru.

"Keep monitoring the situation from a distance, she's dangerous," I said.

Marshall Smith gave me a puzzled look.

"And call Steve Thomas. Let him know I'm being arrested."

Chapter 35

Eric sat in the car, dumbfounded, as the U.S. Marshal drove away with Billie. If she would have let him switch on the phone call between Ping Lau and The General, she could have avoided this arrest.

An alert light blinked on his laptop, and he logged onto the Signal System Seven software hacking program.

"They arrested Bly," Ping Lau said. *"I captured the whole thing from my drone's camera. They thought they were hidden from view but they didn't realize I could see them every time one of my practice drones made a turn in their direction."*

"Good," The General said. *"Now you can proceed unimpeded."*

"How did you manage it?" Ping Lau asked.

"I have a contact inside. I made a phone call and he arranged for her arrest. The only problem being he didn't want to use anyone from his department, so we had to wait for a U.S. Marshal to be assigned."

"Why the red tape?" she asked.

"My contact didn't want to explain how he learned her location. I've done my part, now you do yours."

Click.

Eric frowned. What should he do? Billie said to notify Lieutenant Steve Thomas of her arrest and keep an eye on Ping Lau. She also told him to be careful.

He didn't consider himself a brave man and he certainly wasn't stupid. He knew Ping Lau was a highly skilled assassin and she was smart. Using her drones, she kept them under surveillance when he and Billie thought they were watching *her.*

No, Billie wouldn't have to tell him to be careful again. From now on he planned to surveil her from his computer and he didn't have to follow her to listen in on her phone. He called up Thomas's phone number and initiated a call.

"Lieutenant Thomas? I have some bad news. Yes, she has been arrested. Can we meet? I have something important I need to share with you."

"You can't do this." Greg Graham kicked a trash can in his hotel room. "Senator Stanton needs security Friday for his Portland visit."

Stanton sat in a chair next to a desk, legs crossed, sipping on a can of Fresca. Visible lines on his face punctuated his displeasure with the conversation Graham conducted with the person responsible for assigning secret service agents.

"What the heck are you talking about?" Graham shouted. "Senator Stanton is leading in thirteen state polls over both Democrats and Republications. He's a major candidate and he needs protection.

"We've had death threats for crying out loud. I've been contacted by a reliable source who says she's convinced an assassination attempt could occur in Portland. You've been ordered to do what?

"Christ." Graham slammed the hotel phone down on its cradle.

"Can you believe those frigging morons at the Secret Service?" he said. "They're reassigning the twelve agents we had to an emergency in Seattle."

"Why?" Stanton asked.

"They don't know," Graham said.

"The agent I talked with said it's a bureaucratic screw-up and it could take days to countermand the order."

"Stay on it," Stanton said. "In the meantime, place a call to the Portland Police Bureau and the FBI headquarters there. See if they can spare the additional manpower to cover for our missing security."

"I'll try," he said. "The last I heard, the police were worried about how to control the large crowds they expected."

"Success does have its downside," Stanton said.

He leaned forward over the desk and continued drawing on a hotel notepad. The image of the blonde detective, who had warned him of a death threat, emerged on the pad. A miniature helicopter hovered over her head.

"I sure hope she is wrong," he muttered to himself.

Thursday morning, Ping Lau piloted her rental speedboat up toward the seawall on the Willamette River. She anchored the boat and climbed up a ladder with a coil of rope tied around her waist. When she reached the top, she surveyed the area to be sure she was alone before tugging on the rope and lifting two medium-sized aluminum suitcases from the boat.

She walked to another ladder and replicated her efforts. Beads of perspiration rolled from her face by the time she reached her proposed base of operations. As indicated by the property's schedule, the area lay empty before her.

After weeks of practice, Ping Lau set up the three drones in just under five minutes. She looked at her watch. Eleven-thirty-five, twenty-five minutes before Senator Stanton would take the stage in Pioneer Square.

Tomorrow.

Today's practice run-through would be thorough. The sky was sunny, with a few clouds, the wind calm up to three hundred feet, and with Daylight Savings Time in effect, the sun shone into the eyes of any spectator looking east in the sky, in effect blinding them from seeing her incoming drones.

According to her weather reports, the warm, sunny climate would continue tomorrow. The month of May had a history of being unseasonably warm during the last decade and this year was no exception. Already, the temperatures had soared in the low-nineties twice. The forecast for the next five days projected temperatures in the low eighties.

Ping Lau strapped a pair of video goggles on her head to shield her eyes from the sunlight and watched from the first drone's camera as it lifted off and flew over the river. A magnificent birds-eye view rewarded her efforts.

The river, the bridges, sailboats, and a waterfront park all lay below in a brilliant blush of colors. She controlled the helicopter with a handheld remote-control unit, her fingers nimbly adjusting the craft's height and direction.

Today, the copter held the real payload instead of rocks or pinecones. In the basket under the drone, rested two live grenades. It cruised down the waterfront park and she saw bicyclists and people jogging along the seawall sidewalk.

On the return, the camera caught the rooftops of both the Portland Marriott Downtown Waterfront Hotel and the RiverPlace. She directed the copter over the river and it swooped low over a large sternwheeler, the Portland Spirit, before ascending to two hundred feet.

No one seemed to have noticed her acrobatic stunt and the drone responded well to her commands, even with the added weight of the grenades, which was precisely why she added the live rounds today.

She directed the aircraft toward Pioneer Square, eight blocks from her base, for a brief flyover. It hovered high above the brick-laden plaza as she angled the camera and caught scores of lunchtime pedestrians below.

Some sat on the layered brick shelves, which offered bench-like seating, eating their lunches. She zoomed the camera lens enough to determine a middle-aged man with white hair, eating a hotdog with all of the trimmings.

Ping Lau smiled. It would be perfect. Everything fell into place. The sun would block any searching eyes if they heard her birds approaching. She had attempted looking into the harsh sunlit East sky days ago.

The drones flew perfectly, no one noticed her on her perch, and even the meddlesome Billie Bly would be out of the way.

Chapter 36

I sat at the defense counsel desk in a federal courtroom Thursday morning, the day before Senator John Stanton might meet his death.

I spent a sleepless night in the Justice Center lockup, not because of the proximity to hardened criminals or even the snoring and cries of junkies in the night. My restlessness stemmed from knowing a planned murder might succeed and I could do nothing about it.

Somehow, Ping Lau maneuvered me into jail.

When I spotted Angel being walked up the aisle in handcuffs, my heart skipped a beat. Did they catch her too? How? She took a seat next to me and offered an uneasy smile.

"I'm sorry, honey. I dropped my guard and they snuck up on me."

"Dropped your guard? Oh, please don't tell me Chris is involved."

"I got lonely," she said. "One thing led to another and . . . you know?"

I sighed. "This is why I wanted you two to remain apart until after this thing was finished. Chris distracts you in the worst ways."

"I know and I'm sorry."

Our attorneys joined us and spent the next ten minutes going over what to expect.

I watched as Steve and my brothers entered the court and sat in the back. Agents Thom Miller and George Nelson waited for them to be seated and scurried up to the prosecution bench to meet with a young lanky man with blonde hair.

A woman in a black robe entered the courtroom and the crowd hushed. A clerk announced her as Federal Judge, Annette Sarandon. She was petite with red hair and in her late forties.

"We're here to find just cause for holding these two defendants, one Billie Jean Bly and one Angela G. Lemon, over for a grand jury, is that correct?"

The blonde-haired lanky man rose. "We're holding Miss Bly for a grand jury scheduled on Monday," he said. "The determination of any charges against Miss Lemon as a co-conspirator will also be made then."

"What is Miss Bly's role in the grand jury inquiry?" Judge Sarandon asked.

The prosecutor picked up a pair of reading glasses and glanced at his notes.

"The FBI suspects she might be involved in a bombing and the death of Mr. Benjamin Knowles last month. At the very least, they think she might have relevant information to assist in the federal prosecution's case."

"I see," the judge said, "And Miss Lemon?"

"We arrested her for obstruction and interference with an ongoing investigation. She led the FBI and other federal agencies to believe Miss Bly had taken flight to Los Angeles to avoid the grand jury subpoena."

Judge Sarandon lowered her reading glasses. "Mr. Adelman, there is no law stating the illegality of avoiding a subpoena."

"I'm aware of this," he said. "At the time, Miss Lemon held two pieces of identification. One of her own and one belonging to Miss Bly, which was later determined to be a forgery.

"The officers confronted Miss Lemon in Los Angeles and took her into custody until they could determine her true identity."

"And brought her back to Portland to do so?" Judge Sarandon asked.

"Uh, yes, your honor."

"Then why is she still in custody?"

"The office of Homeland Security thought she might be a threat."

"Oh, they did, did they? On what grounds?"

"I have not been apprised by Homeland Security," he said.

"Your honor, if I may? My name is George Nelson, of Homeland Security."

"This is convenient, isn't it? So, do you have proof this lady might be a security threat?"

"Not yet," Nelson said. "We wanted to subpoena her for the grand jury trial next week and keep her in custody. We feel she is also a flight risk."

"Have you served her with a subpoena?"

"Not yet," Nelson said.

"Do you have one today?"

"No," he said, meekly.

"Well, this is an easy one to solve. The court rules for the immediate release of Angelica G. Lemon. Bailiff, release her please."

"But, your honor," Nelson said.

"Next is the hearing for the continued incarceration of Miss Bly, pending a grand jury hearing."

I cringed. I was happy Angel was released and prayed this judge might free me too.

"Your honor?" My attorney, Elizabeth Bailey, is a slender brunette in her early thirties, a tenacious advocate, and apparently not swayed by a federal hearing.

"Yes, Ms. Bailey?"

"I believe my client's situation is similar to her assistant's. She has been in plain sight in Portland during the entire time, with the exception of a twenty-four-hour period when she flew to Florida. The subpoena could easily have been served if they had only looked for her."

Miller and Nelson emitted a chortling sound in unison over at the prosecutor's table, followed by low mumbles back and forth. Nelson looked visibly upset about something.

"Gentlemen?" the judge said. "I'm going to give you the benefit of the doubt though you have disrupted my court. Is there something you wish to add?"

Nelson conferred with Adelman. "If I may address your question?" Nelson said.

She nodded.

"Miss Bly, concocted an elaborate ruse to mislead process servers by allowing her assistant to travel to Los Angeles under her identity. When we were unable to find Miss Bly after a few days, we ran a check on her credit cards and her driver's license and learned she had flown to Los Angeles.

"Believing Miss Bly to be in LA, the FBI wasted enormous resources in a fruitless search for the defendant."

Judge Sarandon smiled. "Congratulations, Miss Bly. I'm impressed. Two women managed to outsmart the FBI and Homeland Security, for *how long*?"

"About a week," I said.

"Did you break any laws?"

"None I'm aware of," I said.

"I don't think you did either. Your assistant most likely did if she flew under your identity, but you didn't."

"Your honor?" Prosecutor Adelman said.

"Has Miss Bly been served with a proper subpoena?" she asked.

"Yes, your honor."

"Is there any reason I shouldn't release her on her own recognizance, until her hearing next week?"

"Your honor?" Nelson stood. "We would like to be sure Miss Bly is available for testimony next week. We believe she is a flight risk. She's already demonstrated her ability to avoid a grand jury trial."

"Your honor, I must protest," Elizabeth said. "My client has already been subjected to one night in jail. Her further incarceration will impede her ability to work on a very important case."

"Is this so, Miss Bly?" Sarandon turned her stern gaze in my direction.

"Yes, your honor. You see, I'm working on . . ."

"I don't need to know the specifics of your caseload, Miss Bly. I'm sure it is important but the prosecution has made a point. I will set bail for Miss Bly at twenty thousand dollars, refundable if she attends the first grand jury trial."

"Judge Sarandon, I must protest," Nelson said. "Miss Bly is involved in a very serious crime. A crime so violent it threatens the future security of the nation. We must keep her quarantined until the grand jury meets to keep her from contaminating other potential witnesses."

Elizabeth stood and argued against Nelson's request. The two of them went back and forth while a surprised prosecutor and judge let them continue until the gavel finally pounded.

"I think I've heard enough," Sarandon said. "The federal court does have the leeway in certain matters involving Homeland Security. When would your hearing proceed, Mr. Prosecutor?"

Adelman conferred briefly with Nelson. "It could be in session as early as Monday."

"Make sure it is. This court orders the defendant bound until Monday when she shall be delivered to the federal grand jury, here in Portland. Once the hearing begins, or if it doesn't begin, Miss Bly will be released from custody."

"Thank you, your honor." Nelson still stood.

"Your honor?" Elizabeth said. "Portland's Mayor and Police Commissioner have requested a meeting with Miss Bly for about an hour after the proceedings. It appears the police also have some questions and although it appears the federal agencies have taken over the investigation, the city still has jurisdiction."

"This case gets stranger by the minute," Judge Sarandon said. "So ruled."

Chapter 37

I was ushered from the courtroom by a sheriff's deputy, a six-foot African American man with muscles on his muscles and a toothy smile.

He steered me to a conference room where I met with my three brothers, Mayor Jackson, Chief Hardy, and Detective Steve Thomas. The federal offices had a modern feel compared to the mid-century walnut décor of the Multnomah County Courthouse.

The modern oak conference table took up most of the room. A large window on one side of the table made me think of escape. The Bailiff, his hand on my arm, guided me to a chair.

"How are you holding up?" my older brother, Dan, asked.

"I'm okay."

"Only you could get yourself involved in a mess like this," Jason said. His role in our relationship is to point out my inexplicable ability to land in a quagmire.

"I love you too," I said.

"We'll get you out of this," he said.

Dagwood towered behind Jason and offered a sweet "Hi, Sis."

"Bailiff? Would you mind waiting outside," Mayor Jackson said, "This is a confidential meeting."

"Be right here if you need me," he said.

Eric scurried past the bailiff at the door. "Sorry, I'm late." He sat next to me and opened his computer.

"Now, Billie, Steve tells me you have a strong case to present regarding a possible terrorist attack tomorrow," Chief Hardy said.

"It's not a terrorist attack, per se. It's more of an assassination attempt. This is what it's been about all of the time."

"And your suspect is this Chinese woman you've mentioned in the past?"

"Yes, but we have more proof now. Eric, did you play the phone conversations for them?"

"Steve and I met with them yesterday and they heard all three recordings," Eric said.

"Three?" I said. "I knew of the second one but I was arrested before I could hear it."

"You should have let me monitor it," Eric said. "Ping Lau called The General because she spotted us following her. He told her to go on with what she was doing and not to lose us."

"They set me up?" I asked.

He nodded.

"It sounds like the Feds have screwed up this investigation." Hardy, sitting directly across from me, rolled his eyes.

"I'm not so sure they've dropped the ball on the Knowles murder as they've covered up what's really going on," I said.

"I'm listening." Hardy brushed lint from the sleeve of his dress blue police uniform.

"I believe his murder has been a practice run in preparation for killing the presidential candidate, Senator John Stanton, tomorrow at Pioneer Square. I think someone has targeted Knowles to weaken the Democratic fundraising efforts.

"When I met with Knowles, he told me about an acquaintance, Dave Lambert, who died in a scuba diving accident the week before. Lambert was a major fundraiser for the Republican Party.

"I thought this an interesting twist of fate when Knowles also was killed, but after meeting with Stanton last week I learned something which tied these two deaths together."

"You met with Stanton? Where?" Mayor Jackson asked.

"In Florida, during one of his campaign stops," I said. "I told him of my theory and at first he scoffed at it. But when I described the assassin, who I now believe is named Ping Lau, he changed his tune.

"A woman matching her description had been introduced to him by a man named General William Pace. He's commonly referred to as The General in political circles. Stanton believes The General is trying to put together a coup to steal the November Presidential Election.

"He's been pursuing Stanton, trying to get him to switch from Independent to the Republican ticket in the primaries. My guess is The General has some Super PACs behind him, which could make it difficult for any of the other primary candidates to beat his candidate.

"But Stanton refuses to play ball so The General might have to look at other options."

"Are you saying this General person is behind a plot to kill Stanton so he can get his selected candidate elected?" Hardy said.

"I've done some preliminary research and most of the polls show Stanton is ahead of both Democratic and Republican candidates in the Oregon Primary," Eric said.

"Is that so?" Mayor Jackson said.

"Yes. In fact, Oregon could be the first chance the polling could translate into a win for Stanton."

"It would explain why Stanton wouldn't cancel his visit here when I warned him of a possible assassination attempt," I said.

"They're definitely plotting something," Hardy said.

"Billie, maybe you should hear the phone call Ping Lau made after your arrest," Eric said. "Listen."

"They arrested Bly," Ping Lau said. *"I captured the whole thing on my drone's camera. They thought they were hidden from view but they didn't realize I could see them every time one of my practice drones made a turn in their direction."*

I gasped. "The bitch."

"Good," The General said. *"Now you can proceed unimpeded."*

"How did you manage it?" Ping Lau asked.

"I have a contact inside. I made a phone call and he arranged for her arrest. The only problem being he didn't want to use anyone from his department, so we had to wait for a U.S. Marshal to be assigned."

"Why the red tape?" she asked.

"My contact didn't want to explain how he learned her location. I've done my part, now you do yours."

Click.

"That's it, Eric said.

"With your permission, Chief Hardy, I think we should arrest Ping Lau immediately," I said.

"Do you know her location?" he asked.

I started to nod until I noticed Eric's long face.

"She skipped out on me," he said. "I got suspicious when there was no phone activity yesterday and her phone's location didn't change. I went to the hotel this morning and tracked her phone to a hotel dumpster."

"She must have switched to a burner phone," Steve said. "She probably figured out you were tracking her phone."

"Did you check the hotel?"

"She's checked out," Steve said. "I made calls to the other hotels she's frequented but they haven't heard from her."

"It just keeps getting worse," I said. "Have you traced The General's calls?"

"He hasn't made any to the Portland area and he's still in Washington, D.C."

"Keep a watch on him and let us know if he winds up in Portland."

"He said he's coming," Eric said.

"We can't be sure of anything," I said. "It's getting close to D-Day and they will be playing it safe."

"Maybe we should contact the FBI," Mayor Jackson said.

"Hell, no. They screwed the pooch on this one," Hardy said. "This is supposed to be our investigation and it's up to us to arrest this Chinese Mata Hari."

"I have to agree with the Chief, although for a different reason," I said. "This last recording suggests someone inside the federal investigation might be a mole. If we share this information with the FBI it might get to The General and we may never catch them."

"Maybe it's for the best," Steve said. "It might scare them off and Stanton would be safe."

"It also might accelerate their plan," I said. "The crazy bitch could throw a grenade at the airport when Stanton gets off the plane, killing hundreds of bystanders there. At least, this way we have an idea of what to expect."

"Do we?" Mayor Jackson said. "This is a public relations nightmare. If this woman drops a bomb on thousands of people it would be a catastrophe."

We sat at the table in silence for a minute, contemplating the implications.

"No, we have to do something," Mayor Jackson said. "I'm going to notify the council members we're raising the threat level around Stanton's appearance."

"Our department is stretched, but I'll call in additional officers to patrol the staging area and handle crowd control," Chief Hardy said.

"What about Billie?" Steve said. "She knows Ping Lau better than anyone. If we're going to have a chance to catch her we need to get Billie out of jail."

"Leave it to me," Chief Hardy said.

"You can't break her out." Mayor Jackson said. "She's a federal witness."

"Nah, the Sheriff owes me a favor," Hardy said. "Because of overcrowding, we have to release some of the low-risk prisoners into the population to make room for the weekend junkies and thieves we arrest.

"I'll see Billie is on the release list tomorrow morning. She should be out by nine o'clock."

"I guess I can manage one more night in jail," I said.

Chief Hardy smiled, and I knew he was enjoying my imprisonment, no matter how temporary. He really dislikes me.

"Now, what are we going do to stop this calamity?" Mayor Jackson said.

"Eric has been working on what we believe would be the prime areas for Ping Lau to stage an attack," I said. "My brothers are here because I want them to supervise some of our stakeouts. If we're going to catch Ping Lau, we'll need every person we can spare.

"We'll do anything the Chief wants us for," my older brother Dan said. Dagwood and Jason nodded from the far end of the table.

"Let's hear what she suggests," Chief Hardy said.

"Eric was able to trace Ping Lau's phone activity during the past month. She has stayed at five hotels, most of them along the waterfront. Originally I believed she would use the rooftop at Portland City Grill to launch her attack.

"But when Brett and I spotted her working there as a waitress, we might have spoiled her plans. The recording Eric just played confirms my fears. I think our best bet is to check the rooftops of these five hotels and any other hotels within a one-mile range."

"You want us to stake out, what, twenty hotels?" Chief Hardy said. "We'd need a minimum of five officers for each hotel and things could get pretty dicey if we stumble onto her."

"I didn't say it would be easy. First, we need to do a recon and see if any of the hotels have a rooftop suitable for Ping Lau's purposes.

"The prime spots would be closer to Pioneer Square. I believe The RiverPlace Hotel, The Marriott Downtown Waterfront Hotel, and

The Residence Inn Marriot are likeliest if she plans to attack from the river direction."

"There are also four hotels located within a three-block radius," Eric said. "I believe the most likely site would be The Nines Hotel. "I've been to The Departure Lounge on the top floor. The balcony looks right onto Pioneer Square. The view is breathtaking. If she could get to the roof, she could practically throw the grenades herself."

"I'll take The Nines stakeout myself," Hardy said. "She's not going to blow up people right under my nose."

"One more thing," I said. "You might want to put an all-points-bulletin out on The General if he plans to be in Portland tomorrow."

Chapter 38

Ping Lau looked at her watch again for the fifth time in the last twenty minutes. Waiting was not one of her virtues, especially on the day of a hit. Ten-forty-five. Still, an hour-and-a-half before Senator Stanton would take the stage in the open-air venue.

The drones had been set up and ready to go for an hour. A slight breeze off the river still chilled her. Portland mornings in May started cool but managed to heat up between eleven and one.

She had sent a drone up to survey Pioneer Square thirty minutes ago and things looked calm. A half-dozen police officers milled around The Square watching a few hundred early Stanton supporters.

But her last loop revealed scores of people exiting one of the light-rail trains and scurrying along sidewalks toward the event. She heard on the radio crowds were estimated from 80,000 to 100,000 people.

This Stanton character certainly had the power to draw people, she thought. Perhaps this is why The General wanted him dead. He also had the power to scuttle the old fart's dreams of owning a president.

She lined up her batteries and went over the programming of the drones again. Hover, wait for the command, swoop and kill. She felt the warmth of the sun on her back and looked over her shoulder. The orb was bright but not quite high enough to interfere with the sightline of her attacking aircraft from the ground.

It would be by noon, she thought. Sometime between 12:15 and 12:30 p.m., all hell would break loose. She pulled a cellphone-sized device from the pocket of her windbreaker, turned it on, and made a call to Billie Bly's phone.

She flipped a switch on her jamming device after Bly's phone returned three rings. Two rings later her phone died. She tried calling The General and heard nothing but static on her line. The jamming program had enough strength to interfere with all cell phones and police communications within a one-mile radius, perfect for her needs.

But she would need to wait for a call from The General on her new burner phone first. Then it would be lights out.

It was nearly 11:00 a.m. before I left the Justice Center and I was frustrated. The early release paperwork didn't arrive until 10 a.m., an hour later than Chief Hardy indicated, and it took another hour to process me through the bureaucratic system.

I threw open the front door, rubbing my wrists after spending an hour in handcuffs. Angel and Chris stood away from the door on the sidewalk. I was too angry to even address the fact Chris tagged along again when he knew he was a persona non grata.

"Billie, finally," Angel said. "We were afraid they wouldn't release you."

"Me too," I said. "Update me."

"The hotels in the immediate area are being watched," Angel said. Dagwood, Jason, and Dan are staking out the waterfront hotels with backup cops in plain clothes. Steve is covering Portland City Grill, and Chief Hardy has people watching The Nines Hotel rooftop and its Departure Lounge terrace looking down on The Square.

"Here's a radio. They've been reporting in every ten minutes on a secure network. You can hit this button and ask for a check-in."

"This is Billie, can I get an update?" I asked.

"Dan, here, no activity at the RiverPlace."

"This is Dagwood. I'm at the Marriot and we have no activity here, either."

"Still quiet as a mouse here," Chief Hardy said.

The roll-call continued until twenty units reported in. Quiet as a mouse everywhere, I thought. Too quiet. Something had to be going down today. What had I missed? Certainly, the shortest distance would come from one of the four hotels near the waterfront surrounding The Square.

I thought about the riverfront area. Eric had checked all possible locations. The only other possible venue would be in the middle of Tom McCall Waterfront Park, and there would be scores of pedestrians and bicyclists there during the lunch hour.

Or would there be? Would everyone rush up to The Square to hear Senator Stanton speak? Would she merely look like an amateur hobbyist flying her remote-control drones until they started exploding eight blocks away?

"Where are you going?" Angel said, struggling to keep up with me.

"To the riverfront," I said.

"Hey, wait for me," Chris said. "What's at the riverfront?"

"Maybe our elusive drone flyer," I said.

"At one of the hotels?" Angel asked. "But no one has reported seeing anything."

"They aren't looking in the right place," I said.

"What's the right place?" Chris asked.

"In plain sight."

We covered the five-block distance in minutes. The park is narrow but stretches one-and-a-half miles along the Willamette River. It has a substantial open stretch of park between the waterfront-area hotels where Ping Lau could set up her drones.

Trees blocked a park-long view so I started jogging down the sidewalk toward the Morrison Bridge.

"What are we looking for?" Angel said.

"Ping Lau may have set up her operation right here in the park," I said. "I centered on the hotels because she stayed in them long enough to case the roof access. I thought maybe she was practicing on one of the hotel rooftops.

"But maybe she is just brazen enough to do it in front of an audience. Who would know what happens half-a-mile away?"

"I don't see anything." Chris bent over and held his knees to catch his breath.

"Neither do I," Angel said.

"She has to be here somewhere," I said.

We spent the next twenty minutes searching the park area without any luck. I looked at my watch and sighed. Fifteen minutes until noon. Senator Stanton was scheduled to take the stage at 12:15 p.m.

I had failed.

We stood in front of the Salmon Springs Fountain, in front of the Portland Spirit, a 150-foot cruising yacht catering to tourists. It featured three decks and was tall enough I couldn't see its entire top deck from the ground.

A sign hanging on the upper gang plank stated the boat was closed for maintenance repairs and a little alarm buzzed in my brain. The boat was moored with heavy ropes, but several feet separated it from the seawall and the gangplank was raised. I guessed it might be operated by some sort of remote control.

I walked a few hundred feet down the sidewalk until I could see behind the superyacht. A fifteen-foot motorboat bounced on the waves on the far side of the Portland Spirit. A rope connected it to a ladder on the side of the boat.

A wonderful thought occurred to me. Ping Lau could have rented the motorboat and used it to board the vacated cruiser. I had to know for sure. It might be my last chance to stop a catastrophe.

"Angel, are you carrying?" I said.

"Always. Do you want my Glock or the revolver? I have my Derringer reloaded, too."

"I'll take all three. I don't know how much firepower she has."

"Do you think she's on the Portland Spirit?" Chris asked. "That would be too much."

"Why is he here, Angel?"

"He wants to help. He feels bad about getting me caught in Los Angeles."

"Tell him to stay out of my way. I took her Glock and tucked it into the waistband of my blue jeans. The Derringer went into my right stocking and I tucked the revolver into my pocket.

"I hope none of these go off," I said.

"The safety is on the Glock and the Derringer and the revolver doesn't need a safety," Angel said.

I sighed. "You have the wireless radio. Put out the word we think Ping Lau is on the Portland Spirit."

"Hello, I have an update," Angel said. The radio squawked with static. "Hello, can you read me?" More static.

"This thing doesn't work," she said. "No one answers."

"Try your cell phone."

"I'll call Lieutenant Steve," Angel said. We waited for what seemed forever. "My phone is dead."

"Let me try mine," Chris said.

"This can't be good," I said. "Keep trying."

"My phone is dead too. I can't get a signal."

"Crap, someone is jamming our signal," I said. "Go to the RiverPlace and tell my brother, Dan."

I jogged toward the south end of the park to the marina, with all three guns digging into me. Ten minutes later I stood at the slip of a sailboat. It had an engine but I have sailing experience and my plan was to sail quietly to the back of the yacht, climb the ladder and arrest Ping Lau if I found her.

I loosened the rope and jumped into the boat. We drifted away from the dock until I got the sails up and caught a wind. It took minutes to reach the Portland Spirit and I took one last look at my watch as we approached. Five minutes after twelve. Stanton could take the stage as early as 12:15.

A faint hum sounded from above, and I glanced up to see two remote control helicopters hovering a hundred feet above. It was my first ray of hope. If she wasn't on the high deck of the yacht, she had to be close.

Looking into the sun burned my eyes, and I realized it would provide excellent cover for the drones, as they approached from the river. Anyone searching for them would be blinded by the glare.

I lowered the sails and glided toward the yacht, colliding with the motorboat and bouncing into a gentle nudge against the hull. I managed to grab the ship's built-in ladder and tied a rope to it.

The splashing of the waves against the Spirit drowned the sounds of the circling drones above and I prayed they hadn't been deployed. I reached for the ladder, as the sailboat drifted away, and I almost plunged into the river.

The sailboat drifted until the rope became taught and once again it returned to the ladder. I jumped and clung to it as the sailboat wandered from beneath my feet, leaving me hanging. The wet steel made for a slippery climb.

My cold hands struggled to hold onto the cross bars and my feet slipped from the rungs beneath me. I kept going hand-over-hand until I reached the rail and slid over it to land on the deck.

I lie there a minute wondering how could I have gotten out of shape so fast? I grabbed the rail and pulled myself up, standing still, waiting to regain my sea legs.

Ping Lau didn't hear Billie climbing onto the yacht. She remained engrossed with watching a video scene play out in her goggles. The camera looked down at the Portland Pioneer Square stage from above.

It had been delivered by a six-inch drone to the roof of the very Chase Bank building she had attacked a month ago and killed Benjamin Knowles. The irony appealed to her. The murderer returning to the scene of the crime to commit another murder.

The small drone carried a powerful adjustable camera with a telescopic zoom which allowed her to see the mole on the cheek of Greg Graham, Senator Stanton's campaign manager.

She had flown the miniature drone to the rooftop at 10:00 a.m., and its small size had eluded officialdom. She turned the drone off to save its battery until noon. She couldn't believe so many people could fit into a one-city-block area. The crowd mushroomed down the streets in eight directions for blocks.

A sound system boomed so loud she could hear the bass reverberation eight blocks away. She watched and waited for the presidential hopeful candidate to emerge. If only he would take the stage. She wondered if the sheer numbers of people and cars might have blocked his arrival.

Her one hope was seeing Graham below. Stanton must be nearby. When he finally showed his face, the fireworks would begin. She would then take the motorboat across the river to her waiting new rental car, drive to the airport, and get away on one of the three-afternoon flights she'd booked under Brett Wright's credit card.

The final hilarious irony.

Chapter 39

I spotted a stairway inside the Spirit but opted to sneak up on her by climbing the outside ladders to the second and third decks. I stopped just below the top level and peeked over the edge, to see if it was safe, before proceeding.

Ping Lau stood aft with her back to me, wearing goggles to watch and control her drones. There were batteries, some tools, and two empty aluminum-shelled suitcases splayed open.

One of the larger drones waited on deck for its assignment. I looked over my shoulder and could make out two copters still circling and waiting for the final command to attack Senator Stanton.

I produced Angel's Glock and the revolver and climbed the last few steps to the very top of the Spirit. The aft portion of the boat had no side rails, apparently because it was off limits to passengers.

I stood fifty-feet above the seawall and stepped carefully toward Ping Lau, still engrossed with the images displayed in her goggles. Stanton must not have made his appearance, yet. I would have told the cops to keep him away if we had working communication.

I looked toward the RiverPlace hoping to see Dan and a couple dozen reinforcements running up the park. No cops in sight. They're never around when you need one. I took a deep breath and pointed both guns at Ping Lau.

"Turn around slowly and take off those goggles."

Ping Lau turned and lowered her headgear with one hand, while still holding a remote-control pad in her other hand.

"You. You're supposed to be in jail."

"I got a *get out of jail free card*," I said.

"What does it take to keep you down?"

"I don't know. I haven't been there, yet."

She took a step toward me and I aimed both guns straight at her head. She stopped and gave me a wicked smile.

"I suppose you plan to take me to the cops."

"Unless you force me to shoot you."

"Good going, Billie. I knew you'd catch her."

I turned to see a waterlogged Chris standing behind me. "How did you get here?"

"Followed you, of course. I had to steal a boat and then I slipped off the ladder into the river, but I made it."

I turned back just in time to see Ping Lau's sedentary drone rise and attack me. I fired a wild shot at it but missed and the damn thing's blades bit my hand, knocking my Glock from my grip.

I aimed the revolver at Ping Lau and squeezed off another round. The drone took a swipe at my left hand and sliced my wrist. The pain seared and I couldn't maintain enough pressure on the trigger to fire another round.

Ping Lau lunged at me knocking the revolver into the river. We struggled at the edge of the rooftop and Chris joined in the melee. Ping Lau stepped back and hit him with a karate chop across the side of his head.

He reeled and tumbled backward over the edge. I kicked Ping Lau in the face. She tumbled backward, giving me a chance to look to where Chris went overboard. His arms chopped at the water as he tried to swim toward one of the boats about twenty feet away.

Ping Lau recovered quicker than I expected and pushed me overboard too. I tried to straighten my body to avoid a gigantic belly flop from a height of fifty feet and hit the water at a semi-vertical angle, curving below the boat's underwater hull.

The waves from a passing barge pinned me to the underside of the boat. I tried holding my breath long enough to escape this death trap and saw bullets cutting air pockets in the water where I initially landed.

Ping Lau was trying to aerate me from above. I changed my plan from holding my breath and hoping to escape my water prison, to diving deeper and swimming under the Portland Spirit.

The hull was deeper than I imagined and although I filled my lungs with air on the way down, I gasped during the initial plunge and gave up half of my stored oxygen.

Loose jeans and tennis shoes didn't make it any easier for me to swim. I dove deeper, swinging my arms moderately to preserve my strength.

A miracle of sorts occurred after I cleared the middle of the shell. My back glided up the other side of the hull. The momentum and remaining air in my lungs propelled me like a submerged ping pong ball. I popped up, gasping for oxygen, on the dock side of the boat.

My first thought was getting out of there before the waves pushed the Spirit against the seawall and crushed me. I spotted a ladder on the seawall and wearily started climbing. Across from it was another ladder on the boat. I climbed a few more steps on the seawall turned and leaped to the boat's ladder.

I could imagine myself missing the ladder or slipping from it before I jumped, but I caught a rung squarely with both hands and locked my feet on a lower step. I climbed the ladder, cursing under my breath. I smelled like seaweed and musty carp. Ping Lau would have to pay.

My thoughts momentarily went to Chris. Did Ping Lau shoot him or did he drown? Chris, somehow, always came out of a dicey situation in one piece. I prayed to the God of absurdity to spare him, so he could continue to be a pain in my . . . side?

My watch was waterlogged, but the hands on its face stated the time at 12:25. Senator Stanton must be in front of the crowd by now. My adrenalin kicked in and I flopped over the main deck rail like a landed fish.

No time for subtle sneaking up on Ping Lau. I ran inside and took the stairs two at a time. I reached the top of the boat and spotted Ping Lau watching the birds as they circled, still awaiting the kill.

She tapped at the console in her hand and I looked up to see one of the drones breaking formation. I ran and sprang from fourteen feet, landing on her back with all the subtlety of a rhinoceros.

We hit the deck together and I grabbed her hair and smashed her head into the deck. She managed to roll on me and I found myself on the bottom. We rolled again until I was on her. We slugged and poked fingers into eyes and she managed to get her hands on my throat.

All I could think of was getting free of her grip to stop the drone. I clapped both fists on her ears. She released her grip and grabbed her head. I rolled away, grabbed the drone controller from the deck, and struggled to my feet.

"You can't stop them," Ping Lau said. "At twelve thirty-five, they are automatically programmed to fly over the stage and drop three grenades each. Stanton and thousands of people will die."

I kicked her in the face and studied the control unit. I checked my watch: 12:31. No pressure. The console apparently operated all three drones. This moment is the reason I spent the last month learning to fly remote-control drones.

Jack and Mary O'Reilly had tutored me at *Flying Circus Aeronautics,* and I soaked it in like my life and thousands more might depend on it. Catching Andrea and Gerald Green doing the nasty with their lovers only occurred to me later.

The drone had moved from above the river to a position about four blocks away from us. It appeared to be in another holding pattern. I hoped the settings still operated the misbehaving helicopter, loaded with grenades, and changed the settings to manual.

The drone returned, buzzing over our heads. In the periphery of my vision, I saw Ping Lau groggily getting off the deck. I turned the lever and the drone dove at a high speed toward an unpopulated zone in the water.

I ducked toward the deck as the copter splashed into the river and sank into its ignominious grave without exploding.

Ping Lau crawled to a knapsack next to the luggage and I panicked. Her gun. Where was mine? She must have picked it up. I felt for my ankle to see if I had lost the Derringer Angel gave me.

It was gone. No. Wrong ankle. I reached for the other ankle and found a little clump of steel tangled in my dripping stocking. I tried to unravel it as Ping Lau raised a Glock with a silencer and aimed it at me.

I rolled as bullets whizzed around me while still trying to wrestle the damn Derringer from my sock. Chris must have lent me some of his luck because I landed behind a huge venting pipe and found cover long enough to untangle the Derringer. I fiddled to release the metal pin on the safety lever.

I knew Angel loads the double-barrel monster with three-fifty-seven magnum rounds so I expected a recoil. I leaned around the venting pipe in time to see Ping Lau coming steady, with her Glock held in two hands.

A slight snort riffed in the air and a bullet ricocheted from the venting pipe two inches above my head. The huffing noise from the guns echoed in the air like cicada mating calls.

I rolled to the other side of the pipe in a prone position and aimed the four-and-a-half-inch Derringer, aptly nicknamed The Slayer, between Ping Lau's shoulders. I shifted my aim slightly to her right side and pulled the trigger.

Ping Lau fell to the ground writhing in pain, cursing me with every word in her vocabulary. I bounced to my feet and flew toward her, kicking the Glock across the deck.

"It's too late bitch, Stanton is dead."

I ran to the remote-control pad as drone number two broke formation and soared toward Pioneer Square, probably to wait for the third drone's arrival before all three dropped their payloads, as programmed.

I found the digital setting for Nighthawk, as it was named, and manually steered it back toward us. But I must have hit a wrong button because three objects dropped from its basket over the Willamette River. The grenades blew a hole in the middle of the water which, fortunately, held no boaters.

Ping Lau scooted across the deck away from me toward the port side of the boat. The third drone took off over the starboard side and sliced its way through wind currents toward Pioneer Square.

This one didn't stop at the halfway point and I imagined the other two were supposed to join it in the mission. I struggled to regain control over Nighthawk Three in the manual mode. It seemed to want to defy me.

I grabbed the goggles Ping Lau discarded earlier and pulled them over my head. The camera showed an overhead panoramic shot with Pioneer Courthouse Square on the horizon and closing fast.

I threw off the goggles and manipulated the hand controls. I spotted the preset program and managed to delete it. I thought. A minute later I spotted the helicopter floating back to me.

Did it still have its payload? I hadn't heard an explosion. When it got closer I brought it lower and spotted the basket, definitely still full.

I steered it upward, above the river, hoping to get it to follow its predecessors when the damn lever snapped when my excited hands applied too much pressure.

Nighthawk three hovered for a minute, two hundred yards across the Willamette, turned and headed West again to cause mayhem. I panicked and remembered Ping Lau's Glock resting on the starboard side of the deck where I kicked it.

I ran and picked it up and tried to sight the moving drone. Its flight path would carry it right over the ship, a hundred yards away and closing. The target would be a difficult head-on shot.

I would have to lead it and hope the copter's path met my oncoming bullet. I pinged an early shot to get a feel for how fast it approached and where to aim ahead in the wild hopes of hitting it.

I had no choice other than this crazy Buffalo Bill shot. The first round preceded the Nighthawk Three by two feet. I adjusted my aim ahead of the bird, which I now realized traveled much slower than the bullet.

I've spent thousands of hours at the practice range, firing off all sorts of weapons over the years, but never have I hunted, let alone shot at birds on the wing. I said a prayer and held my breath.

Time seemed to freeze. I lifted the Glock, steadying it with both hands, and aimed it with the awkward length and weight the suppresser provided. I closed one eye and sighted down the barrel, held my breath, and squeezed the trigger.

The first round punctured the sky a foot in front of the drone, but I held the trigger on the semi-automatic and the third bullet struck it. The helpless bird floundered in circles and gradually descended.

But the wounded aircraft dipped toward the Portland Spirit and more importantly toward us. I launched curse words which made Ping Lau sound like Mister Rogers and ran to her on the port side.

She was bleeding pretty good, but she would survive if the grenades didn't kill us. I had winged her on the right shoulder bad enough she would never shoot a gun again unless she had reconstructive surgery.

Right now, I was more concerned with being able to do anything again as the whirlybird meandered toward us about twenty feet above. The copter released its grenades, albeit a bit later than 12:35.

Yes, I stopped to look at my watch. I was curious, okay. It was 12:42 p.m. and all were safe. Well, all would be if I could get us off this ship.

I grabbed Ping Lau by the waist and heaved her as hard as I could. She didn't struggle. She saw the impending death too.

Two grenades bounced on the deck and one slipped to either a lower deck or into the river. Ping Lau had rigged the grenade pins to be released before they dropped from the drone.

I had seconds to move. I tossed the Glock aside and dove head-first into the polluted Willamette, the heat of the thunderous explosions roasting my legs on the way down.

Chapter 40

The General stood, gazing from his hotel room window in The Nines Hotel across from Pioneer Square. He had waited for the thunderous explosions to rain down on Senator Stanton and the thousands of fools cheering for a candidate about to die.

But anxiety crept into his confidence. Ping Lau said she would send the drones within twenty minutes after Stanton had begun speaking. The candidate had been talking for thirty minutes and nothing had happened.

He checked his watch again and put his nose to the window glass, trying to will the drones to come. He also worried because there was a strong police presence in his hotel. His plan to cancel the Secret Service detail did not take into consideration the Portland Police would step in to protect Stanton.

Between the thick crowds blocking the streets and the extra police patrols, he worried about making his connection at the airport by three o'clock. He sighed. What happened to Ping Lau? Did she change her mind about when she would launch the drones? Maybe she had technical difficulties.

A nagging thought plagued him. What if she had been found out? They had agreed not to contact each other until the day after the deed was done but he had to know. He dialed the new number on her latest burner phone and waited. It rang once and the phone went dead. He forgot about her jamming device.

Now he wondered if Billie Bly had somehow escaped and thwarted him. Ridiculous. He had been assured she was locked up tight at the Justice Center.

Who else could have found out about their plan? Only one person and he was being paid to keep quiet.

He squinted through the window, searching the sky for three remote-control helicopters, carrying six grenades, wondering when or if they would arrive.

Ping Lau sank like a stone. I realized this when I surfaced and she didn't. I dove underwater in an attempt to find her. The frigid river was clear today since we had little rain during the month of May to muddy the waters.

I made out a murky figure below me and swam toward it. The Chinese woman drifted motionlessly, and I grabbed her under her good arm and struggled toward the surface. She seemed to come to and offered a subdued kick to help me.

The sunlight reflected on the surface above us and I flailed toward it with one arm and two thrashing legs. In the last possible seconds, before I would either pass out or swallow water, we broke the surface.

Ping Lau vomited water, and I grabbed her by the waist and squeezed hard to facilitate the evacuation. The upper decks of the Spirit were on fire and splinters of the decking and rail littered the water around us.

She rested her chin under the crook of my arm and I swam around the back end of the boat to the ladder. Ping Lau went unconscious during the last leg of our journey.

I grabbed the ladder, exhausted, with one hand and held onto Ping Lau with the other. Voices pinged off the water and I realized someone stood above us.

"It's Billie," Dan said. "She's down here."

He climbed toward me on the ladder. "Hang on. We'll get you out of here."

"Take her first," I said. "She's taken in a lot of water."

"Collins, Smith, get down here," Dan said.

He lifted Ping Lau from the water and handed her up to another police officer a few rungs above him. A third cop grabbed her and climbed the few steps to safety.

"I'll get you," Dan said.

"If you can pull me up to the ladder, I think I can climb the rest of the way," I said. "What took you so long?"

"Angel went to the wrong hotel and we had to fight through a crowd," he said. "When we got here, Angel found a drenched Chris lying in the middle of the grass, mumbling you had been killed."

"Sounds par for Chris," I said, and climbed up the ladder after Dan.

The General got out of the cab and tipped the driver five dollars. He approached the airport security area and took the express line dedicated to frequent business flyers and flashed his Maryland driver's license to an agent.

He didn't slow down until the agent barked at him. "One moment sir. I need you to step back here behind the yellow line."

Yellow line? There is no yellow line for express. All of the fliers are cleared in advance.

"I'm in a hurry," he said. "My flight is boarding now."

"I'm afraid you may miss your flight."

He started to reprimand the agent until he took a closer look. The guy wore a brown sports coat and standing next to him was a geeky looking kid with a laptop in his hands.

"I'm Detective Steve Thomas with the Portland Police." He flashed his badge. "I'm afraid I'm going to have to ask you to come with me."

"What is this about, officer," The General asked, as politely as he could manage.

"It has to do with an attempted assassination," the cop said.

"Assassination? Look, I'm a busy man. I have to get back to D.C. to meet with a high-ranking official."

Detective Thomas shook his head.

"Do you have a warrant?"

The cop looked at the kid. "Show him the warrant."

The kid opened up the laptop and shoved it in his face. It displayed a warrant of arrest for William A. Pace, also known as The General.

"Is this a joke. You can't show me a warrant on a computer. You have to serve me."

"Eric?" the cop said to the kid.

Eric handed the computer to him.

"You've been served." The cop shrugged. "What can I say? We're becoming a paperless society. Give Eric your email address. He can send it to you and you can forward it to your lawyer. See? Convenient."

I sat across from Senator John Stanton on the outdoor terrace on the top floor of The Nines Hotel. FBI Agent Miller, Fire Tobacco and Explosives Agent Sanchez, and Homeland Security Assistant Director Nelson attended my little get-together at the urging of the Portland Mayor and Chief of Police.

"I was certainly relieved to get word from you everything was all right," Stanton said. "And you caught the suspect?"

"Yes, it was as I suggested," I said. "Ping Lau and The General colluded to remove you from the presidential race."

"You mean they meant to assassinate him," Chief Hardy said. "I would take this moment to point out Billie Bly tried to get you Feds to look at another suspect and you ignored her."

"We had a prime suspect," Agent Miller said. "The FBI exhausted all leads and Miss Bly's theory didn't pan out. It was a dead end."

"Not so dead," Mayor Jackson said. "We've arrested Ping Lau, who admits to trying to kill Senator Stanton, and Retired General William A. Pace, who apparently wanted to influence the upcoming presidential race."

"Well, kudos to Billie," Sanchez said. "Thanks to her, we didn't have any explosions killing hundreds or thousands of people. My bureau will track down whoever sold the remaining grenades in Ping Lau's possession. We must stop the unauthorized flow of munitions in our country."

"Do you have anything to say?" I asked Nelson.

He seemed lost in thought. "Me? Oh, yes. Homeland Security is certainly grateful for your contribution, Miss Bly. You are to be commended."

"I understand Homeland Security is in charge of the Secret Service now," I said.

"Yes, we took it over from the Treasury Department after Nine-Eleven," Nelson said.

"I was wondering why Homeland Security would withdraw Secret Service protection from Senator Stanton's appearance today?"

"You know, Billie, I was wondering the same thing," Stanton said. "Could you enlighten us, Assistant Director?"

"I'm certain, I don't know, but I'll find out when I get back to Washington."

"We have some recordings suggesting The General has had contact with one of the three of you," I said. "He apparently called someone in this investigation and tipped him off as to my location. A short time later, I was apprehended by a U.S. Marshal.

"When we learned Senator Stanton's Secret Service detail was suddenly rerouted to a supposed terrorism investigation in Seattle, and I heard a recording detailing my approaching arrest after The General contacted someone in the federal investigation, it got me to thinking.

"Which one of you is working with The General in this plot to assassinate Senator Stanton?"

"This is preposterous," Agent Miller said.

"I'm not so sure," Sanchez said. "We've been concerned about some improprieties in our investigation. Think about it. The suspect falls into our laps. There is pressure from Homeland Security in Washington to wrap it up, yet Nelson sticks around Portland."

"I've been instructed to supervise the trial proceedings. The home office doesn't want another botched FBI investigation."

"If you ask me, I don't think one hand of Homeland Security knows what the other hand is doing," I said. "Ever since you've taken over the Secret Service, they've had nothing but scandals erupting in the news."

"She's not wrong," Agent Miller said.

"But in this case, I think Assistant Director Nelson has had a direct hand in the Secret Service's failure to protect Senator Stanton," I said.

Mayor Jackson and Chief Hardy turned toward Nelson. "Is this true?" the Mayor asked.

"Of course not," Nelson said. "It was probably a paperwork error."

"Was it also a paperwork error when you directed U.S. Marshal Levan Smith to arrest me?" I said.

"I did no such thing."

I signaled Steve, who stood in the wings, and a moment later he ushered in a tall man, wearing a brown sports coat with a five-point bronze-star badge pinned to it.

"Marshal Smith, would you repeat what you told us earlier this evening?"

"Yes, ma'am. Police Chief Hardy called me and asked me who requested my services when I picked you up earlier this week. I checked with dispatch and called him back. The request came from an Assistant Director of Homeland Security, a Mr. George Nelson."

"Thank you, Marshal."

He nodded and stepped back to the terrace entrance next to Steve.

"He's mistaken," Nelson said.

"I don't think so," I said. "In fact, I knew what the answer would be before Chief Hardy made the call. You see, I rode with Ping Lau in the ambulance on her way to the hospital. We had a nice little chat."

Nelson wriggled in his patio chair. "I don't have to listen to this from a second-rate P.I. who got lucky."

"Ping Lau was grateful because I saved her life twice this afternoon. I pushed her off The Portland Spirit just before a drone dropped three grenades on us. I also found her near the bottom of the Willamette River and plucked her sorry ass from a watery grave."

Agents Miller and Sanchez shifted wide-eyed stares between themselves to me. Chief Hardy displayed a genuine smile in my direction. Stanton simply grinned. Mayor Jackson sat back in his chair, content to watch the proceedings.

"You see, Ping Lau was very grateful. She admitted she had worked with The General to assassinate Senator Stanton if he wouldn't respond to The General's advances."

Nelson patted his suit jacket where his gun likely was holstered. His eyes glanced around the terrace and to the only exit, populated by the two cops.

"She told me about The General's contact inside the federal agencies. I know the identity of his paid conspirator. We have the phone number The General called frequently to get his information and give his orders."

I turned my gaze to FBI Agent Thom Miller and to Agent Lou Sanchez of the ATFE. They returned questioning looks and I nodded.

"Just kidding," I said. "Tag, you're it." I slapped Nelson's arm.

"I'm not going down for thirty-years because of a little bribery," he said.

But he stood up anyway and retrieved a forty-five from his vest. He grabbed me from my chair and used me for a shield.

"Everybody just sit tight. She and I will be leaving and if you will all be good boys and girls, I'll release Billie safely outside."

He doesn't know me very well. "I don't feel so good," I said and started to faint.

I keeled over and he didn't try to stop me. "If I can just stay like this for a minute, I think I'll be okay."

I reached between my legs and grabbed Nelson's ankles and yanked as hard as I could. I heard a thud, which turned out to be Nelson's head making contact with the railing on the terrace.

"Oops, sorry. Did I do that?"

Steve and Marshall Smith came forward and handcuffed the groggy Nelson.

"Nice work," Agent Miller said. "I don't know how you managed to get a confession from Ping Lau. Professional killers typically don't turn on their clients."

"I may have stretched the truth a bit. You see, Ping Lau wouldn't give me the time of day."

"You bluffed Nelson?"

"Of course. It was the only way to get him to admit his role in this whole mess."

"I don't believe it," Agent Miller said.

"If you knew Billie the way we do, you would," Mayor Jackson said. "She's fooled us more than once."

"You may have your work cut out for you in court," I said. "Unless you can turn The General or Ping Lau. But his confession should help and there is the matter of his phone number in The General's speed dial."

Epilogue: The Final Problem

Chris, Angel, and I sat in padded chairs in the lobby of Crowe Realty. A statuesque blonde with green eyes wearing a short black miniskirt eyed me warily from behind her reception desk.

Her phone buzzed and after a quick conversation, she directed us to Gerald Green's office. Angel and Chris followed me with downcast eyes. This would be their punishment and hopefully a valuable lesson.

Green sat behind a stately walnut desk. I noticed his wavy sandy-colored hair was immaculately combed but thinning on top.

"Sit down," he said, grinning. "Coming to beg a little? Or maybe you decided to take me up on my offer."

"You should join us, Veronica," I said.

"I don't want to interrupt." Her right eye twitched,

"I think you might want to see this," I said.

Reluctantly, she sashayed to the other empty chair in the office, sat and crossed her legs provocatively. I thought, how else could she cross her legs in that short mini-skirt?

"I took your advice and conducted an investigation," I said. "I thought you might like to see the results."

Angel offered me her laptop and I sat it on the desk for Gerald and Veronica. Angel and Chris had already seen what I was going to show the illicit lovebirds.

"Oh, a movie? Did you bring popcorn? I'm going to love dropping this bomb on my wife."

I queued up a video and waited, as my helicopter camera displayed aerial footage of a two-story home, wandered around the house and eventually stopped outside a kitchen window. Gerald's eyes grew larger.

"Christ, this is one of my client's homes. What were you doing there?"

"Not Veronica, like you were," I said.

The camera zoomed in on man and a woman going at it on a kitchen island. It caught them in several risqué positions and showed them laughing and teasing each other.

"Eeep!" Veronica cried. "She's filmed *us*."

Gerald turned out to be anything but dismayed. He scrutinized the video as it ran and asked me to rewind it and pause it a few times.

"So," he said when it finished. "How much is this going to cost me?"

"Not as much as you think," I said.

"Do whatever she wants," Veronica said. "We could lose our jobs."

"I repeat, how much?"

"Right now, it's posted as private on my YouTube channel. If you drop the charges against Angel and Chris, this video will never see the light of day."

"I want the video and any copies you made and I also want you to take it off YouTube," Green said.

"Sorry, it stays on my private YouTube account. Nobody can see it but me. Think of it as insurance."

I had another copy of Andrea and her friend, stashed away for a rainy day, in case she followed through on her threat to sue me. Otherwise, I'd keep it as my little secret. No use in causing trouble unless I have to.

"How about a personal copy for me," Gerald said. "You know, to remind me to stay on the straight and narrow."

"You're a pig," I said. Chris giggled from behind. "You're a pig too, Chris."

"It's a deal if you provide me with a copy." He offered a handshake, which I ignored.

"Veronica, you should really contemplate your poor choice in men. This guy will drop you when somebody new comes along. In fact, I'll bet he's seeing other women behind your back."

"I know," she said.

"And Green, I'll expect to hear you've dropped the charges by Monday."

"It will be done. I know when I'm licked."

"He can't afford the exposure," Veronica said. "No Realty brokerage in town would hire him once its known what we were doing in his clients' homes."

"Thank you, Billie," Angel said, once we were outside. "I know we screwed up royally and I wouldn't blame you if you never used us as operatives. I guess I'll never become a private investigator."

I hugged Angel and whispered in her ear.

"Really. Woohoo," she hollered.

"What?" Chris asked.

"She's going to help me get my P.I. license."

Angel has her own quirks but they are manageable. She's always been by my side and at times put her life at risk for me. I don't know what I would have done without her. I figured it was time for me to reward her loyalty.

"What about me?" he said.

"Chris, you remind me of my Uncle Pete."

"Gee, thanks," Chris said.

"He drove our family crazy with his zany ideas and his knack for getting into trouble. I'm afraid letting you become a private investigator would be akin to setting my home and business on fire."

"So, is that a maybe?"

"Not in this lifetime. You'll just have to be satisfied with getting Angel into trouble and driving me nuts."

"I guess I can do that," he said. "Hey Angel, she said I can be your assistant."

"Chris?" I shook my head. "No."

He sulked and followed Angel to her car.

Brett, standing by his Mercedes, gave me a hug. "He didn't look too happy."

"He's like a puppy. After a minute it's all forgotten and he's ready to play again."

"Speaking of playing, I thought we could spend a few days at the beach. I'd like to have you all to myself so I can thank you properly for all of your hard work to free me."

"I'd like to be alone with you too," I said. "It's been over a month since we've been together."

"It's settled then. I'll book us a cabin close enough for walks on the beach but far enough from killers, politicians, and crooked cops so we won't be disturbed. The only investigation you should pursue now is me."

We kissed in the parking lot, and I have to admit he might be the one. I thought Steve Thomas had been the one all of the years during and after I left the Portland Police Bureau but he couldn't commit to an intimate relationship.

Brett commits and I know he's in our relationship for the long haul. I was ready to take the next step in our relationship. I was ready to call him my boyfriend. Baby steps.

But my commitment phobia incurred a sudden snag.

"You aren't going to try and fly us to the beach in a hot air balloon, are you?"

"Like you said to Chris, not in this lifetime," he said.

"Take me, I'm yours."

www.ingramcontent.com/pod-product-compliance
Lightning Source LLC
Chambersburg PA
CBHW071300250626
47159CB00004B/1253